MOVIE MOGUL
MAMA

Connie Shelton

Books by Connie Shelton
THE CHARLIE PARKER MYSTERY SERIES
Deadly Gamble
Vacations Can Be Murder
Partnerships Can Be Murder
Small Towns Can Be Murder
Memories Can Be Murder
Honeymoons Can Be Murder
Reunions Can Be Murder
Competition Can Be Murder
Balloons Can Be Murder
Obsessions Can Be Murder
Gossip Can Be Murder
Stardom Can Be Murder
Phantoms Can Be Murder
Buried Secrets Can Be Murder
Legends Can Be Murder
Weddings Can Be Murder
Alibis Can Be Murder
Holidays Can Be Murder - a Christmas novella

THE SAMANTHA SWEET SERIES

Sweet Masterpiece   *Sweets Begorra*
Sweet's Sweets   *Sweet Payback*
Sweet Holidays   *Sweet Somethings*
Sweet Hearts   *Sweets Forgotten*
Bitter Sweet   *Spooky Sweet*
Sweets Galore   *Sticky Sweet*

Spellbound Sweets - a Halloween novella
The Woodcarver's Secret

THE HEIST LADIES SERIES
Diamonds Aren't Forever
The Trophy Wife Exchange
Movie Mogul Mama

CHILDREN'S BOOKS
Daisy and Maisie and the Great Lizard Hunt
Daisy and Maisie and the Lost Kitten

MOVIE MOGUL MAMA

Heist Ladies Mysteries, Book 3

Connie Shelton

Secret Staircase Books

Movie Mogul Mama
Published by Secret Staircase Books, an imprint of
Columbine Publishing Group, LLC
PO Box 416, Angel Fire, NM 87710

Book layout and design by Secret Staircase Books
Cover images © Aleksey Telnor and Sandra Stajkovic
Cat silhouette © Jara3000

First trade paperback edition: November, 2018
First e-book edition: November, 2018

Publisher's Cataloging-in-Publication Data

Shelton, Connie
Movie Mogul Mama / by Connie Shelton.
p. cm.
ISBN 978-1945422553 (paperback)
ISBN 978-1945422560 (e-book)

1. Heist Ladies (Fictitious characters)—Fiction. 2. Arizona—Fiction.
3. Hollywood movies—Fiction. 4. International money laundering—
Fiction. 5. Women sleuths—Fiction. 6. Con men—Fiction. 7. Mystery
caper—Fiction. I. Title

Heist Ladies Mystery Series : Book 3.
Shelton, Connie, Heist Ladies mysteries.

BISAC : FICTION / Mystery & Detective.

813/.54

Author's Note

As always, I have a huge amount of gratitude for everyone who helped shape this book into its final version. Dan Shelton, my husband and helpmate for nearly twenty-nine years, is always there for me. And thank you Stephanie, my lovely daughter and business partner, for giving my business and writing career a burst of fresh new energy this year!

Editors Susan Slater and Shirley Shaw spot the plot and character flaws and help smooth the rough bits in the prose. And topping off the effort are my beta readers, who drop everything in their own lives to read and find the typos that inevitably sneak past me. Thank you for your help with this book: Christine Johnson, Marcia Koopman, Lisa Train, and Isobel Tamney. You guys are the best!

Chapter 1

Gracie Nelson folded the last of the five pink cloth napkins, checked the table centerpiece—a mass of casual flowers in shades of vivid purple, yellow, and red—and turned toward the kitchen. Her cell phone buzzed on the countertop. Her mother's fifth text message of the day. Gracie ignored it.

A three-tiered plate held cupcakes, each frosted lavishly and decorated in the same reds and purples as the flower arrangement. She carried it to the table, frowning. The pink napkins were all wrong—too pastel and not at all in keeping with Amber's personality. She set the cakes in place and picked up the napkins. She owned a set of bright yellow ones; maybe she could find them before the guests arrived. A tight pain formed between her eyebrows, and the thought crossed her mind that this was the worst day of the year for her to have agreed to host a party.

But it was done. Amber Zeckis's birthday happened to coincide with the long-awaited cooling trend the Phoenix weather folks had been promising for weeks, and Gracie had leaped at the chance to invite her four closest friends to celebrate with an autumn afternoon of poolside chat. Their last real gathering had been nearly eight weeks ago when, at the height of the triple-digit temperatures, all they could think of for an activity was to see the newest Drew Barrymore chick-flick at the mall theater with the most ridiculous air conditioning. Bundled in sweaters and lap blankets, they'd laughed for two hours. Phoenix area businesses seemed to think if it was 120 outside, it should be 60 degrees inside—there was simply no reasonable way to dress for the contrast, so everyone carried jackets when they went anywhere. Gracie needed to leave early that day to pick up her kids from day camp, and she'd missed the Heist Ladies' social camaraderie.

Her phone buzzed again; this time the text was from Scott. She would have to deal with this issue—soon. But the doorbell rang and saved her having to make an immediate decision.

Sandy Warner stood at the door, a brightly wrapped package in hand. Her blonde hair curved neatly behind her earlobes and she wore an attractive blue tunic top Gracie hadn't seen before. Aside from her hair being slightly longer, something else was different. She started to ask if Sandy had lost weight, but the arrival of another car at the curb distracted both of them.

"Mary's got a new car," Sandy commented. "Boy, a lot can happen during the long, hot summer, can't it?" She chuckled, but Gracie didn't pick up the mood.

"I guess the fitness business is going well," she said.

Mary Holbrook had joined the group fifteen months earlier when she'd been ripped off by her ex-husband, who left her almost penniless, and the Ladies had helped her get back her share. Resemblance to the dumpy, homeless woman who'd entered Sandy's bank that day was completely gone. The happy side effect of Mary's newfound confidence was business ownership, a trendy haircut, and a fit new body.

"Hey, you two!" Mary shouted. She trotted up the sidewalk and gave Sandy a hug before the two of them entered Gracie's foyer.

Gracie stepped aside and ushered them through to the patio, where sandwiches and chilled Sangria waited. Mary and Sandy set their gifts on a side table; Gracie told them to help themselves to the wine while she attended to the front door once again.

Amber was bouncing on her toes when Gracie opened the door. The youngest of the group, her petite frame conveyed nearly electrical energy. "Woo-hoo!" she said. "Be sure to congratulate Pen." She glanced over her shoulder toward the tall blonde who was locking her Mercedes at the curb.

"I heard that," Penelope Fitzpatrick said. She balanced a huge box while shifting her purse strap to her left shoulder.

"What's this about?" Gracie asked.

"I just finished my latest manuscript and hit the Send button. It's off to my editor."

"Ooh, I can hardly wait!" Gracie remembered the first time she'd met her favorite novelist at a luncheon gathering where Sandy introduced them. It was at the beginning of the first case the Heist Ladies had undertaken. Since then, she'd become slightly less star-struck around dignified, British Pen but she still ran out to buy each new book the moment it came out. She congratulated Pen on the book and Amber on this being her birthday.

"Hey, I just think it's cool you guys would take an afternoon off work to celebrate." Amber's dark, springy curls bounced as she practically danced her way out to the back deck where Sandy and Mary had already poured sangria into five glasses.

"I just assumed everyone would be up for wine," Sandy said. "An afternoon away from the bank is celebration enough for me."

Mary handed a glass to the birthday girl. "Hey, I'm always up for someone else's birthday party. We can ignore mine though, thank you very much."

Pen laughed. "I outrank you by a good twenty years, Mary, and I could be Amber's grandmother, so let's don't talk about ages and forgetting birthdays. I'm actually flattered you lot want to hang out with me."

"Absolutely." Gracie loved the easy banter among the friends who had grown so close in such a short time. "And, hey, what's this new bling, Amber?"

With her hair pulled on top of her head, it was hard to miss the sparkle of diamond earrings.

"A little birthday thing from my parents. They're abroad this week, and this was their way of saying sorry for not visiting me." She preened a little. "Gorgeous, huh. Although I wouldn't have minded going to Australia with them instead."

Pen raised her wine glass. "Here's to our birthday girl, to our lovely hostess, and to great friends."

"And to your new book," Gracie added. "Just because you have a dozen of them doesn't mean this one isn't just as special as all the others."

Five glasses clicked. Five shouts of "Cheers!" and some hugs. Gracie heard the phone ring in the kitchen.

"Sorry, I've been ignoring this all morning. Maybe I'd better take it. Help yourselves to the food, and there's plenty more sangria if we polish off that pitcher."

She hurried to the marble counter where she'd set her cell phone earlier. Six missed calls showed on the screen, and the current one was from her husband—again. She picked it up.

"Honey, sorry. I've been busy getting the party ready for Amber."

"Gracie, you'd better sit down. It isn't good news. I've just got off the phone for the third time with Ken Yearout."

The loan manager at their credit union. Although she had a pretty good idea what Scott was about to say, she sat.

Chapter 2

Gracie? What the hell?" Mary was the first to spot Gracie as she walked through the dining room and came out the sliding door to the patio. The others looked toward her.

Gracie jammed the tissue into the pocket of her white capris. Amber's birthday party really wasn't the place to get into this.

"Your eyes are red and your nose looks like a clown-face reject," Mary said. Hard to believe she'd once been shy about speaking out. "You were gone ten minutes and something has obviously happened."

Pen reached out and took her hand, drawing Gracie to sit beside her on the cushioned swing.

"Tell us about it," Sandy suggested. "Maybe we can help."

Gracie felt her eyes well up again. She blinked hard and

took a deep breath. She didn't see any way out of the mess at this point.

"My mother's going to lose her house and take all our savings along with it," she said.

"Oh, no."

"How the hell did *that* happen?" Mary burst out.

"Mary!" Sandy put a restraining hand on her friend's arm. "It's not really our business."

Gracie sniffed and tried for a smile. "No, it's okay. I wish I could say someone did this to us." A glance at Mary. "It's not as if I have a rotten ex, like yours. Scott has been so great, and the whole thing is my fault."

Sandy's banking experience had revealed all types of financial mishaps, but from what she knew of Scott and Gracie Nelson and their personal situation, she couldn't imagine their falling into any of the usual traps. People typically either bought way more than they could afford, or they encountered a terrible setback such as the loss of a job—neither was the case here—or they borrowed against their equity and spent the cash on an extravagant vacation or some other luxury, then regretted it later. She knew of nothing like that in Gracie's life. She and Scott were the epitome of stable, settled suburban life—he with a lucrative career, she a stay-home mom, and two high-achieving kids in school. What could Gracie be talking about?

"How is it your fault?" Amber asked. The question seemed pointed but was asked with such genuine concern, no one took exception.

"Well, you've already heard the bottom line, so I might as well start at the beginning," Gracie said.

She smiled when Mary handed her a fresh glass of wine. The others settled on chairs all around.

"So, it started a couple of years ago with my sister.

Hannah is three years older than me, two kids, divorced from a guy who did okay paying his child support until he had a bad accident and never went back to work. Hannah's got a decent job but they live in California. Things are expensive there, and she didn't make enough to stay afloat without Jay's help. Two years ago she moved in with Mom, since her kids weren't in school yet. Daycare cost was eating her alive, so they decided Mom would babysit and they'd pool their resources until Hannah figured out what to do next. She has applications in with companies all over the country, but so far nothing's worked out."

A ripple of impatience crossed Amber's smooth forehead as she clearly wished Gracie would get into the nitty-gritty.

"You have to know Hannah and Mom to get the full picture," Gracie said. "My sister has always been a dreamer. It's why she married a movie stuntman. Jay is gorgeous but way too daredevil to be married with kids. He made great money when he worked, but Hannah never did consider what might happen to all of them if he didn't. Mom and Dad had some money—he did well for himself when he started a restaurant, opened several more, franchised the whole lot of them and sold to a corporation. But they spent like crazy, too. Lots of overseas travel, big house, even bigger vacation house, fast cars, loose women ..."

She blushed. "Sorry, that's more than you wanted to know. Long story short, Dad took off with a French model and continued the high life. Mom tried to keep up her lifestyle but soon ran low on funds. To keep living that way, she got a huge mortgage on her house and tried various investments to keep up with the payments. Some worked out, others didn't."

"I get the feeling you and Scott got yourselves pulled

into one of those?" Pen asked the question gently.

"Not directly, thank goodness." Gracie realized her wine glass was empty. She set it on a side table. "What happened was, one of Mom's less-brilliant ideas basically left her strapped. By then she had Hannah and two toddlers living with her. When she begged me to help out, I asked Scott. We borrowed against our retirement funds and gave Mom the cash. We could afford it and she assured me she would soon get her money back and would repay us with interest and then some."

"But she didn't." Mary recognized desperation. She'd been there herself.

"She didn't. She still swears she'll get her investment back, but Hannah's told me differently. The money is most likely gone forever." Her voice went a little ragged. "Even that setback wouldn't have killed us, but now her mortgage company has merged with another and they're calling in the loan. They want it all, in full, in thirty days."

Penelope had been quiet. "Let's talk about this. I'd like to help."

"Pen, I can't let you …"

"Temporarily, Gracie. I know you don't want a handout. But we can't see your family booted from their home. Let me see what I can do. I'll talk to this loan manager … perhaps a portion of the loan amount would satisfy him …?"

Sandy looked skeptical. "I don't know about that. This mortgage thing has blown up. It's made the national news, and your mother isn't the only one affected."

Gracie's face crumpled, but Pen put a reassuring hand on her knee. "We'll work it out."

The older woman stood and walked the length of the patio, then turned and approached the group once more.

"We'll sort it out," Pen announced, "then we'll catch

up with this investment firm, or whoever it is, and we'll get your mother's money so she can keep her home and repay you. We've done it before, we can do it again."

Amber sent Mary a high-five.

Gracie spoke up. "When I met you, I mentioned one of my reasons for helping was because I felt my family had been taken in by someone. I thought joining all of you to solve crimes where con artists had taken advantage of an innocent person would somehow ... maybe ... make up for it. I really wasn't thinking of dragging you all into my personal troubles."

"We are not being dragged," Pen said. "We are leaping in."

"Scott and I don't even know what kind of deal it was or who this guy is that Mom 'invested' her money with."

Sandy took a deep breath. "What *do* you know about it, Gracie?"

"It's got something to do with producing a movie."

"Wait—your mother's in California. So this is a Hollywood movie? Are there famous people involved?"

"I think so," Gracie said. "Are you all really sure about—"

Amber's eyes sparkled. "Well, *yeah*. Absolutely sure."

Mary paced, appearing ready to punch someone.

Sandy's conservative banker face was on.

Pen seemed stoic. "I'm sure I've untangled much trickier plots in my novels. I say the Heist Ladies get back to work!"

Chapter 3

Birthday gifts forgotten, the Ladies fortified themselves with chicken salad sandwiches and iced tea, deciding the rest of the sangria was best left for later.

"Let's see what you got in writing," Sandy said.

"That would be a good start," Gracie admitted. "I'll get my file."

By the time the others had helped themselves to chocolate cupcakes with mounds of frosting, she had returned with a slender folder. Sandy wiped her fingers on her napkin and opened the file. Her mouth twisted in concentration as she paged through the sheets.

"These look like standard mortgage documents," she said, looking up. "They asked only the most cursory of questions about where the money would go, but I don't see anything naming this Hollywood connection."

Gracie looked ill at ease. "I realize now that I should

have asked a lot more questions. Scott and I just took Mom's word for it that she desperately needed the cash. And Hannah played on my sympathy for her and her kids. I just couldn't envision all of them suddenly homeless."

"Okay, we can't focus on emotions or blame," Pen said. "We need facts. Can you call your mother and get something for us to go on?"

"If we had the name of the person who accepted her money, even the name of the film they were financing … I can fill in a lot of the other details," Amber said.

The other four looked at her. Their young cohort had unearthed amazing amounts of data in their previous cases. Mary and Sandy were nodding.

Gracie picked up her phone and tapped a number. The voice at the other end went on nearly five minutes while Gracie nodded and inserted an occasional half-word. To the other women it sounded like chipmunk chatter. Amber raised her palms in a *what* gesture and Gracie took charge.

"Mom. Mom! I know all that. Listen a second, will you? I think I have a way to help us all out of the situation, but I need information from you."

She put the phone on speaker and set it on the table. The others gathered closer.

"Mom, I've got some friends here who know how to track down money. Sandy, Pen, Amber, and Mary are on the line. If you can tell us something about this investment you got into …"

"Oh, hi, girls!" came a smoke-roughened voice from the speaker. "I'm Janice."

Greetings all around.

"Janice, can you tell us who you invested with? Gracie says it's something to do with a movie production. We need some names and addresses if you have them," Sandy said.

"Well, how it all started was through a woman at my club. A bunch of us play bridge on Thursdays—well, every alternate Thursday, actually."

Sandy's gaze went skyward. "Is your friend the one you gave the money to? That's what we *really* need to know. Who took your money?"

"Oh. I see Gracie has already confided some things."

Pen took charge. "Your home and your daughter's savings are at risk, Mrs.—um, Janice. She needs to act now, and we've offered to help. If she can't get help through her friends, she may need to report this to the authorities. Various agencies regulate investments, but they tend to act slowly. We want to help now." Emphasis on the final word was subtle, but effective.

"Oh, yes, well all right."

"Start at the beginning, but try not to digress," Pen said.

"Right." They could almost imagine Janice sitting up straighter, taking them seriously. "My friend from the club had invested in an earlier film and she was thrilled with the results. The movie had apparently done very well at the box office and her returns were to start coming in at any time."

Pen's alarm meter began a subtle buzz. Returns had not actually been paid to the friend.

Janice continued. "Patty introduced me to her producer at a party. Nice man—*so* personable. Young, as they all are out here, and really good-looking. He actually thought I was Patty's daughter—of course he told me that when she wasn't standing there."

"Mom! Stay on topic. His name?"

"Yes, right. It's Robert Williams—well, he said to call him Rob. Tall, dark hair, neat goatee, looks like a runner or fitness expert with that nice body of his."

"What's the name of his production company?" Sandy asked.

"Um … let me think. Something adventurous. That's because the film is an action picture. He told me George Clooney and Brad Pitt were being considered for the lead roles—two men who go after the same treasure, but one's a—"

"Mom. Focus. The company name?"

"Intrepid Dog Pictures. That's it."

"Never heard of them," Mary said.

"I hadn't either, but the website gave a list of their film credits. Plus, he's also been associated with several other companies."

Amber was tapping busily on her phone's browser.

"He told me the project was open to a very limited number of investors. Patty was going to get in on the ground floor, and we would get a higher return for our money by signing on early. Later investors would have to settle for a smaller percentage. We had walked out to the terrace, and he pulled out this little tablet device and played the advertisement … whatever they call it … a trailer, I think? Anyway, oh my gosh, it sounded fantastic. Well, in fact, he had some review quote on there saying it was going to be the best film of the year. There was George, there was Brad—how could I resist those two?"

"Did you receive a copy of that movie trailer?" Pen asked.

"Oh, yes. I've watched it a lot of times. Hannah and the kids loved it too. She's so excited that I'm an investor. We're getting red-carpet treatment and tickets to the premier. It's where everyone who's anyone in this town will be, come next April."

Amber was looking at something on her phone screen,

shaking her head.

Gracie spoke up. "Mom, what other information did he give you? Surely you didn't send money based on a two-minute video."

"Of course not, Grace Ann Nelson. I wasn't born yesterday." Janice cleared her throat for the third time and went on. "There was all kind of investor information on the website, including charts with the returns on his previous films. People are making profits of forty and fifty percent. Try getting that at a bank these days. This is the investment of a lifetime."

"I found the movie trailer," Amber said quietly, holding up her phone.

"Did you actually speak with some of these other investors, the ones who collected their returns?"

"Yes—Patty. She's very pleased."

Pen remembered Janice's previous words; Patty's investment returns were *due* to come in soon. She raised an eyebrow toward Sandy, who mirrored the skeptical look.

"Janice, did you get anything in writing?" Sandy asked. "Do you have a contract? Were there printed brochures or a prospectus describing the investment, his commitment to pay, a payment schedule—anything that would help us form a complete picture?"

"Well, yes, I'm sure I have the information here somewhere."

"Mail it to me, Mom, please." Gracie sounded harried. "I'll talk to you later, once we have a chance to look it over."

She ended the call and the women sat there a full minute, silent, as each dealt with her thoughts. Amber was the first to speak. "I smell scam all over this thing," she said.

Chapter 4

Amber held up her phone and played the video, but it was hard for everyone to see.

"We need a bigger screen," Grace said. "We'll bring it up on my computer."

Snagging a cupcake and napkin for each of them, Sandy and the others followed her inside. They stood around the large desktop screen and watched as the canned voice, familiar to every moviegoer in America, began the spiel: *"In the high-stakes world of antiquities, one artifact stands out ..."*

An actor who might have been George Clooney stood in the shadows as ominous music rolled. A beam of light caught the gleam from an object on a pedestal across the room. The scene flashed forward to the Brad Pitt character in a sleek car, racing away from pursuers on a rain-slick road. The music reached a crescendo as the narrator finished with the clincher question: *"This time ... will the forces of darkness win?"*

The women watched the short film twice.

"Okay, it does look pretty exciting," Sandy admitted.

"That's because it's a mishmash of actual movie clips, movies that *were* exciting," Amber said. "The shadowy opening scene—that's not Clooney, but that scene came from one of the older Indiana Jones films and the guy in the shadows was one of the bad guys. The car racing in the rain? That came out of James Bond. It can't be Brad Pitt. The guy built this trailer from clips he found elsewhere and pasted together."

"You're so right." Gracie said, her hand to her throat. "The beam of light on the object—I remember that from somewhere, not sure which picture."

"They're calling this movie *Fraction.*"

"Which means what—the numbers we had to learn in elementary school?"

"It's just a word. But a familiar word people can picture in their minds, a concept we're all familiar with, and presumably something that relates to the plot."

A message appeared in the corner of the screen.

"Email from Hannah," Gracie said. "Let's see if she's already sent something."

When she opened the message, it contained nothing but a link to a website: fractionthemovie.com. She clicked the link and a glamorous set of graphics appeared. The same fast car, the same shadowy villain, and the same unidentified object on a pedestal, along with some explosion effects, starbursts, and a matrix of numbers to put the viewer in mind of complex computer formulas.

It was all there: the cast list claiming A-List actors, the racy buzzwords from the plot, and a huge "Coming Next Spring" banner.

"When did your mother give this guy her money?" Mary asked.

"Three years, or more. Scott and I got into this whole bailout thing with her more than two years ago."

"So, 'next spring' could really mean anytime, couldn't it?" Mary said.

The five exchanged glances. "It really could," said Pen.

Amber had taken over at the computer. She scrolled to the bottom of the page, where very small letters formed a link that said "Investor Inquiries." She gave an evil little chuckle and clicked.

"Let's just see what the pitch really says," she said.

The next page opened with three paragraphs of tightly packed small print. Amber leaned forward and read aloud. "In connection with an equity financing of at least ten million dollars, the Company may convert the investment into shares of non-voting preferred stock (Conversion Shares) at a price based on the lower of (A) a 20% discount to the price paid per share for Preferred Stock by the investors in the Qualified Equity Financing or (B) the price per share based on a $30 million valuation cap ..." She turned to Sandy. "Do you have any idea what that means?"

Sandy blinked, moved in closer and read the paragraph for herself. "Vaguely. An investor might or might not own non-voting stock in the company when all is said and done."

"And what does that mean?" Gracie asked.

"I suppose if the movie became wildly successful and showed a profit, investors would get a share, although without the ability to vote, any distributions would be entirely left up to the directors of the company."

"Does this tell us anything about the actual company?" Pen asked.

Sandy asked Amber to scroll the screen down a bit more. "Let's see ... goals seem to be along the lines of 'creating elaborate sensory experiences in the expectation of capturing an audience's attention' and 'engaging with customers by using branded campaigns.' There's more but it's really couched in a lot of marketing-speak."

"Made to sound important in such a way the average person has no clue," Mary said. "Well, in my opinion."

"Yeah, pretty much."

The women exchanged glances.

Sandy went on. "All companies that need to raise capital for their projects and for expansion create business prospectuses, and I'm sure many very legitimate ones use similar language. Gracie, did your mother have any of the materials reviewed by an attorney before she signed up?"

Gracie sighed. "I doubt it. Mom tends to flit from one shiny bauble to the next. It's how she ran through all the money she got from the divorce. And, trust me, a project that might link her name to George Clooney's—that would be a shiny bauble to her."

"So even if she did have an attorney review the contract, she might have signed over the money anyway?" Mary asked.

Gracie nodded.

"Okay, so then what can be done about it? I have a feeling the law wouldn't prosecute in a case where a person of legal age signed a contract. There must have been wording to inform investors there were no guaranteed returns," Mary said.

"No doubt." Sandy rubbed her back where it had cramped from bending near the computer screen.

The group had become quiet, each with her own thoughts about what to do next, when Gracie's phone rang.

"Hannah—hi. What did you find?" Silence at Gracie's end while her sister talked. "Nothing? What about contacting Mr. Williams's office and getting a duplicate? Really? Well, shit."

She hung up and looked around the room. "They can't find the contract. Mom remembers it as a couple of pages with a blue cover sheet, but she's been through all her papers. They even thought of asking the producer's company to send a duplicate, but Hannah was told Mr. Williams is the only one who can provide it. He's filming on location, but they didn't say where."

"That sounds like a handy answer when you don't want to be found," Mary commented.

Amber had continued clicking various links on the website. "Hey, this might be a lead."

The others gathered closer again.

"I'm still in the investment section, and it's talking about an investor event. It's this weekend, in Rhode Island."

"Hmm?" Gracie's surprise was evident. "What on earth would Rhode Island have to do with anything?"

"It doesn't matter," Pen said. She scanned the page Amber had brought up. "I think I should go."

"Seriously?"

"Why not? I have the credentials, if they want to check my background. I can always say I have a secret desire that Mr. Williams turn my latest book into a movie, and I'm willing to invest the cash to make it happen."

"Well, it would sound plausible," Sandy said.

"I should take an assistant—two sets of eyes and all that."

Amber almost jabbed Pen in the eye, in her haste to raise her hand. "Pick me, pick me! I'd love to go … and it's my birthday." She was bouncing in her seat at the computer desk.

Pen laughed and glanced around at the others. Mary and Sandy had business obligations at home. Gracie was in too emotional a state; she was likely to punch Rob Williams in the face if she met him. Amber truly was the logical choice for the trip.

"All right, all right. You shall go."

Their youngest member beamed. "I'll make a great assistant, Pen, and I won't let you down."

Pen squeezed her hand. "Now, we must look at this logically. A one-line mention of this investor meeting on the website is not exactly an invitation. We'll need a way in. Plus, we need to be a bit more specific about the location, other than just Rhode Island. Granted, it's a small state, but really."

Amber already had her phone out. She pointed to a number on the screen then began tapping the digits.

"Is this the office of Intrepid Dog Pictures? I'm calling on behalf of the bestselling novelist Penelope Fitzpatrick. Yes? I see. Ms. Fitzpatrick received word about an investment opportunity—something about raising venture capital for films—and she is most interested in speaking with Mr. Robert Williams about participating. I've located information on your website about an upcoming investor meeting?"

She listened, nodding now and then.

"We're in Arizona but we can be on a plane in the morning," she said to whomever was on the line, raising a questioning glance toward Pen at the same time. A smile spread across her face but she kept her voice neutral when she spoke again. "Yes, thank you. That will be very satisfactory."

When she ended the call, a huge grin broke out. "We're in! The presentation is being held at someplace called The

Breakers in Newport, Saturday evening. Our invitations will be held at the door for us."

"The Breakers," Pen said. "We must plan to dress."

"Oh, definitely," Sandy said. "I've heard of that place. One of the Vanderbilt family's 'cottages.' The Gilded Age, when summer homes were enormous mansions. By which I mean, my entire house could probably fit into the kitchen of the place."

"That's the one," Pen confirmed. "I've been there once, on a public tour, when I needed background for one of my historical novels. Evidently, the property can be rented for special occasions, and I must admit I'm faintly impressed. The fact Intrepid Dog Pictures has the money and clout to use The Breakers says something."

"Don't become too impressed," Sandy cautioned. "Keep in mind, it's likely Janice's money and other investors who are footing the bill. And *don't* let the man talk you into giving him any more."

"I'll keep her purse under control," Amber said. Her dark eyes sparkled.

Chapter 5

"You look amazing," Amber said when Pen emerged from the bedroom of their suite wearing a pale lavender sheath dress and gold accessories. Her blonde page curved neatly to her chin, held above one ear with an understated gold clip.

"Thank you. And I must say I wholeheartedly approve of your outfit, as well."

Amber, who normally stayed in yoga pants and a loose t-shirt all day, had found a cute dress that reflected her personality but was also appropriate for an assistant to a wealthy woman. The eggplant chiffon flattered her dark skin tone, and her choice of bright pink bangle bracelets and dangling earrings added the right touch of fun.

"I even got a leather portfolio so it can look like I'm carrying all your important papers," she told Pen. "What they won't know is that I ran a little remote-cam device through the spine of the notebook and it's recording to my phone which is here." She lifted a triangular flounce at the waist of her dress, to reveal her phone in a trim little case. "Everyone's got a phone on them nowadays, so even if it's spotted, it won't be out of place."

"Well, dear, I must say you've thought of everything."

"I may only end up with pictures of that fabulous mansion," Amber admitted, "but you never know. If I hear any juicy tidbits of conversation I might grab those as well. And, if Brad Pitt is there, I'm definitely whipping out the phone and getting a selfie with him."

Pen laughed. She'd been very fortunate in her writing career, having met a number of celebrities and nearly all the authors from the *New York Times* list. She'd forgotten how easily star-struck she'd been at Amber's age.

They had arrived the day before, settled in at a nice hotel, got to bed early, after Amber checked in by email with Gracie, Sandy, and Mary. This morning they'd driven around Newport. Amber had found a narrated audio tour, which she played from her phone, so they could learn a bit about the area. She was astonished at the number of mansions along the southern and eastern shores.

The audio spoke of the area history, which included rum-running, a slave trade, British and French military troops, and onward to the gilded age when fortunes were made on everything from railroads and oil to canned soup and the paperclip. Along came the likes of Doris Duke, the Kennedys, and the notorious Von Bulows. In more recent times, mansions and exclusive properties were being bought up by television, film, and sports celebrities. Concepts such as 'old money' and 'new money' were still quite important here when it came to admission to the exclusive clubs. Amber just smiled and shook her head.

Pen put on her poshest British accent and said, "Good to know all this. I must drop a mention of my grandfather's ties to the tsar."

They drove past the entrance to The Breakers, where at midday tourists flocked through the gates to obtain tickets for the tour.

"Just think," Amber had said, "we'll be back this evening, eating off the fine china and hobnobbing with the rich."

Now, dressed in their finery, they stepped out of the hotel to the limousine Pen had hired for the evening. "One, in case we can't find our way back in the dark," she'd said, "and two, to make an impression. To get the real nitty-gritty, as they say, we want these people to believe I'm able to make a substantial investment."

"Remember what Gracie said. Do *not* actually sign anything."

Pen patted Amber's hand as the car pulled onto the long gravel driveway. After tour hours, the huge home had been transformed. Soft lighting illuminated the landscaping and stone walls of the house, and uniformed attendants indicated the way. The limo pulled up to the impressive entry, and the ladies stepped out.

White-gloved attendants accepted their wraps, while others showed them to an elegant great hall with carved pillars, red carpets, gold rococo embellishments, and massive chandeliers hanging from chains twenty feet above. Tables sparkled with crystal and cutlery, and roving waiters offered glasses of champagne.

Taking a glass, Pen scanned the room. She did some quick math and calculated the number of expected investors to be at least eighty. If half actually invested—

she expected it would be more—and with an average investment of two-hundred thousand, Williams's company easily stood to receive eight million dollars. With high-pressure sales techniques and generous investors, that amount could potentially double.

"Pretty amazing, huh?" Amber said. She pointed out where red velvet ropes remained at the top of the grand staircase and across a few other doorways. Other doors were closed. Apparently, renting the facility for an evening did not include unlimited access to the seventy rooms. It would be interesting to see how the evening unfolded.

"Yes, indeed."

"My parents hang with a pretty well-off crowd in Santa Fe," Amber said behind her champagne glass, "but I tell you, it's nothing of this caliber."

Pen chuckled softly. "There's not much of this caliber in the world anymore, if you're referring to the mansion," she said under her breath. "It's a bygone era. As for the guests, I sense a fair number of people somewhat out of their depth. These aren't donors who can freely give money in the millions, but they'd love the opportunity to rub elbows with Hollywood, perhaps visit a movie set or attend a premier, in exchange for a hundred grand or two of their hard-earned savings." She passed along her quick calculation of what the crowd might be worth.

"Whew!" Amber almost said it a bit loudly. She lowered her voice. "So, you think it's all about the star power."

"Look closely. Off-the-rack tuxedos, dresses from Nordstrom, not Versace. I'm not saying that's a bad thing. These people are simply at a different level financially than those who pull in millions a year."

"That makes me feel better—less out of my depth," Amber said. "Although I still fit in better at a Beyoncé concert."

Pen was about to respond when one of the young women dressed in black, with an Intrepid Dog Pictures logo on her jacket, approached. With a warm smile, she offered to show them to their table. Place cards dictated that they would be seated at a five-place table with a couple from New York and a single woman who introduced herself as Maisie Brown. The husband and wife pair—Joe and Virginia—seemed a little quiet, as if the whole experience was a shade beyond their experience. Maisie fairly bubbled with excitement, however.

"I just can't wait to see what Rob has in store for us tonight," she said.

Five waiters, with plates in hand, set a salad before each of the diners at the same moment.

"You appear to be familiar with Mr. Williams and his business," Pen said to Maisie. "You know him personally?"

"I feel like I do," the other woman said. "This will be my second picture with him."

"You're an actor?" Amber asked.

"Oh, heavens no! I'm purely an investor. I love being involved, but from the sidelines. I tell you, there's nothing like attending a premier. We all get flown to Hollywood, and there's a red carpet, and the stars come. I mean, the stars of the movie, of course, but a lot of their friends come too, and they sit in the audience right with the rest of us. Even though everybody's all dressed up, we get popcorn and Cokes, and we laugh together …"

Joe and Virginia were a little wide-eyed at this point.

"I mean, it's really a special experience," Maisie said. "My friends back home can't believe I get to do this. And, you know, I tell Jane Simmons … I say, well maybe if you'd saved more back in your days as a banker, well maybe you'd be investing in Rob's films now, right along with me."

"So, the return on your investment in the films has been good?" Pen asked.

"Oh my." Maisie raised a hand to her chest, her gaze rising. "I can't even tell you."

The main courses arrived just then, exactly as ordered when they had procured their tickets, salmon for Amber and a fork-tender filet for Pen. Conversation waned for a few minutes, until Pen turned to Maisie once again.

"I'm curious about something. A friend invested in one of Rob's films a couple of years ago, but she hasn't heard much about the finished picture."

Maisie laid down her silverware and wiped her mouth with her napkin. "You know, I'm still not sure how that works. It does seem to take awhile to produce these things. Tell her to be patient. If Rob Williams is behind it, it's going to be a great movie."

Amber caught Pen's eye as the waiters again appeared and began removing plates. Obviously, her young cohort wanted to discuss something she couldn't say at the table. They were about to excuse themselves to the ladies room when the lights flickered and a voice came through on a speaker.

"Ladies and gentlemen. In a moment, over your desserts, we'll begin Mr. Williams's presentation."

Precisely on cue, plates containing slivers of a rich chocolate cake, drizzled with an attractive ribbon of raspberry puree, appeared from each diner's left side. Pen noticed the red decoration had been formed in the shape of a strip of film. In the uppermost frame of the filmstrip was a tiny, almost imperceptible dollar sign. She wouldn't have noticed if she hadn't looked directly at it before the lights dimmed.

At the end of the room a white projection screen

began to lower from the second floor balcony's stone balustrade. Sparkles and crisscrossed klieg lights showed on the screen, and an extremely handsome man in tuxedo stepped into the spotlight beneath it.

An unseen announcer said: "Ladies and gentlemen—Mr. Robert Williams!"

With the collective intake of breath, it felt as if the air had been sucked from the room.

Chapter 6

Williams took a bow, his hands in prayer position, and gave a tiny salute to the audience. "Thank you. Thank you *so* much." His voice cracked the tiniest bit, right on cue.

Pen tapped Amber's leg beneath the table. Amber casually laid her notebook beside her dessert plate, shifting herself and her place setting slightly to aim the hidden camera toward the speaker and the oversized screen. She gave a slight shrug to Pen. *I don't know if we'll capture anything.*

"We are all so honored to welcome you here as our guests," Williams continued. "Isn't this a special place?"

Across the table, Pen saw the New York couple nodding, soaking up all that honor. Maisie Brown seemed starry-eyed.

"The Breakers is a very special place to me, because …" a long pause "… because this is where we'll be filming a large part of our next production! Yes, folks, you heard it here first because this is a new announcement. Trust me, the networks will be all over this in a few days, but you— *you*—are the first to know. And you're the first to know because you will be a part of it."

He turned, one arm upraised, sweeping the large room with his gaze.

"We're signing a full cast of A-Listers for this one, folks. Liam Neeson, Kate Winslow, Julia Roberts, Sean Connery. That's right." His tone dropped to an intimate level. "I know—can you imagine what the premier's going to look like? I know a lot of you in this room have been with me on previous films. Some of you have been on the set, a lot of you have been to premier night. Yeah. *Yeah!* You know the excitement, that feeling of sitting next to Julia or Sean in the audience."

Scattered applause went up, joined in a moment by nearly the entire audience. At their table, Maisie was practically on her feet.

"Okay, I know—*you* want to know. What's the story line? What are the roles? What's going to draw millions of people and hundreds of millions of dollars in returns for our investment in this film?"

Pen recognized the familiarity as a common sales pitch—*our* investment, *you* know the excitement … The guy was very good at this.

"Hey, everyone—let's not wait any longer!"

The spotlight went out, the screen brightened, and dramatic music filled the room, reverberating off the stone walls and marble columns. The familiar recorded voice began the litany, the setup for a psychological thriller pitting two sisters against an evil, shadowy father. The setting in the background did, indeed, appear to be the famous mansion where the party had convened. Pen had a momentary thought that perhaps this man was for real, that a couple of the big movie stars might step into the spotlight at the moment the trailer ended. She shook off the thought—these were skilled Hollywood production people. They could make their viewers believe anything.

Amber had lifted the cover of her notebook and tilted it, getting a good angle on the screen. If the images came out halfway decently, the Heist Ladies could take their time and analyze them later. To cover her movements, she'd pulled out a pen and was making notes on the page.

The music rose to a crescendo, then dropped off abruptly.

"Wow," came a woman's voice through the microphone. The screen withdrew and the spotlight was back. This time an efficient-looking brunette woman in a perfectly tailored business suit stood in the light, holding the microphone. "Does this look like an Oscar winner, or what!"

Many in the audience cheered.

"All right, the big moment is upon us, and Rob and his associate producers are available to meet with you, one-on-one, and you'll surely want to have your checkbooks ready." The brunette delivered her lines with a quirky smile. "Meanwhile, finish your desserts and enjoy this beautiful place, and soon we'll have carriage rides around the grounds—it's just beautiful out there on this crisp autumn evening."

The lights came up, and within moments young men and women in the black uniform with the logo began appearing beside the diners.

"Ms. Fitzpatrick?" said a twenty-something girl with blonde hair in a tight bun. "Come with me. Your assistant is welcome to join a group for the mansion tour."

With subtle assurance, the girl guided Pen from the table and made sure Amber was steered to another assistant who already had a group of about ten he was leading toward the grand staircase. Amber gave a backward glance at Pen, her eyes conveying that she would learn as much as she could.

Very efficient management of our movements, Pen thought as she was escorted down a marble corridor to an elegant sitting room. Six small round tables had been set up, each with two chairs on one side and a tuxedoed man in another chair facing them. Couples sat at four of the tables and another single woman at the fifth. Pen was taken to the sixth. Because of the size of the room, she realized right away that conversations could not be overheard between them. A boiler room, billionaire style.

By the luck of the draw, she was seated facing Rob Williams himself. He'd apparently consulted some kind of cheat-sheet because he greeted her by name and knew she was a novelist.

"You know, Ms. Fitzpatrick, we're always considering new material for scripts, and I have a feeling your book could be our next big find."

Master flatterer. "Oh, which title are you most interested in?"

His research hadn't gone quite that deep, but he was smooth. "They're all good. Why don't you send me the one *you* would most like to see brought to film."

She sent him a tight smile.

"Meanwhile, I know you're here because you know a great investment when it's presented." Repeating two or three of the same points he'd made during the presentation, he pulled out the contract. In less than thirty seconds, he had filled in her name on the blank line near the top.

"Well, Mr. Williams—"

"Please. It's Rob."

How apt, since it's what you do. "Yes, well, Rob. I'm *very* intrigued with this. One of the women at our table just couldn't say enough about what a wonderful opportunity it is. And I'm sure that's true. All I need to do is take the contract to my business manager, have him review the terms, and a check will be coming your way."

Not signing on the spot was obviously a common objection because Rob was ready with an answer.

"Mm, that's too bad," he said. "You did understand from the presentation that this is an extremely limited opportunity. The terms we set forth here …" He turned the contract to face toward Pen, but kept his Montblanc waving back and forth across the page just enough to make it impossible for her to focus on the print. "These types of returns don't come along often, and for you to be included on the initial offering, I'm afraid we must have your commitment tonight. Surely you understand." His face rendered a perfect sympathetic smile.

Oh, I understand. More than you know.

"The contract appears to be quite concise," she said. "Shall I just give it a quick read, then?"

She'd gripped the edge of the pages before he could react. As she suspected, the two-page document was short on promises and vague on payouts and timeframes. She reminded herself the goal was to get out of here tonight with a copy of the contract, no matter what it took. She set an eager expression on her face.

"Is a credit card all right as a deposit? I assure you, it has a six-figure credit limit, with the full amount available right now. A letter of credit or wire transfer shall follow for the balance, Monday morning when the bank opens."

"Absolutely. Just fill in your banking information

here … and add your signature at the bottom." He handed her the Montblanc pen.

"Just one thing," she said, lowering her voice. "Penelope Fitzpatrick is actually a pen name. I'll just need to—"

She blacked out the space where he'd written her name and filled it with the name of one of her fictional characters, Clarissa Claremore. A random string of digits went into the spaces for banking information, and she signed the bottom line—C. Claremore—in an unreadable flourish. In the space labelled Amount of Investment, she wrote $200,000. There—that should make the man extremely happy.

"Thank you so much, Ms. Fitz—um, Ms. Claremore. I assure you, you will be among those most handsomely rewarded when the box office returns come in. *And*, I shall personally make certain you have a seat at Julia's table on Oscar night."

He reached for the contract, but Pen managed to be quicker.

"Oh, don't worry, we'll mail you a copy of this in the morning," he said.

No way. This must be exactly why Janice had no copy of the document she had signed.

"I'm sorry. That doesn't work for me. This is a mansion, granted, but there's a business office attached somewhere. We'll simply go there now and make the needed copies." She gripped the contract and stood up.

Rob's mouth pinched tightly in a straight line, but Pen still had the upper hand. She noticed the turnover at other tables. Couples who had completed their contracts had been escorted out and new faces were coming in. In fact, the same young woman who had escorted her into the room was standing at the doorway with new customers.

He wouldn't want a scene.

"Shall we find that business office?" Pen pressed.

Rob signaled his employee over and told her to show Ms. Fitzpatrick to the copy machine. He muttered something that sounded like a demand that the girl bring back the original, not the copy, but the moment he looked up he was once again all smiles. All those zeros were counting for something.

"A pleasure," he said, even as he was walking toward the new victims waiting at the door.

Although her escort had been sent with orders about getting the contract original, she'd also been well schooled in politeness. Pen had no trouble keeping control of the document as they walked to a narrower corridor and into an office. She operated the copier herself, rather than turning the pages over to the employee. It was crucial that no trickery occur.

Her handler stayed with her throughout the process, saying something into a previously unseen microphone. The only part Pen caught was her own name. They left the office area, traversed the great hall again, where all signs of dinner had vanished, leaving only the white-clothed tables and red floral centerpieces. Beyond the great hall, doors opened to a wide veranda where a few people milled about.

Pen's escort touched her elbow and indicated Amber standing near the edge, with a white horse-drawn carriage coming to a stop in front of her. One of the uniformed escorts was standing beside her.

"How was the tour of the mansion?" Pen asked, as the two were handed up into the carriage.

"Wow," Amber said. "It's the most amazing place. Hard to believe people actually lived like this. It seems like a fairy tale."

"It does, doesn't it? And to think I'm now an investor. Rob told me I'll be hearing from him and we may be invited to come to the set sometime," Pen said with a wink, assuming the coachmen were part of the enemy camp.

The carriage ride lasted no more than ten minutes, ending at the front of the property where Pen's hired limousine waited, idling. Incredible timing, she thought cynically. She thought back to the subtle hand signals, the brief radio exchange, the many escorts who made certain every guest was exactly where he or she was supposed to be. Nothing had been left to chance, and she supposed that's how it had to be with such big money involved.

Chapter 7

I could use a cup of tea," Pen said.

Back at the hotel, each had changed into something soft and comfortable and they'd met in the suite's sitting area. Pen had set the contract on the coffee table and was figuring out the instructions for the room's little beverage device.

"I'm definitely too keyed up to sleep yet," Amber agreed. "Is it too late to call Arizona? Maybe we should report to Gracie."

Pen looked at her watch. "Ten o'clock here, so it's only eight there. Let's do it."

Pen brought up Gracie's number on her mobile phone and set it where both could hear over the speaker.

"What's happened?" Gracie asked immediately. "How did it go?"

"Well, I can easily see how your mother got hooked into this, and why she can't find any paperwork other than the glossy brochures. The guy is a master at the game," Pen said. She described the intense atmosphere of the boiler room, even though it had taken place in a dazzling setting. "Even easier to intimidate average people when you put them into surroundings like that."

"The couple from New York, Joe and Virginia, they were really out of their element," Amber said. "After you were taken away, they were looking around for the exit, but one of those assistants practically jumped right on them."

"I saw them in the sales room," Pen said, "but you know who I didn't see ... the other woman, Maisie Brown. I was thinking about that during the carriage ride. I have a very strong feeling she was planted there among the rest of us. Did you notice that? Each table had one or two who were the most enthusiastic, the ones who always started the applause or the cheers when Rob Williams appeared."

Gracie's voice came over the line. "So, you think my mom was steered in the same way? You don't suppose her friend Patty ..."

"Does Janice know this Patty very well?"

"I don't really know ... I mean, she talks as if she does, but Mom is one of those who instantly becomes friends with everyone. She doesn't have good radar for spotting phonies."

"It would have been difficult in this group tonight," Pen assured her. "They blended in very well."

"But, Pen, I think you're right," Amber said. "I never did see Maisie or the other couple after the presentation. Once the selling began, these people were very cautious to keep us separated. They didn't even let me go in with Pen. I noticed that couples were kept together. I guess, obviously, husband and wife will make joint decisions, but people like me—P.A.s or business associates—anyone who might talk the *real* investor out of signing—we were kept away until it was a done deal."

"But you got a much better look at the mansion than the rest of us," Pen said, with a grin toward Amber.

"Well, yeah. And, I did get a few juicy tidbits of conversation here and there. They might have tried to keep us apart, but they don't know that I have excellent hearing."

Pen looked at Amber over the top of her teacup. "Excellent … do tell."

"Well, the brunette who came under the spotlight after Rob showed the movie trailer … her name's Abby. While he was in the other room getting signatures and money she was steering the various gofers to their positions, and she seemed pretty friendly with one guy. Anyway, I was with a group being shown the billiard room, and while our guide was going on about the amazing tile work and the fact there's some inconspicuous little turtle in a mosaic on the ceiling, I edged closer to Abby. I still had my camera going and I tilted it her way.

"She's telling the guy things about Rob, kind of personal stuff, and I caught something about France. Well, my ears perked up at that. You *know* I've always wanted to go to Paris …"

"Amber!" Grace's impatience came through.

"Okay, I know. So, the thing that really stuck with me was when Abby said Rob puts down the rich people all the time. Loves their money but is sick of dealing with them calling the office and pestering."

"What! The rat! That would have been my mom."

"Yes, and he apparently also told her once he has enough money, he's going to vanish. To hell with everybody in the movie business. He's out of there."

"Oh my god," Gracie said. "He really is going to take the money and run."

"Did you manage to record that part?" Pen asked, glancing around for the notebook with the camera.

Amber crumpled. "No, unfortunately not. I'd left the camera on too long and my battery died. It's charging in my room right now. We can look at the footage and see what I did get later."

"So, we don't have enough to turn him over to the law?" Gracie asked.

"We might. We've got a good start with the contract. I gather I was one of the few to get out of the building with a copy of what I signed. As contracts go, it's really pitiful. Two pages, all of it in favor of the production company, nothing in the way of a guaranteed return. No recourse for the investor if every cent of the money is lost."

"That's horrible."

"But probably not uncommon. Most investments involve some degree of risk—your stock broker won't guarantee much of anything either. Every investor is supposed to make his or her own informed decisions. But this differs radically in the contrast between what the sales pitch, the website, and the video trailer promise and what the contract says. There's nothing naming these A-list actors they promised; loopholes allow them to change the script, the location, all of it. Not to mention the way investors are pressured. He wouldn't let me take a copy of the contract for review by my attorney—insisted the offer was only good tonight."

"If we turn it over to the law, will they just shake their heads and say it's a case of Buyer Beware?" Gracie asked.

"I don't know, but I'm going to do my best. I'll run

it past Benton when I get home," Pen said. The retired district attorney was a close friend and confidant who had advised her on legal matters a few times.

Gracie thanked them and they hung up.

"Let's see what we got on video," Pen suggested. "Can we watch while it's plugged into the charger?"

They went into Amber's bedroom and she brought up the camera program which had transmitted to her phone. First impression of the video was a garble of noise. The dramatic music from the movie trailer was overwhelmed by chatter—Pen recognized the voices of their table companions—and by dishes clattering as the waiters picked up dinner plates and delivered desserts. It was the only part of the whole production which had not been choreographed quite closely enough.

Once the noises abated, the soundtrack quality improved. There were still a couple of interruptions when a waiter passed between their table and the projection screen, but much of the trailer came through. They sat close, squinting at the small screen.

"I don't know," Pen said when it finished. "Do you think anyone else will be able to grasp it? We know what was said because we were there. I'm afraid others may find it hard to follow."

"I'll see what I can do with it once it's transferred to my computer. I've a pretty good editing program."

Pen still had the two-page contract in her hand. "I'm disappointed we didn't get more. I've no idea if this skimpy document and our dubious video will be enough to convince the law to pursue a case."

"What about if we could find other so-called investors who would join in?"

Pen thought about it. "I like the idea. We could ask

Janice who, besides her friend Patty, was at the presentation she attended. I'd want to talk to others—I have a feeling Patty may have been put into the audience just as our Maisie was."

"So, a couple of us go to California while Rob is out here, filming on location, and we break into his offices and find the other contracts. We could contact each investor, say we're just checking up to see if they've been pleased with the return on their money. I bet we'd get an earful." Amber had a devilish look on her face.

"No doubt." Pen laughed as she left for her own bedroom.

In the morning they treated themselves to a room service breakfast. Amber appeared in a long t-shirt and robe, her wild curls in complete disarray. She downed two cups of coffee, then her eyes brightened and her customary smile came back.

"I was thinking most of the night," she said.

Pen smiled as she cracked her soft-boiled egg. "I'm not surprised. And what did you conclude?"

"Rob said his crew is filming at The Breakers this week, right? It was one of the reasons he hosted last night's gathering there. So, maybe we go there again this morning and see who's around. Some of the investors from last night may have shown up to watch the action—in fact, we could use that as our own excuse—or, I might spot Abby or some of the other gofers and blatantly listen to the gossip some more."

"Why not? Our flight doesn't leave until this afternoon."

"If I get the chance, at least this time I have a fully charged phone for recording and filming what's going on." Amber laughed and lifted the cover from her plate of blueberry pancakes.

An hour later they were in their rental car again, having packed and checked out of the hotel. They could spend the morning watching how film production worked and still make their flight easily. From Bellevue Avenue they made their way through the neighborhood of huge homes, turned on Ruggles, and made a left on Ochre Point. The street in front of The Breakers was clogged with tour trollies, but the parking lot across the street still had spaces. They parked and walked among a stream of people headed up the long drive toward the ticket counter.

"Rather a different picture than last night," Pen commented. "Arrival at the front door by limo sort of spoiled me."

"Yeah. I'm kind of surprised," Amber said. "How can they be filming with this many people milling around? Looks like we'll have to buy a ticket if we want to get beyond the front door."

"Maybe we misunderstood and the filming only takes place early or late in the day, outside tour hours." Pen looked around and spotted a door marked Office. "Let's check with someone."

Pen tried the door. It opened to a small reception area with a slender young man seated at the desk. Beyond, she saw another room and heard female voices. Presumably, this was where the ticket proceeds were brought and counted. It certainly wasn't the management office she'd been taken to last night in order to make her photocopy.

"We're not here for the tour," she began, "we need to speak with Rob Williams, the producer who's filming here. Where might we find him?"

The desk guy gave her a completely blank look.

"Movie?" Amber said. "They're shooting a movie here. Is it inside the mansion or out on the grounds somewhere?"

His mouth opened and shut a couple of times before words came out. "I have no idea about that. Let me call Ms. Blanchard." He picked up his handset.

They waited nearly ten minutes before an efficient-looking woman in a navy suit bustled in.

"Harriet Blanchard, estate manager," she said, extending her hand. "I'm afraid I didn't understand the question about some sort of filming …"

Pen repeated what they'd heard the previous evening, Rob's claims about the mansion being used as a movie set for his current production.

Harriet's eyebrows pulled together in front. "What was the name of the production company?"

"Intrepid Dog Pictures," Amber said. "Robert Williams is the producer."

Blanchard shook her head. "I'm afraid there's a misunderstanding. Mr. Williams rented a few of the rooms for a social gathering last night. He catered a dinner for his guests, and they had access to a few of the ground floor rooms afterward. But that was the extent of it. They paid for the use of the space until ten o'clock. Everything was cleared away by eleven, and the entire house was reset for tours again well before we opened the doors at nine this morning."

"So, even outdoors on the lawns—no filming?"

Blanchard made an impatient gesture. "No. As I said, there are no film production companies with access at all right now. It's something we plan well in advance. There are arrangements to be made, legal contracts, permits issued and deposits paid, clearances for all their staff. This man you're talking about has never filmed a movie here."

Chapter 8

So, I wonder how many other film locations Rob Williams has claimed, places he's never actually made a movie?" Sandy mused.

The team had assembled the following morning, choosing one of their favorite breakfast places for an early meeting. Mary's jujitsu class would come to her gym at ten and Sandy needed to be at the bank for a client meeting, so seventy-thirty for omelets and coffee worked for all.

Amber, looking far more bright-eyed than Pen after their quick East Coast trip, held up her phone for all to see.

"I couldn't sleep last night," she admitted, "so I started checking. Rob Williams's website claims he was producer or executive producer on five films, dating back about eight years. But that's *his* word. He doesn't even have a Wikipedia bio, and I'm not finding much of any Hollywood connection prior to his own listings."

"Because he was probably in grammar school," Pen mumbled. She'd drained her first cup of coffee and was working on the second, but her flawless English complexion seemed more drawn than usual.

Mary and Gracie chuckled at her comment.

"I tell you, you cannot believe how young he is," Pen said.

"According to his website, he's forty." Amber squinted at the phone.

"He began producing movies in his early thirties, then," Sandy said. "That does seem young to have gotten such a head start in the business."

"What did I tell you? A baby," Pen said. Her poached egg and toast had arrived, and she spread marmalade on one of the whole-wheat triangles. "It's the trouble with these new up-and-comers, they want instant fame and fortune without putting in the years to earn it—present company excepted, of course."

Amber gave her a sweet smile.

Gracie, halfway through her Denver omelet, set down her fork. "What did Benton advise? You saw him last night, right?"

"Yes, he picked me up at the airport and we had a quick bite on the way home. I showed him the contract and filled him in on our visit to Newport. He said, and I quote, 'I don't see how throwing a party in a mansion while claiming something more can really be construed as illegal, actually.' He did admit such false claims are on the shady side, but it's almost always up to the investor to check out the claims and the company they are signing with."

"But did he have any advice for what might be done now?" Gracie asked.

"He said, based on what I told him, he would recommend that we find more victims of Williams's before we try taking it to the law. It will be up to the prosecutor's office to decide whether to pursue criminal prosecution, and that will likely depend on the amount of money involved. If they won't pursue it, there are the civil courts, but we would spend a great deal on lawyers if we go that direction. When he asked whether any of the plaintiffs have money to go that route, I had to admit we only know of your mother so far."

Gracie's mouth pursed and she nodded.

"We actually met very few of the guests at the dinner, and those were introduced by first names only."

"Other than Maisie Brown," Amber reminded. "I'm going to see if I can search her out."

"She wouldn't be of any help. She swore she'd made a lot of money from her film investments," Pen said. "And when I mentioned her to Benton he made the very valid point that perhaps it was true. Maybe Maisie really did earn an impressive return."

"Even if she didn't, would she admit it to us? She was glowing with excitement at the chance to invest with Rob again," Amber said.

"Unless, as I suspected, she might have been planted in the audience to help drum up enthusiasm." Pen popped the orangey bite of toast into her mouth.

"Okay, so if this Maisie Brown proves to be a dead end, victim-wise, what about others? Who else's names do you remember from the gathering?" Sandy asked.

"I talked with one of Rob's assistants, a thirty-something woman named Abby. Unfortunately, she and the others who were part of the show only gave first names."

"A first name is a starting place. We can find out more

about anybody," Mary said. "Look, I can take some time away from the gym. Billy took his vacation last month and he's been pushing me to do the same. If we have to go somewhere to track down this Rob Williams, I'm in."

"A new face would be good," Pen said. "I fairly well burned my bridges, if it comes to doing anything sneaky, since I got a little confrontational with him at the contract signing. He *might* remember Amber, but he's never seen the rest of you."

"So, here's what I'm thinking," Sandy said, pointing with her pen at the yellow pad of notes she'd been taking. "We locate Abby whatshername and Maisie Brown. Figure out where we'd need to go to talk with each of them face to face. If we can get any kind of admission from Abby, or some kind of paperwork from Maisie … well, it would give us that much more evidence."

"Where are the offices of this Intrepid Dog Pictures—somewhere in California?" Mary asked with a chuckle. "Sorry, that name is just too funny."

"Yeah, it's in the Los Angeles area," Amber said, smiling back. "I can get an address."

"Okay, do that," Sandy said. "Then let's look at the next steps. If we can somehow get in there—maybe with this Abby as a contact, maybe not—at least we can try to get a look through the records and find out how many victims were scammed. According to Benton, the more the better because the law can then build a stronger case."

"And at least we'll find out that my mom isn't alone in this thing."

"She's not alone, I assure you," Pen said. "That huge room was full of new takers for Rob Williams and his offer. In the room where the hard-sell pitch was made, I personally witnessed at least five other people signing up."

"We have to take this guy down," Mary said, her eyes bright with moisture. "We just have to."

Chapter 9

Rob Williams sat back in his first-class seat, eyes closed, savoring the past few days. Newport had gone well. And The Breakers—nice. He could get used to a lifestyle like that. Yeah, easy.

He felt movement at his wrist. The flight attendant had picked up his empty scotch glass. When he opened his eyes she asked if he would like another.

"Sure, hon."

She gave him a look but headed to the galley to get the drink.

Hon. His father's way of addressing women. Rob's years in California had taught him better but he sometimes forgot to watch his mouth. Robert senior had never sat in first class on an airplane, had never walked into a mansion like that one in Newport, was probably sitting in some

Milwaukee bar right now, wondering if it was going to snow tonight.

Rob put the picture out of his head, his old man with stained dungarees and a beer gut that grew bigger every year. His mom, the longsuffering quiet one, until she just gave up and died last year. Cancer. Now, Pop didn't even bother to go home for dinner, just ate pork skins and pickled eggs at the bar and called it food. Whenever Rob (he'd ditched childhood-cute 'Robbie' the minute he left their home) talked to his dad about his unhealthy lifestyle, Pop either went on a rant about what a young ingrate he was, or the phone line got real quiet and Rob felt bad for lecturing.

Screw it, he decided. His world and his father's were so far apart they'd never mesh. Let the old man do whatever he wanted. Rob knew what he wanted for himself, and it didn't involve the Midwest—at all.

He'd been fourteen when he filmed his first movie— four minutes of footage in which he and Mom had dressed the family cat in baby clothes and watched its cute antics as it wrestled its way out of a tiny buggy and ran behind the couch. No plot, no acting—but, oh, the feeling of that camera in his hands!

At nineteen he'd snagged a summer job on a documentary, working with the sound crew. The director captivated him. Everything to do with movie making was about turning reality into fantasy, about controlling the angles, the lighting, the script and the players. By September, he knew his life's calling—he would become a film producer. He watched the executives come and go in their limos, wearing their tailored suits and fat diamonds on their pinkies. As much as he loved the creativity, he craved the lifestyle.

He combed garage sales and pawn shops, and he came up with a couple of decent professional cameras, some editing equipment, and even a canvas director's chair which he had embroidered with his name on the back. Then he discovered he would need money. Big surprise that even unknown actors don't work for free, and the ones he'd heard of were completely inaccessible to him. It didn't stop Rob Williams.

He moved to California, sneaked off a studio tour bus, and prowled through garbage bins, coming up with snippets of film that he pieced together to make his first movie trailer. Up in Silicon Valley he found young guys with so much money they didn't know what to do with it, and he got them to invest. Meanwhile, the documentary he'd worked on the previous year earned a couple of Oscar nominations, one being for sound effects, and Rob could legitimately link his name with that of the famed golden statue.

He put together a short film and netted $10,000 after a year of hard work.

After that, his fundraising efforts took on a whole new dimension. He learned the value of the crowd mentality. Get one or two people in a room interested in a project and others would leap aboard. When his first gala-style fundraiser netted nearly a million dollars, his future was sealed. To hell with the work of hiring and funding and filming—he could make more money by simply pretending to do those things.

He sighed happily in his first-class airline seat.

When the flight attendant came back with his third scotch he thanked her respectfully and got a smile. Always worked. Treat 'em like you're a gentleman and they'll act less and less like a lady. Like that little blonde he'd picked up after the investor dinner night before last. She'd eyed his tuxedo and the fresh trim on his goatee—he'd even had a facial that day—and she'd been *so* ready to hop into his bed.

He'd slipped her a business card with his mobile number written on the back. After that, all he had to do was get Abby on the redeye flight back to L.A. and the blonde was all his for the next twenty-four hours. She told him she was a college intern working a semester for the Historical Preservation Society, majoring in some stupid art-preservation subject. He'd continued to pour the wine, nodded at all the right places in the conversation, and proceeded to enjoy every inch of that twenty-year-old body. Yum.

When she started making noises about coming out to L.A. sometime soon, he shut her down with the news that he'd be out of the country, filming on location in eastern Croatia or some such thing. He couldn't actually remember what had popped into his head at the moment. But he'd sent her away with a smile on her face, after a room-service breakfast.

Now, it was back to business. He pulled out his tablet and checked his bank accounts. All the investor receipts had cleared except the one from Clarissa Claremore, the older woman who told him she was a bestseller novelist, who wrote under the name Penelope Fitzpatrick. He remembered her. Classy, like some actress from the '40s, the kind that wore her hair and makeup subdued, her clothes well tailored in classic styles. Funny that her bank hadn't transferred the funds. He would have Abby check on that.

He sipped his Glenlivet and thought ahead to his next money-raiser. The setup was simple: create a beautiful movie trailer, imply that a number of big names were already attached to the picture, throw in a mention of the long-ago Oscar nomination, keeping it vague, promise substantial returns—something around a double on their money (he'd discovered people became hesitant when the number was too outrageous), bank the money offshore, and do it all again.

Abby was a heck of a researcher; she had a real knack for finding people with spare dollars in their accounts. Sometimes a friend-of-a-friend got invited along, but they had to be good for at least a hundred grand before they got in the door.

Average take for an evening like they'd just staged, after expenses for renting the location, catering the dinner, and hiring young locals as escorts and pages ... usually in the high six-figures, sometimes more. California was the hot spot—all that Silicon Valley money in the hands of inexperienced investors, living close enough to the film industry that nearly everyone "knew someone who knew someone" and thought they had an 'in' with the business.

But some government office in southern California had already been prowling around his finances, and he couldn't afford to hold another party there. Rhode Island had taken him completely out of his own backyard, a good thing. He'd hit the West Coast plenty of times, the East Coast a couple ... now, maybe somewhere in the middle. He brought up a map and set his wheels in motion to find a city with a lot of moneyed folks. Vail—too small. Dallas—possible. Scottsdale—that sounded about right. People in the nearby Phoenix cities called it Snotsdale. A town where everyone tried to outdo the others was perfect for his purposes. He added it to Abby's to-do list. Find the location and set up the next investor party.

He didn't want to wait too long. He'd already found a superb villa on the French Riviera—in one of his corporate names, of course—and his lifelong dream was about to come true. He was still two mil short of the asking price. Thirty-three million was just the start, he knew. He'd still need an operating fund. If he could clear ten at the Scottsdale party, it would set him up with household staff, gardeners, and pool cleaners—the life he'd always wanted.

One thing he'd learned from watching the Hollywood crowd—they didn't actually spend much of their own money. Once they were in, everything just flowed their way, gratis. Those ten-grand a night hotel rooms? Freebies, just so the hotel could claim famous guests. The private jets? On loan from a corporate mogul who loved dropping, "Oh yeah, Angelina flew with us last trip." Once Rob moved into that neighborhood, he'd be doing all the same things.

He grinned and drained the last of his scotch.

Chapter 10

Gracie carried dirty cereal bowls to the sink, giving them a quick swish of water and loading them into the dishwasher.

"Kids off to school?" Scott asked, walking up behind her.

"Yeah. We're going to keep this financial thing off their radar, aren't we?"

"That's my vote. Until we know what'll happen with your mother, we'd better just keep this to ourselves."

"Except for the Ladies. We agreed on that."

He grimaced. Agreement had come only after Gracie managed to blurt out the family secret in front of her friends.

"I'm sorry," she said, turning toward him and wrapping her arms around his waist. "It's just—"

"I know. You helped a couple of them with problems, now they want to help you. This club, or whatever you call yourselves, started as a scratch-each-other's-backs deal. Everyone helps everyone else."

"Yes, we do. And now it's our family's turn to be on the receiving end. You have to admit, we solved a couple of cases already when the law couldn't help. This time, I really believe if we just gather the evidence the law *will* be able to act."

He grumbled a little, looking around the room for his keys.

"Honey, don't be mad. Please. I'd do *anything* to get back in your good graces."

"*Anything?*" He crooked one eyebrow upward in the way that always made her smile.

Her hands worked their way downward. "Um, as long as we're done in an hour. I have a meeting."

He kissed the top of her head. "Well, sadly, I have a meeting sooner than that. I gotta get to the office."

They exchanged a promising kiss and he turned away to reach for his jacket.

"You're the best husband on the planet," she said. "My mother has even said so."

He rolled his eyes. "Just get her out of this jam as quick as you can, you and your friends."

An hour later Gracie was rolling up in front of Pen's spacious hilltop home, where Amber's Prius and Sandy's Mazda already sat in the circular driveway. The group had decided they could speak more openly and have use of a better internet connection here than in a public place. Pen had promised authentic English scones and tea.

Mary pulled up a few seconds behind Gracie, and they walked to the front door together. Through the beveled glass they'd been spotted. Amber opened the door and the scent of recent baking wafted out.

"All right, everyone," Pen announced. "You'll want to get your scones while they're warm. The teapot is just here—milk, sugar, lemon … however you like it."

Gracie admired the lovely china cups, wondering if they had been in Pen's family a long time. The five women took seats in the living room that overlooked a good portion of Maricopa County.

As usual, Sandy brought out a yellow pad of notes. "Okay, what's the latest news?" she asked.

Amber wiped crumbs from her mouth and raised her hand. "I called Intrepid Dog Pictures. Abby wasn't in, but the receptionist very kindly allowed me to leave a message on her voicemail."

"What did you say?" Gracie asked.

"I didn't actually plan to say anything. Her recorded message gave me the info I needed." She mimicked another voice. " 'You've reached Abby Singer's desk. Please leave a message. If it's urgent, speak to my assistant at extension 327.' "

"Abby Singer," Sandy said. "I wonder why that seems familiar."

Blank looks all around.

"Well, maybe it will come to me. Or maybe it's my overactive mind messing around with me."

"Anyway," Amber said, "the next thing I did was scout around on social media. Between Facebook and Instagram, I now know her favorite food—pizza—and her favorite Italian restaurant. There are also a couple bars where she likes to hang out. One seems like her after-work happy hour choice. The other is a hopping place on Saturday nights. Several times, she's posted pictures of Rob Williams there with her."

"So they're a thing?" Mary asked.

"Kind of looks that way."

"Not just friends with benefits?" Gracie asked.

"He's her boss," Pen pointed out. "Is it possible to be boss and friend? Sorry, I've been outside the office world too long and things have changed."

Pen and Sandy looked toward the younger members, but Gracie just shrugged and Mary rolled her eyes.

"So … we have an address for Intrepid Dog's office and we have some options for ways to meet up with Abby and ask some questions. Next decision is, who should make the trip to California?"

Gracie sighed. "I should probably go along. If nothing else, touch base with my mom and sister. Maybe I can learn more about their situation by being there in person. And on the more useful side of things, I do have experience rifling through files in search of juicy tidbits."

Sandy laughed. She and Gracie had gone through the office of the museum director, and nearly been caught at it, during their first case together.

"I don't suppose there's any chance of coming up with a reason to request copies of the contracts, or …" Pen's voice trailed off. "No, you're right. There's no way Rob Williams is going to willingly share information with us. What *was* I thinking?"

Sandy set down her teacup. "We'll see what we can learn from Abby. And I think Mary's the one for the job."

Mary sputtered. "I don't know …"

"I thought about suggesting Amber for this, but she's already had a conversation with Abby and the odds are too great she would remember. It's a little too coincidental for Amber to have *happened* to be at the meeting in Newport and then just drop into Abby's favorite bar in California. She needs to think she's talking to an absolute stranger if we hope to get her to confide anything. Plus, Mary, you're fit, hip, and appear younger. With the hair and the tan, you have the California look. You'll be a natural."

Mary blushed to the tips of her frosted, spiky hair. "Well, okay then."

"Fine," Pen said. "that's set. How soon shall I get your reservations?"

The group had fallen into the routine where Pen advanced money for expenses, being repaid from the proceeds of whatever they recovered. It seemed the most businesslike way to handle it, without the actual formality of forming a business for their endeavors.

"One of the bits I overheard, while Pen was receiving the hard-sell for her investment money, was that Rob was going out on a film location somewhere in Europe within a few days," Amber told them.

She picked up her phone and dialed the number for Intrepid Dog Pictures again. "Robert Williams, please. Amber, with Direct TV."

She listened for a few seconds.

"And when do you expect him back? Really, that long? No, no message. I'll just check back later." She turned to the group. "Sometimes, sounding like you're selling something is the best way. He's leaving town this afternoon and won't be returning for eight weeks."

All five ladies smiled. "While the cat's away …" Amber said, her dark eyes sparkling.

Chapter 11

Southwest flight 1613 touched down at LAX at precisely 2:41 p.m. Mary and Gracie retrieved their small carry-on bags and wheeled them to the rental car transport van. Paperwork done, they found their white Toyota in the lot.

"Do you want to touch base with your mom? Let her know we got here?"

Gracie ran her hands through her long hair. "Not yet. I can't handle her right now. Plus, she's out in Pasadena and the traffic will be horrid this time of day. Let's take care of business first, and maybe we'll have some answers before I have to face her questions."

Mary patted her friend's shoulder. "I get it." She programmed the GPS with the address of their hotel. Pen had made reservations for them just a few blocks from both the Intrepid Dog Pictures offices and the hangouts where Amber had determined Abby Singer liked to go.

"How do you want to work the meetup with our quarry?" Mary asked as she steered through traffic. "I can go by myself, but I sense that a drink would add to your 'happy' right now."

"No kidding. I'm—never mind." No reason to get into the tension at home as she was packing for the trip. "Yeah, I'm up for a drink. We can head straight to the bar, for all I care."

"You'll need to reprogram our little buddy then. I can't imagine taking my eyes off the road at the moment."

"This is fine. We'll go to the hotel, freshen up. Then we can locate the bar. Might be a good idea for us to walk in separately and not sit together. If Abby takes a seat at the bar, as Amber says she seems to do in her photos, you can try to sit next to her and with luck I'll get close enough to overhear. Or not. Let's play it by ear."

It was five-thirty when Mary walked into Zeb's, an office worker hangout with a modern exterior and a dim, noisy interior. Tables around the perimeter held groups of four and six, guys dressed in youthful corporate attire—jeans or slacks, jacket, white shirt unbuttoned at the top—women in fitted dresses with contrasting jackets and impossibly high heels. Seriously? They worked all day in those things?

She looked around, tagging herself as most likely the oldest person in the room. She lifted her chin and held her shoulders back. Everyone at the gym told her she looked twenty years younger than her actual forty-seven, and she was determined to pull it off here, as well. She spotted Abby sitting at the bar, dangling a beige-heeled shoe off the footrest of her barstool, chatting quietly with another young woman. Neither appeared to be scouting out the males. Abby laughed suddenly at something her friend had said, throwing her head back. Clearly, she wasn't on her first drink of the evening.

Mary stepped up to the bar behind Abby, smiling an apology to the man on the left whose elbow she had bumped. She glanced at Abby's glass. Some kind of whiskey, neat. She caught the bartender's eye and ordered a bourbon on the rocks. When it came, she made a small production of swirling the ice, clattering it in the glass a little more than necessary. When Abby turned to glance at the sound Mary spoke.

"Abby? Abby Singer? Oh my gosh, I'd forgotten you work in this neighborhood."

Abby turned her chair, staring with incomprehension.

"Sorry—last June? Crystal and Josh's wedding … we sat there laughing over that old couple dancing, so cute."
Be careful what you post on Facebook, especially with a comment like 'how wasted was I?'

"Yeah, yeah, the wedding." Abby was clearly searching her memory for the connection.

"Hey, I gotta go," said the friend. "Catch you later."

Mary deftly slid around to take the empty stool. "Mary Holbrook. We met over the shrimp on the buffet, and … well … Some party that was. So, anyway, I'm at Holmes-Barney now." She waved vaguely over her shoulder toward what could have been any office in any building in the area. "Are you still working with Rob Williams?"

"Yeah—actually, I am."

"It's going good? I remember you talking about how much you liked it, but I forget what you said you do there. All I know about him is that he's a pretty big-name producer, right? It must be amazing, you getting to hang around all those movie stars all the time."

Abby brightened a little, downed the rest of her drink

and ordered another. "It's okay. Yeah … and he's doing good. We're still a couple, I suppose."

"Oh, gosh, that sounds a little lukewarm."

Over Abby's shoulder, Mary saw Gracie approach the bar and order a glass of wine. She left it where the bartender set it and pulled out her phone. She was merrily texting away with her thumbs, and Mary flicked her attention back to Abby.

"It's getting that way," Abby muttered, taking a hefty slug of her new drink.

"Are we talking the job or the boyfriend?" Mary leaned in closer, speaking confidentially.

"Mostly Rob. I—shit. I think he's cheating on me. We just got back from this trip to Newport, and I really, really did think he planned to propose. I mean, it was this romantic place with a huge mansion and fantastic gardens where we did our presentation together. Any spot there would have been a perfect setting. And, we stayed at such a cute little guesthouse hotel nearby—*so* New England, with gingerbread trim and all. *That* would have been a perfect spot for a proposal. But, *no* … We finished the presentation that night, and he hustled me off to the airport in an Uber car, not even taking me himself. Said I needed to be back at the office in the morning, but then it really wasn't even anything that important." She downed another hefty gulp.

"God, Abby, that sounds rotten." Mary gently touched her arm.

"But then he gets in the next day and he's all lovey-dovey again. The office was mostly business as usual, but he sneaks me off to the art director's room, which has no one in it right now, and he wants to jump me right there on the desk. What's with that?"

"Woo—were there a lot of other people around? I

mean, that had to be kind of weird."

"Well, it's not a big office. The two of us and a couple of admin assistants. When we're in mid-production, I guess it gets more crazed. I've only been there two years, but Rob talks about back in the day, having screenwriters, storyboard artists, and a full crew working all hours, and how nuts it can be with location shoots and deadlines."

"So, nothing currently in production, I guess?"

"There's always something on the horizon, but nothing's going on right now."

Mary caught Gracie's glance for a fraction of a second. Abby's statement didn't sound at all like what had been presented to the investors, including both Janice and Pen.

Abby's glass was empty and she looked at it, considering another. Decided against it. "Look, it's been fun catching up, but I need to get going."

"Yeah, hey, good luck with the …" She pointed to her ring finger.

"Thanks." Abby slid off the stool and walked a little unsteadily toward the door, fumbling in her purse.

Gracie edged onto the empty seat and picked up her wine glass. "Hmm—interesting."

"We learned a few good facts. Such as, there won't be a lot of people around the office, and it doesn't sound as if there's any overtime happening at all. But our other intel is a little off. Amber said he was leaving town yesterday and wouldn't be back for awhile. Abby says he was there this morning. I wish I'd thought to ask if he was leaving again soon—maybe they both are. Or … I don't know … maybe he's skipping out for some time with someone else."

"When it comes to a showdown, Rob's own actions might be the best way to get Abby on our side," Gracie said.

"Were you here for the part where she talked about expecting a proposal and not getting it?"

"Oh yeah, got the whole thing right here." She held up her phone.

"I thought you were texting someone back home."

"Ha—taking notes, and adding a few impressions of my own." Gracie sipped her wine while Mary pulled over a basket of some kind of crackers that looked like straw and tasted like dust.

"So, what's our next step?" she asked, after working to chew one of the flavorless tidbits.

"Since I'm not super eager to have face time with my mother, let's go break into Rob Williams's offices." Gracie drained her wine and stood.

Chapter 12

Gracie brought up the address for Intrepid Dog Pictures on her phone's map. "It's about four blocks away. Maybe we should take the car."

Mary flexed her leg muscles and gave her a look.

"Well, in case we find something we want to take with us. We'd look pretty funny walking down the street with our arms full of file folders."

Another look.

"Okay, you're right. We're not out to burgle the place, just to gather information." They set out walking.

Six downtown California blocks turned out to be a lot shorter than what they were used to in Phoenix. A couple of blocks east of the bar, three blocks south—they were there in less than ten minutes. The neighborhood was noticeably lower-rent than what they'd passed through earlier, on their way to the bar, although Mary commented that probably nothing in the entire metro area was truly affordable.

The high-rise at 300 Cranberry Avenue lacked the sleek steel and glass façade of those farther west. It had a definite '60s look about it. The lobby doors were unlocked but no one sat at the desk. From the thin layer of dust, it appeared no security guard had manned it for some time. It was a little after six o'clock and the lobby had a hollow feel.

Gracie consulted a directory where white plastic letters stuck into a black velvet background spelled out the names and suite numbers of the tenants—two law offices, an architectural design firm, a copy shop, and a few with hyphenated names similar to the one Mary had invented for her conversation with Abby. Intrepid, Inc. occupied a suite on the second floor.

"I suppose this must be the corporate name for Intrepid Dog Pictures?" Gracie said with a shrug.

Mary pressed the elevator button. When the doors slid open, a man wearing khakis and a knit two-button shirt stepped out. His eyes were fixed on his phone and he didn't even bother with a nod toward the women. They kept an eye on him until he pushed his way out the front door. Surely, whoever was last to leave the building at night must need to lock up. But this one didn't.

"What's our plan if it turns out Rob Williams is actually at the office when we arrive?" Mary asked as the elevator whirred softly on the upward trip.

Gracie's eyes widened. "I don't know. I hadn't thought about that."

Suite 2-G was at the far end of the hall. Mary noted a lighted exit sign and a door marked as a stairway. Good to know—just in case.

Gracie was eyeing the plain wooden door, the basic lock, and the narrow window beside it with "Intrepid, Inc." lettered in black. A glance through the window showed a reception area, unoccupied, with a small lamp glowing softly on the credenza behind a secretarial desk. No hours were noted on the sign, but it appeared they had arrived after everyone had left for the day. Lucky. She pulled out a set of lock picks.

"Amber's really the whiz with these," she muttered as she fumbled the tiny torsion wrench into the lock and inserted the hook pick.

"You practiced with them at home, though, right?" Mary was keeping an eye on the hall and ears tuned to any little sound.

"I was able to get into my son's bedroom."

"Way simple."

"Well, and I did manage my own front door. Just keep watching, okay?"

She continued to fiddle with the tools, feeling the tumblers move slightly then slip back into place. She began to wonder if it wouldn't just be simpler to come back during business hours and talk their way in.

"Hurry up!" Mary hissed. "The elevator just went down to the lobby. Somebody's coming."

Gracie dropped the hook pick and had to start over, but this time she managed to get the pins to drop into place on the first try. The elevator dinged, one floor down, then started moving.

As she pressed the door handle down, the elevator doors slid open, not more than twenty feet away. Both women practically fell into the office. Gracie grabbed the door as it swung closed, barely stopping it from slamming. Mary ducked to the side of the window and craned her neck to get an angle on the view of the narrow hallway.

"I can't see a damn thing," she whispered.

They held their breath for a full minute.

"I think they went the other way," Mary said.

Gracie pressed the door to be certain it had latched, then turned the lock to secure themselves inside. "Whew!"

Eyes adjusting to the dim lighting from the night light, they surveyed the room. The receptionist's desk was a high-end Mayline, which Gracie recognized from reading lots of decorating magazines. The guest chairs she knew, also, carried high price tags, and a Surya rug wouldn't have come cheap. On the walls hung framed movie posters bearing titles neither of the ladies recognized; the thing the posters had in common was Robert Williams as producer.

"Looks like he really did attract some big-name talent," Gracie said, pointing out that every film boasted at least two or three A-listers.

Moving through a set of double doors, they walked into a foyer that branched off with a narrow hallway to the right, and a solid door to the left. A gold plaque with Robert S. Williams, Reliant Fox Productions, engraved on it announced that this was the executive office.

"Mmm?" Mary ran her finger over the unfamiliar production company name. "I wonder what that's about."

Gracie leaned close and whispered. "Let's make sure we're alone."

She gently twisted the knob on Williams's door. It was locked. Nodding the other direction, they tiptoed down the carpeted hallway. Four doors branched off it, one being a bathroom. The first office on the right was clearly Abby Singer's. Good furnishings, a brass nameplate facing the door. The desk was another Mayline, the chair a quality ergonomic model. A laptop computer sat in the center of the desk, closed now. A color laser printer stood on a separate stand, with reams of thick paper in a cream color. Beside the blank paper sat a stack of invitations and matching envelopes.

"Invites to the investor meeting," Gracie said, recognizing the style and content. "It's the one Pen and Amber just attended." She picked up one of the invitations and stuffed it into her purse. "They must produce these right here, from her laptop."

Mary had remained near the door, listening, edgy.

"Okay, on to the other rooms."

The next door down the hall must have been the one Abby referred to as the art director's office. It contained a drafting table, rolls of glossy paper, and a computer with a huge screen. Production for the posters they'd seen out front?

The remaining room seemed to be used only for storage. Three desks and an assortment of file cabinets were jammed into the space. None appeared to be in use; the file cabinet drawers were blocked by other pieces of furniture. If there was good stuff to be had, it must be either in Rob's or Abby's offices.

"You take hers," Gracie suggested. "I'll have to get past the lock on his."

"Okay, but make it quick. We already know someone else is in the building. I don't want to get caught in here."

Nothing like a no-pressure lock job, Gracie thought as she fiddled again with the picks. This lock was of better quality than the one on the outer door, and it resisted her efforts until she was about to scream. She heard footsteps behind her as the last of the tumblers fell into place.

"If there's really important stuff in Abby's office, it's on her computer," Mary said. "I wish I knew half of what

Amber does about hacking."

"We don't use that word," Gracie said, groaning as she straightened her knees. "We just think of it as Amber's talent for data sharing."

"Yeah, well, whatever. I'm not taking a rap for robbery by taking the computer with me."

Together, they walked into Rob Williams's office. The boss had clearly kept the best of the furnishings for his own space. Mahogany desk and credenza, cushy executive chair, an astounding Isfahan rug, and LeRoy Neiman prints. Unlike Abby's office, this one was immaculate— empty desktop polished to a high shine, no papers, printer, stapler, or any other signs of actual work being done. The desk held a phone, a leather blotter, and a Montblanc pen set that must have set him back five hundred dollars. The credenza was topped with framed photos of Rob standing next to various celebrities.

Gracie stopped staring and headed for the drawers. The quality lock on the office door obviously gave Rob confidence that his files would be safe. Except there were no files. She pulled open every drawer in the room. There were crystal glasses and top-shelf scotch in the credenza, a leather portfolio, assorted pens, and a shoebox-sized wooden box of business cards from other people.

"He must keep everything on his mobile or on a computer he takes home with him," she said.

"They say it's becoming a paperless society. Could be this guy is proof—"

Both heads snapped toward the door.

"What was that noise?" Gracie whispered.

"Someone's turning the doorknob at the hall. Shit! Did we lock it after ourselves?"

Not half a breath passed until the rattling sound

stopped. Mary stepped to Rob's partially open door and risked a peek at the oblique angle out to the reception area. She drew back quickly and eased the door space to a mere crack.

"Some guy in a khaki uniform staring in. I think it's a security guard. Or it could be the night janitor."

"Oh shit, oh shit, oh shit …" Gracie poised to dive into the knee space under the desk.

"Wait-wait." Mary signaled with her outstretched palm. "He's moving on."

She tiptoed, although the carpet masked footsteps well, toward the reception area. The uniformed man was whistling some kind of tune; she could hear it when she put her ear to the outer door. Then voices.

"You gonna be much longer?" the guard said to someone a few doors down. Mary couldn't hear the response, but the next from the guard was, "Okay, then, I'm ready to lock up."

She dashed back to Gracie. "We're about to get locked in for the night. Hurry up!"

Gracie grabbed the business cards from the wooden box and jammed them into her purse, shut the drawer, and remembered to twist the locking mechanism on the inner office before she rushed to join Mary at the door to the hall.

She reached for the handle, but Mary put out a hand to restrain her. "That other person is still in the building. I just heard the guard talking to him."

Gracie's eyes grew a bit frantic.

"Hold on." Mary eased the door open and peered down the hall. A door snicked firmly closed, a man sighed, the elevator dinged. "He's left. We gotta go—now!"

"How?"

"C'mon—the stairs."

They backed out of the Intrepid, Inc. office, keeping an eye on the elevator and hall. Luckily, the exit door to the stairway was unlocked. As quietly as possible, they descended to the ground floor and peeked into the lobby. The guard stood at the street door, keys in hand, waiting for the man who was taking his time strolling from the elevator.

"Keep smiling and keep going, no matter what," Mary said.

Hiking her purse strap onto her shoulder, Gracie turned to Mary and made a comment about the weather. They walked purposefully toward the guard at the door.

"Hey, where—?"

"Good night," Mary said. "Have a good one."

Chapter 13

Abby's silver Mercedes convertible was sitting in his driveway when Rob got home. Why had he bought her the toy? It seemed to make her cling to him more frantically. All he'd wanted was a piece of that great body; the car purchase came after one of their particularly lucrative investment meetings, at a moment he'd been feeling generous. No idea what had come over him *that* day.

He pulled in beside the Benz and summoned up a dazzler of a smile.

"I couldn't wait," she said, stepping around the front of her car, her fingers undoing the top button of her blouse. Desperation hung over her, almost as heavy as the perfume she'd liberally doused herself with.

He grabbed his computer case from the passenger seat and ushered her toward the front door. No point in letting the neighbors watch the dramatics. He unlocked the door and pocketed his key. Never again would he make the mistake he'd made once with a girlfriend who'd swiped the house key off his nightstand and had a copy made for herself. Abby wasn't likely to break in and smash all the photos of him with anyone other than herself, but you never knew.

"Want a drink?" he asked.

"Maybe just a mineral water—I had a couple at Zeb's already. I was hoping you'd drop by there and we might go grab some dinner."

"Sorry. I had other things." He poured Dewar's into a glass for himself and handed Abby her mineral water in its plastic bottle. "In fact, I can't really make an evening of it. Brought home too much work." And the flight attendant from Delta would be waiting at Ciro's in an hour's time. But he needed to tread lightly with Abby—she was still a vital part of the investor scheme.

He set his computer on the dining table and shed his jacket. "Look, I really just want to get a quick shower and settle back with the paperwork I brought home."

"If it's about setting up the next gala, I'd be glad to stay and help."

"No, it's not really any one specific project—just a bunch of little details that are hanging over me. Really."

"I'd be glad to stay long enough to help with the shower …" Her smile curved seductively.

"Abby, no." He reached out and took her shoulders, keeping her at arm's length. "Babe, it's not that I'm not interested. I just need a little down time. Look—stay long enough to finish your drink, but seriously, tonight you can't stay."

"*Down* time?" Her brows pulled together in the middle.

"As opposed to all the time you've been spending keeping it *up* recently? I saw that blonde intern giving you the eye in Newport, you know."

Play this cool. She's too valuable a business asset right now. "Hey, Abbs—you know you're the one. You're my right arm. We're a team. Nobody takes that away from us."

Her expression relaxed. "But you sent me home so suddenly."

"Because, if you'll remember, I needed you to handle the meeting with the Sundance people." *And if I actually had a film to enter in the festival, that meeting could have been important.* "Baby, you saw how eager I was, the minute I got back in the office."

He slid his hands from her shoulders to the curve of her waist and pulled her close, kissing the top of her head. She wrapped her arms around his waist and hugged. Crisis averted.

"Okay," he said, stepping back. "I'll see you in the morning at the office."

She picked up her mineral water from the table and raised the bottle. "If you really can't use some help tonight, okay then." She sipped the fizzy liquid, her eyes sliding toward his computer case on the table. Before he could reach out, she'd plucked a printed sheet of paper that was sticking out of the side pocket. "What's this?"

The real estate listing for my dream. Shit. "Oh, that? Just a potential location for one of the films." The seven-bedroom white villa was all angles and light, with an indoor pool, and hillside seclusion just outside Cannes. At thirty-three million dollars it was certainly priced right, and was close enough to afford him access to the famed film festival.

"Gorgeous! Wow—couldn't you just see us living in a

place like that some day?"

Me, yes. Us? No way I'm getting tied down. "Well, it's pretty far away. You'd miss your sister if you had to spend much time in the south of France."

"Well, hey, at least if we use it as a location, we get to stay there awhile, right?"

"Um, maybe. We'll see how it works out."

Again, the brows pulled together.

He sighed. "What I meant to say was, absolutely. You bet. When we film there it'll be the grand adventure of our lives."

"Okay, now you're just teasing. You've told me how it is on location—living in RVs, dusty towns that don't even have internet half the time, local food that sucks. But, surely in France ..."

"Good point. France will have everything we could possibly want." Was she *ever* going to finish the damn mineral water and *go*? He resisted looking at his watch, but the numerals on the microwave beyond the kitchen island told him he now had forty-five minutes to get to his dinner date.

At last, Abby drained the small bottle and set it on his dining table. She took another fond look at the French villa, but at least she handed the page back when he held out his hand. He walked her to the door, kissed her with gusto. The way she kissed back made him almost wish he'd not made other plans tonight. They could have had a good time staying in. He could still ... Who was the flight attendant, after all?

Abby was watching his face closely. He put on the appropriate regretful look and opened the door.

"See you at the office tomorrow. Be ready to fill me in on the venue choices for Scottsdale, okay?"

She shook her head. "I swear, you really do eat, sleep, and breathe business."

"That, I do." He closed the door before she'd quite left the porch, but he heard her car start up a minute later.

As he dashed for the shower, it began to nag at him that Abby was getting too close. Now she knew about the villa. If she put it together—the amount of money they were raking in, the way he kept his expenses cut to the bone, the fact she'd never actually seen him begin production on a movie in the two years she'd been with him … It was about time to get rid of her.

Chapter 14

"It was all I could do not to run the minute we hit the sidewalk," Gracie said, panting, when they reached their rental car. As it was, they had speed walked, glancing over their shoulders the first two blocks.

"I need to get you into the gym more often." Mary fluffed her spiky hair to catch the breeze. Otherwise, she hadn't sweated a drop.

They slid into the car, putting their thoughts together. Mary spoke first. "Did you get the idea that Intrepid Dog Pictures has downsized—bigtime? All that expensive furniture and art but, shall we say, borderline dumpy office suite."

"I thought so. And what's with the other company name on the window? Reliant Fox Productions. Reliant on what—their money donors?" Gracie was rummaging in her bag and came out with the fistful of business cards she'd snatched from the box in Rob's office. "I wonder if these will tell us anything."

Mary craned her neck sideways for a better look. "They seem to be from a whole variety of people. Look, there's a building contractor, here's a CEO of some satellite TV company ... and what's a venture capitalist, anyway?"

Gracie tried to stack the cards, but they became unwieldy and a few flew loose and went between the bucket seats.

"Careful, we don't want to lose any until we can figure out what they mean," Mary said, reaching for the strays.

"Right. We can go through these in our room tonight." Gracie stuffed the cards back into her purse. "For now, we still have the whole evening. If Amber's come up with his address, I say we go check him out. We can surely come up with a good cover story."

Mary was one step ahead, already dialing their youngest cohort.

"Oh yeah, found it easy-peasy," Amber said. "It's scary what information those mapping apps have on us." She rattled off an address in nearby Inglewood. Gracie wrote it down, but Mary was already entering it into their GPS.

Together, they gave Amber the rundown on what they'd discovered so far, and she promised to search for background information on the second company name.

Mary started the car and let the GPS, which they had affectionately named Birdy, talk her through the turns. On the map the distance seemed like nothing at all, but rush hour was still in full swing, and the drive took nearly forty-five minutes. When Birdy told them the destination was two hundred feet ahead on the right, Mary slowed and they both stared toward the house.

Small Spanish colonial with tan stucco and red-tiled roof, a driveway running down the west side to what looked like a detached garage, a small square of lawn out front and two small flowering shrubs against the covered front porch. No lights on inside, no vehicle in the driveway.

"Doesn't look like much, especially for some fancy movie producer," Gracie said.

Mary snorted. "Probably built fifty years ago for ten grand and sells for a million today."

"Seriously?"

"Well, you know how crazy this market is. Your mother lives here."

Gracie nodded. Unfortunately, real estate woes had hit way too close.

"Anyway," Mary said, "it doesn't look like anyone's home. Might give us a chance for a look around."

"And if Robert Williams really is here, I plan to confront him about my mother's investment. Demand that he hand over what he promised she would earn."

"Yeah, well … let's just go see." Mary had driven past the house and parked three doors down.

Personally, she didn't think Rob would be there, but it also wouldn't do to have him come driving up, spot their car, and be prepared to catch intruders in his house. She noticed the other houses on the block showed signs of life—cars, lights, sounds of television coming from behind closed curtains. No one was out and about, so it seemed as good a time as any to do this.

Gracie was out and halfway up the sidewalk before Mary had locked the car and caught up. "I say we try the honest approach first—I mean, he could just be a guy who actually has room in the garage for his car and likes to sit in the dark watching TV."

She walked to the front door and rang the bell. No response but the echo of the chime. She began to dig into her purse for the lock picks.

"Getting pretty confident with those, aren't you?" Mary teased. "But maybe we'd better check out the back first. What if he's out on the patio firing up the grill?"

"Okay. And it might be better if some dog walker didn't spot me down on my knees at the front door."

They put on a little show of disappointment that no one had answered, then walked down the long drive toward the garage. No sign of backyard activity on the plain concrete slab, where a single scrawny palm tree in the back corner provided the only landscaping. The back door had a wrought iron gate over it, as did all the windows. Great neighborhood, Mary thought.

"So, I guess it's the front door, after all," Gracie whispered.

"I could suggest we wait until he comes home and just get ourselves invited inside," Mary said, "but that kind of defeats our purpose of coming up with copies of contracts and proof that he's cheating people. He's hardly likely to hand over any of it willingly."

Gracie was already working on the front door lock. "Probably could have done this one with a credit card. I'm not sure I've ever seen such a cheap lock. Doesn't the guy do anything to keep up his home?"

"Probably a rental."

They stepped into a living room that felt crowded with a sectional sofa, coffee table, and widescreen TV. The latter sat in front of a fireplace, which clearly didn't work. Along the mantle sat more photos of Rob and his celebrity chums. A niche to the right held a dining table and two chairs, and past that was a kitchen with '80s-era appliances.

All this was visible only because of a streetlamp that shone through the open blinds.

Gracie edged her way through the living room, peering through a blocky hall that revealed two bedrooms and a bath. One bedroom held packing boxes, stacked nearly to the ceiling; in the other a king-sized bed took up nearly every inch of the space. This looked like a starter home for a young family, not the digs of an important producer. More than ever, she wondered what Rob Williams's real story was.

"There's a computer," Mary whispered from the dining area. "Should we take it?"

"No!" Gracie stubbed her toe on a hidden leg of the sofa as she hurried toward her friend. "I mean, at this point we haven't actually done anything wrong—"

"If you don't count breaking and entering."

"We've only looked for information. We haven't stolen anything."

"But *he* has! He's taken a whole bunch of money under false pretenses."

Gracie laid a hand on Mary's arm. "And … the law will deal with him, eventually. What we need is to find evidence. We'll take the evidence to the law, and it will turn out all right."

Mary gave her a skeptical look. "You saw how that worked out in my case. Remember?"

Gracie twitched. "Let's just see if we can find some records or something. I brought a flash drive to copy stuff."

She unzipped the computer bag and slid the laptop onto the dining table. Facing the screen away from any windows, she pressed the power switch and the screen lit.

"Well, great, it needs a password."

"Not surprised."

"Call Amber—she knows how to get into these things."

Mary pulled out her phone again and got Amber on the first ring.

"Why am I not surprised to hear from you two again so soon?" she joked. "Did it turn out to be the right address?"

Gracie and Mary exchanged a glance. What if they'd broken into the wrong house? But no—there were the photos on the mantle. Gracie began to giggle. Mary held out a hand to shush her.

"The computer needs a password," Mary told Amber. "Can you get us into it?"

"How much time do you have? I'll need an internet connection and some protocol numbers. If you haven't gotten past booting it up, it's not a quick process."

"Can we copy anything onto a flash drive without logging in first?"

"If you could see my face, you'd know I'm rolling my eyes right now. No. You can't just plug a flash drive into any computer. You have to get logged on and then find the files."

"I suppose I knew that," Mary grumbled. "Just grabbing at straws here."

Gracie tapped her on the shoulder. "Look." She held up some printed pages. "They were in the computer case and they look similar to the contract Pen got hold of."

Amber was talking again. "There's one thing I might try remotely ... let me see ..."

Gracie pulled another sheet of paper from the case, a photo of a huge house. She held it toward the window to read the details, but couldn't see well enough.

All at once, lights beamed across the living room window and shone into the dining room. A car had pulled into the driveway. The photo dropped to the floor.

"Mary—look!" Gracie frantically gestured toward the sleek SUV less than twenty feet away.

"Amber—gotta go!" Mary clicked off the call, pocketed the phone, and slammed the computer's lid down.

"It's Rob," Gracie said. "He's got someone with him."

The producer's face showed clearly in the Land Rover's overhead light. They recognized the dark hair and neat goatee. He got out and walked around to the passenger side, opening the door to a tall blonde with curls that flowed to her waist. Definitely not Abby Singer. Both were laughing and looking only at each other.

"Which way are they going?" Gracie's head whipped left and right as she weighed the options—front door or back.

"They're heading to the front," Mary whispered.

"Come on, the kitchen door's this way." Gracie grabbed the handful of papers she'd taken from the computer bag and headed through the small galley kitchen.

The back door swung open, revealing the inside of the locked, wrought iron security door.

Chapter 15

Birdy calmly guided the rental car back to the Seaside Inn, luckily, because Mary's hands didn't stop shaking until they were safely in their room with the door locked.

"I need a drink," she told Gracie. "What's in the minibar?"

"Those things are *so expen*—"

"I don't care. Two narrow escapes in one evening has earned me a bourbon and Coke."

Gracie went for ice while Mary raided the stash. With two fourteen-dollar cocktails poured, she reached for a teensy can of peanuts.

"Don't. That's where I draw the line. Look at the price list. That quarter-cup of nuts will set you back another thirty. Let's get a pizza delivered—at least it will fill up both of us." Gracie kicked off her shoes and made the call.

"Oh my god, can you believe what we just did? I'm definitely getting too old for this," Mary said. She was finally able to laugh about the escapade.

"That iron door … I was about to throw myself against it."

"Good thing I noticed the little twist lock. I saved you from a row of bruises in the morning."

"I wonder if he'll notice it's not locked. Or, what if he touches the computer and it's still warm? He'll know someone broke in."

"I have a feeling the warm thing he'll be touching right now isn't his computer."

They both screamed with laughter and almost missed the knock of the pizza guy at the door. They settled with slices, conversation waning until they'd each put away two.

"Seriously, he'll know. Look at all the papers I came away with." Gracie nodded toward the pages she'd dropped on one of the beds.

"Maybe he'll be so hung over, his head filled with memories of his date, that he will have completely forgotten which papers he brought home."

"Let's hope." Gracie wiped pepperoni grease off her mouth with a napkin. "Anyway, we should go through our bounty and put it together so we can report to the team."

Mary became pensive. "You know what the sad thing is … Abby was right about Rob cheating on her. She really pinned her hopes on that guy."

"As did a lot of people. And we're going to figure out how to sic the law on him."

Gracie dumped the contents of her purse, gathering all the business cards she had taken from Rob's office, stacking them neatly. Sitting cross-legged on her bed, she began to look carefully at the papers from his computer bag. There were four of the two-page contracts in the same format Pen had showed them. Long on promises, absent any sort of guarantees. Mary had picked up the business cards; she now sat on the room's other bed, sorting and then laying them out in rows in front of her.

"I really wish we'd been able to see what he has on his computer," Gracie said after reading one of the contracts in detail and skimming the rest. "Surely, he has more data than he gives here. I mean, what about the contracts between the actors and his company? Those must be fairly hefty documents—and maybe that's why he doesn't print them out. For his sake, he'd better keep good backups of the computer ..." She looked up at Mary. "Why didn't I think of it? Rather than trying to get into the computer, we should have been looking for backup drives—an external hard drive, flash drives, memory sticks. Right?"

"Are you seriously thinking of going back?" Mary's face was screwed up into a frown as she continued to stare at the cards in front of her.

"Well ... I don't know."

"Take a look at this," Mary said, picking up a card and flinging it across the space between them to land at the edge of Gracie's bed.

Gracie picked it up. "Roger G. Middleton, OB-GYN. Middleton Obstetrics, LLP. Obviously, not Rob's personal physician."

"Turn the card over. See the little numbers written on the back?"

Gracie squinted. "Very small, lower right corner ... 450. So?"

"So, every one of these cards has a number. The smallest three-digit one I've found is 100, the largest 970. Some are in a different format. This one, for instance, is 1.2

and the card comes from a Las Vegas building contractor. I recognize the firm from my old days in the plumbing business. It's a huge company with multi-million dollar casino jobs."

"The numbers represent money?"

Mary nodded slowly. "I'm starting to think so. And I think I have a way to find out. Is it too late to call someone?"

They decided it wasn't, and Mary dialed the cell number shown on the card she was holding. It rang twice and a man answered. "Gil? Hi, it's Mary Holbrook, Holbrook Plumbing Supply in Phoenix."

"Mary—well, it's been a long time. Everything going okay?"

They exchanged a minute or so of small talk before Mary got down to the real question. "Say, Gil, I've been contacted regarding an unusual investment, which I'm seriously considering, and your name was given as a reference as another investor in the same opportunity. Well, this is really outside my expertise, so I thought I'd give a call, you know, just check it out."

"What's that?"

"It's a movie deal, the company is Intrepid Dog Pictures—or it might have been called Reliant Fox Productions. Producer's name is Robert Williams. A friend just got back from a presentation Williams did, talking about what a great investment this would be, and we were told you'd invested something like 1.2 in it?"

A long pause. The sound of something whiskery scraping against the phone. "Well, yeah. Actually, that's right. I'm just, uh, just surprised they shared names and numbers. Not real pleased about that, actually."

"Oh. Well, really, I don't want to get anyone in trouble. I'm afraid I did a little name-dropping here and there, just to see if anyone I knew was already invested. I'm sorry if it's something that's none of my business." *Like hell. I now know you got involved.*

"Well, it's not your fault, Mary. And it's okay. We did business for a lot of years and I trust you."

"If it's not too forward of me ... and don't give numbers if you don't want to ... I completely understand. I'm just curious whether you're happy with the return on the money you invested. I mean, I don't have anything close to that, myself."

Another pause. "Hmm, well, at this moment I can't really say either way. I haven't received my royalty check yet, but it really isn't due until early next year. That's the way my contract was structured."

Mary thanked him and hung up. She related the parts Gracie hadn't been able to hear.

"Same story my mom was told. Promises of payments always seemed to be out in the future somewhere." She brought out her phone and opened the calculator function. "Read me the numbers from the cards."

Mary read out numbers and Gracie added them up.

"More than twenty million dollars. And we haven't yet found anyone who has received a nickel back on the investment. This looks like evidence we can turn over to the law. We need to share it with the group and decide our next moves."

Chapter 16

Amber pulled onto the elegantly curved driveway, swinging her Prius around in an arc so the passenger door aligned perfectly with Pen's front door. She'd sent Pen a text an hour ago: **Exciting news!** They'd concocted a plan to track down the one person who might be able to shed light on the exact investment returns from Rob Williams's company.

Pen appeared at the door, dressed in flattering autumn tan slacks and a matching tunic with a lively patterned scarf draped over her shoulders. Amber looked at her own leggings and t-shirt, hoping—belatedly—that she wasn't out of her depth. Pen joined her in the car and complimented Amber on the way she'd pulled her curly hair into a topknot.

"Sorry I'm so casual, Pen. I was at exercise class when

I got the message with the address."

"Fill me in."

"So, anyway—you know I've been on the trail of Maisie Brown since we got back from Newport."

"Yes. After she sat there at our table and fairly glowed with tales of the fantastic returns she'd received on her investment …"

"And I thought your idea of finding her and asking her to corroborate that with some actual proof was really smart. I remembered at some point during the dinner she said she also lived in Arizona, and while that isn't much info it did give me a good start. Plus, the fact that hers is a somewhat unusual name."

"And you found her?"

"Yeah, I think I mentioned in a message yesterday that I'd located *a* Maisie Brown on Facebook. People can choose whether to reveal where they live, their birthdate, and such. This one shows herself living in Arizona, but not what city. This week, she posted a photo of The Breakers and said she'd just returned from Newport. She's our gal, for sure."

"But her address? There are times when I miss the old days of the telephone directory."

Amber had started the car. "Well, there are better ways now. I started prowling further to find out where she lives, and I came up with an address in Flagstaff. So, if you're up for a drive …"

"I adore Flagstaff—absolutely, let's go!"

Within ten minutes, they were on the 101 Loop, heading toward I-17 north.

"How do we know Maisie will be there when we arrive?" Pen asked, after the question had nagged her for a few minutes.

"Well, I set that up quite nicely, I think." Amber flashed her pretty smile toward her companion. "I called, pretending to have a florist's delivery, and asked if she would be home after noon."

"That's brilliant. I'm so pleased to be associated with great minds like yours."

"Um, well, we'll see. At least we know where we're going and are pretty certain she'll greet us with a smile." Amber concentrated on merging with the heavier traffic on the interstate, then settled back once they cleared the busier exits for Carefree, Cave Creek, and Anthem.

"So, I assume we'll stop off somewhere and pick up a decent little bouquet and talk our way into her house. Do we have a plan beyond that?" Pen asked.

"I'll admit I haven't got quite that far. Could we pretend this is one of your novels and you'll tell me how your characters would decide what to do next?"

"Oh dear. Well, let's see." Pen lifted her sunglasses and rubbed an itchy spot on her nose. Glasses back in place, she said, "What would be wrong with something close to the truth? She'll remember us from the dinner, so there's not much way to claim we're someone else. I could say I was so inspired by her success in the movie investment that I'm considering putting in even more money. But I'm also cautious, so would she mind sharing some data—at least give me an idea of the percentage she earned."

"It would be great if we could get her to show us statements she received with the earnings."

"Yes. I like that idea," Pen said.

They lapsed into silence, each formulating her thoughts on what to say once they cornered their witness. The road began to climb, taking them out of saguaro country and into areas of high-desert vegetation, and finally to mountainous terrain and tall ponderosa pines. Amber exited and spotted a florist.

"We still want to use the flower delivery approach?" she asked as she cruised toward the parking area.

"Why not? Every woman loves to get flowers, and maybe a gift will make her more receptive to our questions." Pen hopped out and went inside, spotting several nice autumn arrangements in the display case. She sprang for a decent-sized one, hoping to impress, and carried it back to the car.

"I think we're set. How's our timing?"

"Perfect," Amber said, pulling onto the main street again. "It's 12:15."

They rolled up in front of a complex of townhomes that sat on a gently sloping hill, fairly new, by the look of the immature landscaping. At a guess, they might have been built a year or two earlier. The chalet-style buildings were clad in wood siding in shades of tan and brown with dark brown trim. Very pseudo-Swiss. The complex backed up to ponderosa forest, giving residents the automatic feeling of being in the midst of nature, while the front yards contained pine and aspen saplings and a variety of native plants that would do well through the snowy winters and moderately warm summers.

Maisie Brown's unit was in the third building, and the driveway in front of her address held a white compact Chevy. The neighborhood and the vehicle didn't exactly scream *wealth*, but oftentimes it was the quiet ones who hid it best. They parked out front and walked up a set of flagstone steps that curved up the slight hill.

The Maisie Brown who answered the door bore little resemblance to the one from the party. Outside the glittering setting, and minus the designer dress, she looked like any other American housewife. Her face registered surprise when she opened the door; clearly, she didn't immediately remember the women.

"Oh! I thought the delivery might be from Carter's Flowers. You aren't …"

"Hello, Maisie. No, we aren't actually from a shop. We met you recently at the dinner in Newport and wanted to bring this little gift, hoping for the chance to visit a bit more." Pen extended the bouquet, just slightly out of Maisie's reach.

What was the woman to do? She couldn't very well grab the flowers and refuse to speak with her guests. She seemed a little confused, but accepted the gift and stepped back to let them in.

Amber, who had sat closest to Maisie, spoke first to break the ice. "I guess I look like a slob compared to what you saw me wearing before. The difference between a fancy dress-up occasion and everyday clothes, huh." She laughed and Maisie did a halfhearted chuckle.

"The flowers are beautiful," she said. "Is there an occasion?"

She walked them through a wide foyer to a spacious living room decorated in white and beige, with accents of darker brown and orange. Pen's choice of flower arrangement couldn't have been a better fit. Maisie set the vase on the coffee table. Pen and Amber exchanged a glance. Now they were here, it was a little harder to know exactly how to begin.

Pen finally took the leap. "Actually, I did want to visit a bit more on the same subject we talked about the other night—Intrepid Dog Pictures and the investment opportunity."

"I've, um, gone the max I can do," Maisie said. "So, I

hope you didn't waste a trip."

She thinks we're with Rob Williams. Amber's eyes spoke silently to Pen.

"Oh, no," Pen said. "I'm merely another investor, like yourself. I put some money into the new film when we were in Newport, and I'm seriously considering a bit more. A larger investment, I mean. So, I wonder if I could get more information from you?"

Maisie shifted from one foot to the other. She hadn't yet invited them to sit.

"What Pen is asking," Amber said, "is not so much any specifics about the amounts you put in or anything. That's strictly your business. As her, um, accountant, I've suggested she compare the ROI—the return on investment—between this opportunity and a few others she has been considering."

Pen's eyes widened a touch, but she played along.

"Yes, Ms. Zeckis is very astute with numbers, so I trust her opinions. She does such a wonderful job of looking out for me. Anyway, we're wondering—checking, really— to see if these movie production investments would pay as well as, say, stock in Apple or Microsoft. Can you share some basic information with us?"

"At the gala dinner, you indicated you'd been very happy with the results," Amber said. "We're just wondering the extent of the returns—are we talking double-digit gains? Triple digit?"

Maisie's hands were fidgeting now. "Maybe we'd best all sit down."

She indicated the sofa for Pen and Amber, taking an armchair near the doorway for herself. The better to escape if punches began to fly?

"I don't know what to tell you ladies. I'm not very

good with financial statements. My Bernie used to handle everything, but he's gone two years now. Heart failure. I've had to do everything on my own. I downsized from our huge old house to this townhouse, and I love it here, really. But when it comes to brokerage statements, bank accounts, CDs, and investments, I just look at the statements and file them away."

"Would you be willing to show me your statements from Intrepid Dog Pictures?" Pen asked as gently as possible.

"There aren't any. I've never received a thing."

"No statements?"

"Nothing." Her face crumpled. "Not a red cent."

"But you said—"

"I know. I feel so bad about that. I got a call from Mr. Williams's office about a month ago, apologizing that royalty payments had been delayed. To make up for it, the lady said they would add fifty-percent to my current royalty balance if I would attend the party and talk to new investors. I didn't even have to make up anything, just tell them how much was coming to me. She named a figure that floored me. Said that much was in my royalty account, and that it was growing every day."

"Did she send you any proof of this?"

"Well, not really, but she gave the figure down to the penny. She was reading it off a printed statement, I'm sure." Maisie was now wringing her hands. "They bought my plane ticket and even had that elegant dress and all the jewelry ready to loan me when I got there. A free trip, a fancy dinner, and all I had to do was repeat what she'd told me about my own investment. Was I dumb to do it?"

"You couldn't have known," Pen said quietly. "Do you think there were others in the audience who were asked to do the same thing?"

"I know there were. We were assigned a dressing room there in the mansion where we chose our fancy clothing from a selection. They set it up where there weren't more than one or two women in there at a time. We couldn't really converse because we were each sent by those escorts to separate tables. I didn't think much of it at the time, but it's been bothering me ever since." Her eyes welled up. "I feel so stupid."

Amber left the sofa and crossed to Maisie's side. "You're not stupid. A lot of people were fooled. We have reason to suspect Rob Williams has been doing this awhile and that he's not using the money to make movies. We think he's stealing it."

"What!—you mean my money's gone forever?" Her jaw had gone slack.

"We don't know. It's why we're trying to find written evidence of the promises they've made or statements to prove they've actually paid out some dividends. If we can get such evidence, we'll compile it and present it to the police in California. With luck, maybe they'll prosecute and get the money back. It's happened with other investment swindles, maybe it will work for us, too."

"Could you? Get my money back? I'm a widow on a pension. I gave him nearly all my spare cash. I'd be so grateful."

"Honestly, we don't know how it will turn out," Pen said, standing up. "We can only work on it, but we will certainly let you know if the money can be recovered."

Tears had tracked through the powder on Maisie's face, and Amber felt her heart go out to the woman. They hugged her and left, exchanging phone numbers so they could keep her posted on their progress.

Out in the Prius, Amber turned to Pen. "I get the feeling this scam is huge. How many other seniors are out there in exactly Maisie's position?"

"I have no idea, but it's frightening."

Chapter 17

I wish I'd taken one of the computers," Gracie said. "These business cards feel like only the tip of the iceberg."

"I'm not sure we should take a chance on breaking in again," Mary told her. "When it comes to getting caught, I have a feeling the third time's the charm."

The two were having breakfast the morning after a restless night. Discovering a number of Rob Williams's likely victims had nixed the possibility of quieting either of their minds enough to sleep.

"I suppose while I'm here in California, it's the time to see my mom and get this discussion out in the open. I sense something like panic in her phone calls."

"When do you want to go?"

"Never. Later this morning? She lives in Pasadena—

we'll need to let the morning rush traffic die down." Gracie couldn't conceal the trepidation on her face. "After more coffee—lots more coffee."

* * *

The modern ranch style home draped itself along a hillside, with native plantings and mature palm trees flanking a wide driveway. Janice Weaver greeted them at the oversized front door, wearing a flamboyant caftan in brilliant rainbow colors, a glass with some kind of clear amber liquid in one hand. Mary immediately saw where Gracie had gotten her dark hair, high cheekbones, and perfectly tilted nose. But where Gracie's smile was open, almost naïve at times, Janice's mouth formed an impatient pout, reddened by lipstick seeping into surrounding lip lines.

"Well, come in," she said. "I was wondering if you'd get out here to see me."

"Hi, Mom." Gracie endured a perfunctory hug, then introduced Mary.

"Scott told me you'd come to California. But that was two days ago."

"We're actually here on a little business," Mary said, as Janice led them through a spacious den and outside through an open sliding door. Below the patio, steps went down to a kidney-shaped swimming pool that glowed with turquoise sparkle in the late-morning light.

"Yes, Mom, we're investigating that movie producer who took your money—our money." Gracie flopped down in one of the cushioned chairs that surrounded a glass-topped table.

"And? Am I getting my royalties, like he promised?"

"Well … it doesn't appear that way yet. We're working on it, but it looks like the police may have to get involved."

"Oh, geez. You can't be serious. If this has to go to court, it could take forever." Janice set her beverage on the table with a clatter, turning to pluck dead blossoms from an exuberant petunia in a nearby pot.

"Yes, Mom, it might." Gracie sent an apologetic shrug toward Mary while Janice's back was turned.

"Well, I don't know what I'm going to do," Janice said. "If they come in here trying to kick me out of my own home …"

"Mother, I don't really think—" The voice startled Mary. A younger, mousier version of Gracie had stepped out to the patio.

"Hannah!" Gracie got up and gave her sister a hug.

Mary sized them up. The older, confident sister who'd escaped their mother and forged a new life. And the faded version with mousy brown hair, no makeup, and a pale lavender sack-like cotton dress, which did nothing to enhance her figure. For the first time, she noticed two toddlers clinging to Hannah's skirt.

Janice spoke up. "I haven't offered you girls anything— can I get you a drink? It's nearly noon, if that counts for something. Hannah's got some homemade juices and herbal teas in the kitchen, if that's more your style."

"I'd love a glass of water," Mary said, curious to see which of the women would go inside to get it. With Hannah tied down on both sides, Janice bustled into the kitchen.

Gracie glanced toward the door and turned to her sister. "So, how is it *really* going?"

Hannah took a seat and herded her little ones onto her lap. "Sorry, the kids are a bit insecure. Not used to being here yet, and J-a-y isn't helping the situation. Totally incommunicado. Mother, well, she's … she's Mother."

"And moneywise?"

"Well, we're not starving and as far as I know the electric bill's being paid. We'll see what happens when the divorce is final, but there won't be much left for me to get a place for the three of us. We lived right up to the limit on credit cards every month." Hannah glanced toward Mary and smiled. "I'm so sorry. You don't want to get dragged into all that."

"Not a problem. A year ago, I was in worse shape than this. By far." Mary looked around at the lush garden and swimming pool, a far cry from the homeless shelter she'd been living in when she met Gracie and her friends.

"Really? You seem so … *together*. I hope …" Hannah sighed.

Janice came back outside, carrying a tray with two glasses of iced water, lemon slices floating in them. "I asked Maria to make some lunch for us. She does a wonderful chicken salad."

Mary saw the incredulous look pass over Gracie's face. Her mother couldn't be in horrible financial straits if she still had her housekeeper. Family dynamics were interesting, she decided as she observed Gracie's family over lunch. Topics skipped around from old friends—Janice seemed to think Gracie would remember all of her mother's old country club crowd—to the upcoming holidays. Wasn't it hard to believe Thanksgiving would be here in less than three weeks, and wasn't the weather still beautiful for this late in the year?

No one mentioned the elephant in the room, the possible financial downfall of all three women. Mary wondered if that was because of her presence, but the more she observed the interaction—especially between Gracie and her mother—the more she decided they were a group that didn't talk about the bad stuff until it was down upon them.

Janice was right. Maria's chicken salad was wonderful, with dried cranberries and walnuts and a touch of something in the dressing—curry maybe? But the minute the plates were cleared, it became evident that Gracie couldn't wait to get away.

Out in the car again, Mary retraced the route toward their hotel.

"You see what I mean? About my mother," Gracie said. "One minute she's whining about how the sky is falling … and then she entertains as if there's not a care in the world. I don't have any idea of her true financial picture."

"But she came to you and Scott for money. It's got to be worse than she lets on."

"Yeah." Gracie's voice cracked. "That's what I'm afraid of."

Chapter 18

Rob sailed into the office, buoyed by what he thought of as *a night of wonder*. His date had gone far better than he'd dreamed, and the woman—Cyndi, which he remembered only because she'd pointed out the unusual spelling—regularly flew in and out of LAX. She'd promised to call him the next time she overnighted here.

"Morning, Rob," greeted his receptionist. Cute girl—all the women in Rob's life were great looking. They had to be. But this one had the brain God gave a sparrow, which he'd realized the first time she messed up the simplest of filing tasks and it took him days to find some important paperwork. Maybe it was time to clean house around here. He rolled past, flashing a quick smile, and unlocked the door to his executive office.

Thoughts about Abby intruded. He'd been pissed and

ready to get rid of her, too, last night when she'd showed up at his door, hinting at staying. That situation was a bit more touchy. As his right hand for the last two years, Abby knew a lot. Most importantly, she knew how Rob thought and what he expected in the business. It would take a long time to train someone else to handle all the little steps it took to put together these investor meetings.

But he was tired of the way she inserted herself into his private time. Sleeping with her had been a mistake. At first, the sex was fantastic, but recently her moves had become repetitive and those once-enticing little moans just grated on his nerves now. How was he going to handle this?

Thinking of the devil … She walked into his office without even tapping at the door.

"Good *morning*, handsome." The sing-songy greeting every day was another thing that was bugging him nowadays.

"Hey Abbs." He shoved the photo of the villa into a drawer and closed it casually.

"You look well rested. Looks like it was a good idea to stay home last night."

If only you knew.

"You have time to go over the Arizona venue ideas?" She had a folder in hand and started to take a seat across the desk from him before he answered.

What if I didn't? But before he could invent some excuse that would keep him in control of the meeting, she'd opened the folder and spread out several printed pages. *Oh, what the hell.*

"We could go with the Royale." She pointed at a swath of lush green lawn leading up to a pale stucco building with impressive archways and red-tile accents. "Or there's the Biltmore or the Grande Palms. They're all five-star properties, even though none has the historic factor we found at The Breakers."

"Great research," he said, admitting even to himself just how good she was at this. "Let me look them over and I'll let you know which one to book."

She pushed the folder toward him and glanced at the half-open doorway. By the look in her eye, he knew exactly what she was thinking. Little make-out sessions in the office had become one of the perks of her working here. She glanced toward the knee space under the desk.

"Babe, wow. I'd love to, but I've got a call from Paramount coming in any minute now."

"Ooh, it could be fun to watch you keep a straight face and talk to the guy while I'm giving you—"

"No! I mean, no, really … I can't." *After six o'clock this morning, I* actually *can't.* "It's an important call, plus you're busy today, too."

She pouted but there was a smile beneath it. She still had plans, he could tell.

"Close the door on your way out."

She flashed him a resentful stare but he was still the boss, and she knew the importance of contact with the major studios.

Okay, how was he going to cover this? He wanted some time to himself. He needed a nap, but that wasn't going to happen as long as Abby was here and felt it her right to walk into his office anytime she chose.

He picked up his cell phone and dialed the office's landline. Lowering and roughening his voice, he said he was Cecil B. DeMille calling for Robert Williams. Birdbrain at the front desk actually buzzed his intercom line and announced Mr. DeMille's call. God—seriously? He hoped Abby wasn't standing right there, but he'd heard her clattering about with the file drawers in her own office.

He picked up line one and uttered a hearty greeting. As long as the light was lit on the panel at the reception desk, he was relatively safe from interruptions. Setting both phones aside, he glanced over the venue selections Abby had chosen. What did it matter? He could have let her pick one. Mainly, he wanted to get this next meeting done quickly. He was only a couple million shy of purchasing the villa and having enough banked away to set himself up in luxury and privacy.

Something nagged at him, something about one of the donors from Newport and how her money transfer had not gone through. He needed to check on that. Now what was her name?

He reached into the lower drawer in his desk, the place where he kept business cards with dollar amounts written on them. He was proud of his little bookkeeping system. What a perfect way to track donors and their contributions (he refused to think of them in terms of investors who would need to be repaid). No one, at a glance, would have a clue what the numbers meant. Every few weeks, he would revisit the box with their cards, call back those who had not given any money, put a little more pressure on them. One of these days, he needed to take the box of cards to the bank and stash them in his safe deposit box, away from prying government eyes.

Money, of course, was electronically transferred immediately to an account in Europe under a different corporate name. The signed contracts, which the donors didn't get copies of, went into the shredder at home. Voila! No paper trail whatsoever.

He lifted the lid on the wooden box and stopped dead. It was empty.

"Abby!" he shouted, forgetting he was supposedly on the phone.

He quickly hung up the receiver when she opened the door.

"Have you been into my desk? This box?"

She seemed genuinely puzzled. "No. What's in the box?"

"Nothing. Well, just some cards I was keeping track of."

She shrugged. "No idea. I haven't seen them."

The fact that his inner office door was always locked whenever he was out meant none of the other part-timers had access. Not that they would dare poke around in his desk. He must have taken the cards to the bank after all. Things had been crazy right before Newport.

Abby was still standing there and he glanced up. "You need something?"

She came to some decision. He could see it on her face. "We need to talk."

Oh shit. That phrase could mean a lot of things, none of them good. *Please don't let her announce she's pregnant.*

She stepped inside and closed the door. "Rob, we've been working together quite awhile, and we've been a couple more than a year. I, um, well, I'd like a commitment. I was hoping Newport might have included a special occasion …"

He pretended not to understand what she was getting at, buying himself a moment to think.

"You're not preg—"

"Oh, heavens no! I'm more careful than that." She actually laughed a little.

Think, Rob, think!

"Well, we're fairly well committed here already, but

I think I can see my way to upping your salary *and* your bonus rate."

The smile stayed on her face for only a nano-second, then her eyes froze. "Robert Williams, I'm asking if you'll marry me."

Huh … why hadn't he seen this coming? Okay, what to say now?

"I think the look of shock on your face and the lengthy pause is my answer. Am I right?"

"Abbs, it's just—"

"No one answers a marriage proposal with 'it's just' unless they're squirming out of it." Tears welled in her eyes. Great. "I love you, Rob, and I've worked my tail off for you …"

"I know, I know," he said, stepping around the side of his desk. A hug, a kiss—those usually fixed anything—but she backed away.

"I want to marry you, and you're offering me more *money*—do you know how that *feels*?"

He went blank. More money always felt pretty good to him.

"I'm done." Her voice was flat, but her eyes sparked with fire. "I am *so* done. Organize your own parties and find someone else to talk about what a *wonderful* guy you are. I can't do it."

He had a feeling his mouth was hanging open as she walked out, slamming the door.

Chapter 19

Their room had been cleaned when Mary and Gracie arrived back at the hotel.

"So. What have we really accomplished?" Gracie asked, tossing her purse onto her bed. "Other than touching base, seeing Mom and Hannah didn't really tell me anything about what's going on."

"Janice seemed a bit in a dither about what she'll do if she doesn't get her money back from Williams. That could be worrisome."

"One thing I've learned about my mother, over the years. Don't go into a panic just because she does. I wish I'd remembered that advice when she hit me up and we raided our savings to help her out. Her situation is still going to come to a head, only now I'm in the midst of it."

Gracie's phone pinged with a message from Amber.

You two up for a meeting? I've got the gang here.

She replied an affirmative and opened her video chat app. Propping the phone upright on the room's small table, she and Mary took seats facing it. In a few seconds, Amber, Pen, and Sandy appeared where they had gathered around Amber's computer screen. Gracie could picture the tiny off-campus apartment jammed with electronic gadgets and friends.

Amber started the conversation. "So … dish! What's going on out there? Is Hollywood super glamorous? Have you seen movie stars on every corner?"

Gracie and Mary both laughed. Mary spoke up. "Well, it's greener than Phoenix—otherwise, the palm trees and oleander look about the same as ours. The movie stars don't seem to hang out on the corners, and I guess we haven't gone upscale enough to find out which restaurants they go to."

"We've talked with Abby Singer. There seems to be a little trouble in paradise with them as a couple," Gracie said.

"Oh, and this girl—" pointing at Gracie "—is getting pretty darn good with lock picks. She's gotten us into both Rob Williams's office and his house."

"I bet that's really something to see," Sandy said.

"Well, not so much. We were both surprised. His house is just really average, and the office isn't a prestigious address." They went on to fill in the Ladies with more details.

"Do we have anything to back up what he says in his presentations?" Pen asked.

"I noticed lots of photos of him with celebrities," Mary said. "It could mean they've done business together … it could just mean he's attended some trendy parties and managed to get himself photographed a lot."

"What about paperwork? Contracts with any of these stars?"

"Nothing. I swear, the man keeps nothing in writing," Gracie said. "In that whole office there were no file cabinets, no drawers filled with folders."

"That doesn't make any sense. A contract with a big-name star is going to be negotiated through his or her agent, and it's got to be a pretty detailed document, something signed in triplicate or some such, with each party getting copies. Those contracts have to exist somewhere." Pen's voice had become no-nonsense. "I've had a book optioned for film, and if the negotiations had ever become serious, there would have been a lot of paperwork. I'll make a few calls and see what I can learn."

"All I can figure is that everything is on his computer," Gracie said.

"Which we were very tempted to take, but we're trying to draw the line about breaking the law."

"Well, kind of. We did get past several sets of locks," Gracie reminded. "The one thing I did take was a stack of business cards I found in a box in one desk drawer." She went on to describe them and how they had added up the small handwritten numbers on the back of each one.

"Twenty million dollars!" Sandy looked as if she might fall out of her chair.

All three in the Phoenix group were a little slack-jawed at the news.

"This could well be the best clue yet," Pen said. "You said you called one of those people and his investment amount agreed with the number written on the card. So, if the police were to contact others and get similar stories …"

"While we're out here, should we contact the police?"

Mary asked. "Do you all think we're ready?"

Sandy looked thoughtful. "I don't know. We've got some good evidence. Pen's contract and those business cards—providing the rest of them check out as investors who were never repaid—Janice's testimony … The video from the presentation is a little iffy, but it would support the rest of the stories. If we just had a way to track the money, find out where it's gone."

"It doesn't sound as if he's spending the money on luxurious living for himself," Pen said. "That's the first thing I would have expected you to find—that he lives in some mega mansion or his offices are over-the-top posh."

"So, if he's not spending the money on his own lifestyle, where's it going?" Mary challenged. "Somehow, I don't see him supporting the homeless or funding a charity. The man we saw giving that razzmatazz presentation does not seem like the type."

Gracie gripped Mary's arm. "That big villa—the picture we saw in his briefcase. Do you think …?"

Amber spoke up. "Let me get on the money angle and the big house. Did you guys grab the picture of the big house? I need something to go on."

"Unfortunately, no. I'd just spotted it when he came home."

"Okay, never mind. I'll see if I can locate real estate records. You said you think it was in Italy or France?"

It wasn't much to go on—they all realized it.

"Meanwhile, we could stay out here a couple more days if that would be helpful," Gracie said. "We'll put together the evidence we have, if you can email us a copy of your contract, Pen, and we'll see if we can find the right person to talk to with law enforcement here."

"What we need is an insider, someone who worked for

him and knows where the dirt is, someone who is open to talking about the whole scheme," Sandy said.

Gracie and Mary exchanged a look. Abby Singer.

"We know where she works and where she goes for drinks afterward. She *might* be a possibility." Mary remembered Abby's disenchantment with Rob the day before.

It was risky, depending on a love spat to turn into actual evidence *and* to make it all the way to a courtroom trial. But it was worth a try. Scorned lovers had a way of harboring grudges for a very long time.

Chapter 20

Zeb's Bar was teeming with people when Gracie and Mary walked in that afternoon. On the way over, they'd discussed the possibility that Abby might not come in. With no idea of her routine, and no home address for her, they had decided it was worth the cost of a couple of drinks to hang out awhile and take their chances. All the cocktail waitresses were rushing about, looking a little stressed, and there wasn't an empty seat in the house.

Gracie pointed out a couple at the bar who were nuzzling each other and practically panting. "They'll be leaving soon," she told Mary. "Let's be ready to get their seats."

They ordered two glasses of merlot, tipped the bartender well, and stood by. It was easy enough to keep an eye on the room while making chit-chat. Scanning the tables, even those in the shadowy corners, neither spotted any sign of Abby Singer. True to Gracie's prediction, the smooching couple shoved their glasses back and vacated their seats, never taking their eyes off each other.

Mary surreptitiously wiped each of the wooden seats with a napkin. "Sorry—habit from the gym."

"Ew." Gracie laughed.

Two other women were eyeing the empty barstools. Not bothering with an apologetic smile, Mary and Gracie took the seats.

"Now—will our quarry appear?"

"Well, at least we can keep these drinks going awhile," Mary said. "Here's to a successful round of evidence gathering." They clinked glasses.

"We did have a good call with the rest of the gang, right? Amber will surely come up with his bank info. She's always been a whiz at—" Gracie's eyes went toward the door. "Oops, there she is. Casually look over her direction and catch her attention. If she acts like she wants to join you, I'll make a deal over leaving and she can have my seat."

"You're leaving me to do all the talking? What if I can't think what to ask?"

"You did fine the other day, but I won't leave the bar. We'll see where the questions go and if it looks like she's open to talking to both of us, I'll come back."

The plan worked. As Abby approached Mary, it was obvious she'd been crying. She had reapplied makeup, but the telltale puffiness and reddened eyelids were still apparent. Mary decided not to ask—just let the conversation go where it would.

Abby sent a small, grateful smile toward Gracie—with no sign of recognition—and took the offered barstool. She ordered a top-shelf scotch and plunked down a credit card, telling the bartender to start a tab.

"We'll see how long this works," she muttered in Mary's direction. "I have had the shopping spree of my life this afternoon."

"Wow, good for you," Mary said. "Yesterday, you didn't seem too happy but, hey, new shoes always brighten a girl's day, right?"

Abby's eyes glittered. "Especially when the *rat* is getting the bill."

"Uh-oh. The guy you told me about?"

"Yeah. It's over. I walked out after proposing to him and getting a blank look in return."

"Ooh—not good. He's the producer you told me about?" Mary took a slow sip of her wine, giving Abby time to answer.

"Yeah … I suppose my one big regret—well, there are a few—but the big one is that I won't get the chance to stay at this fabulous villa he's picked out as a location for the next film." Abby swallowed her scotch in one gulp and ordered another. "Yeah, I know—I should have used his credit card on food and to pay ahead on my rent, since I'm also out of a job."

"But shoes and drinks are more fun."

"No shit. Have another one," Abby said, tilting her head toward Mary's near-empty glass. "I'm buying. No— Rob The Rat Williams is buying." She started to laugh hysterically.

Mary caught Gracie's eye across the room and sent a help-me look.

"Rob Williams … I'd forgotten you mentioned his name yesterday. No wonder it sounded familiar. The woman who was sitting here a minute ago? She was telling me that her mother got caught up in something with him.

It sounds like the guy really gets around."

Abby's eyes hardened and the laugh was gone. "I can't even *tell* you. *Yeah*, he gets around."

Gracie had edged to the bar and ordered another glass of wine, giving Mary her opening.

"Abby, this is Gracie. She's the one I was telling you about. Gracie, Abby's just got screwed over by Rob Williams."

Gracie set her phone on the bar and put a sympathetic hand on Abby's shoulder. "Girl, I feel your pain."

Abby eyed Gracie up and down, and Gracie jumped in to correct the misconception. "Oh, heavens no, not sex. Money. And it's my mom he convinced to invest with him. She hasn't got a dime of her money back yet."

"Well, invite her down. I'm buying drinks on his credit card. In fact, let's have good old Rob buy drinks for the whole house. Bartender!"

"Um, Abby … you might want to be sure you don't hit his credit limit. He'll start getting alerts from the bank."

"Oh yeah." Abby waved off the bartender. She was slumping against the polished bar at this point.

"So, what was your deal?" Gracie asked. "Did you invest with him too?"

"Yeah. Money, yes, but mainly two years of my *life*. Helped him put together these huge gala parties, got up in front of his audiences telling everyone what a *wonderful* guy he is, slept with him. Oh, yeah, even after I figured out he was shagging anyone else he wanted." She downed the third scotch and her words began to slide into a liquid puddle. "How dumb was I?"

"There must have been perks—like hanging out with movie stars and watching the filming, traveling to great places and staying in fantastic hotels."

Abby made a slashing motion with her hand, which almost sent her empty glass flying. Mary caught it just in time. "None of that. Never an actor, never a movie set. I know for a fact that he hasn't produced a movie in several years. You know, his Oscar nomination goes *way* back."

The ladies didn't admit they already knew that little tidbit, or the fact the nomination was for sound effects in an otherwise unremarkable film.

"So, just to be clear … He gets people to invest in movies that are never made?"

Abby nodded hugely.

"Then where does the money go?"

An exaggerated shrug. "No idea."

"You were his top assistant, like, second in command, and he never told you?"

"Nope."

Gracie and Mary glanced at each other over the top of Abby's head. Their witness was quickly reaching the point where she would need to be put into a cab, and they needed some kind of commitment from her.

"Abby," Gracie said, taking the girl's hand and making eye contact. "My mother is out her entire life savings. We're thinking of hiring a lawyer, maybe involving the police. Would you be willing to tell them what you just told us?"

A slow smile crept over Abby's face. "Oh, *absotively*. You bet."

Chapter 21

The massive tires hit the runway hard and the reverse thrusters engaged, sending everyone sliding toward the fronts of their seats. Sky Harbor had plenty of runway but it never felt that way as pilots always wanted to get to the closest taxiway, then the terminal, and make a quick turnaround. Timing was everything in the airline business—at least that's how it seemed to Rob Williams.

Well, timing was everything to him, as well, and being out of the office for a few days right now was a great way to avoid any possible second-thoughts confrontation that could happen if Abby came back into the office. He doubted she would—she'd carried a box of personal items out with her yesterday.

He texted his ride that he'd just landed and should be at the south curb in ten minutes. He dragged his computer case from the space in front of his feet, stashed the few papers he'd taken out to read during the flight, and stood to get his carry-on bag. He'd booked himself at the Royale— mainly because it was tops on the Scottsdale venue list Abby had compiled for him, and secondly because she'd convinced them how important he was. Somehow, it always worked and he got the royal treatment wherever he went.

Abby. What on earth had possessed her to do what she'd done yesterday? Propose marriage? Didn't the girl realize he never intended to be tied down? Hadn't he made it abundantly clear?

He pulled his bag from the overhead bin, chafing at the delay as people ahead of him poked along. Outside the aircraft door, he edged past some doddering old snowbird couple and took off down the jetway at a brisk pace. Stretching his legs felt good. Getting out of sight of the old lady, who looked way too much like his mother, felt better. He felt his eyelids sting and he blinked them fast.

No thinking about Mom now. The only woman in his life he'd loved unconditionally, the only one who promised she would always be there for him. Until she wasn't. Damn cancer. Damn her for getting it. He felt the stupid tingle in his nose, the signal it was turning red and getting ready to drip.

He detoured into the men's room and into a stall. He parked the roller bag and snatched a few squares of tissue from the dispenser, rubbed his nose vigorously. Taking a deep breath and blowing it out, repeating it three times, helped. He squared his shoulders and walked back out to the bustling concourse. He was doing fine without getting attached to a woman.

A pair of tight jeans caught his eye just ahead. That's right—focus on the parts you could see, touch, and enjoy.

Forget about the emotional crap. Love 'em and leave 'em. There was something to that old saying. Do it before they could leave you. He focused on the jeans and ignored every gray-haired woman he passed. Down the escalator, out to the curb.

He texted his ride again, giving the door number where he'd just exited, and the limo with the discreet Royale logo glided up in front of him. The driver greeted him the way he liked to be greeted, taking his bag and stowing it quickly in the trunk while Rob slid into the roomy back seat and eyed the bar setup. He was looking forward to his meeting with the events director in the morning. Meanwhile, he would enjoy some pool time this afternoon, followed by the best dinner on the menu at the swanky hotel—all of it gratis, provided he booked his event with them.

See? he told himself, *I can handle it all just fine without her.*

Thirty minutes later, the limo delivered him to the elegant resort, driving slowly up a lane flanked with royal palms on both sides and a median filled with purple petunias blooming in profusion. The driver opened the car door for Rob, retrieved his bag, and a doorman in purple and gold livery ushered him inside. Inside the spacious lobby, he approached the front desk. Again, the deferential attitude, the employees who were accustomed to dealing with a wealthy clientele. Rob loved it.

"We'll need a credit card for incidentals," the clerk said, *sotto voce.*

"Of course." He handed over his Intrepid Dog Pictures card, hoping the man across the desk noticed he was in the film business.

A moment's delay, tapping of computer keys. "Sir, it appears … Well, we have you down for three nights, and that's the amount we usually use as a hold on the card.

It's not accepting …" The clerk seemed as embarrassed as Rob felt.

"Oh?" Maybe charges from the caterer or the venue in Newport were still coming in. "That's all right. Here's another." He handed over his personal gold card.

"I'm here to meet with Ms. Bradshaw in Events."

"Yes, sir. And your charge amount will be adjusted at checkout, most certainly."

This time there was no question, and he soon had his key and directions to a suite overlooking the golf course. Yes, it was going to be a pleasant three days.

* * *

Cicely Bradshaw was a bit no-nonsense for Rob's taste, although he supposed it was part of the job. Booking large events, working with clients, and being the go-between with staff to set up meeting rooms, dinners, and wedding receptions no doubt required a variety of skills. Still, he had to admit to feeling a little intimidated while the fifty-something woman peppered him with questions.

She sat across the conference table from him, her short frame a bit dwarfed by the size of the room's furnishings, but her severely cut gray hair, charcoal suit, and the steely rims of her glasses didn't suggest a shred of weakness. She'd walked into the room with a folder of papers, shaken his hand with an iron grip, and proceeded with the grilling— what size room, how many attendees, what budget for the dinner, how many tables, what types of centerpieces? His assistant had indicated they would want projection equipment and a large screen—he did understand there were additional charges for those items?

He nodded a little numbly and found himself

repeatedly asking what Abby had originally told them. She always handled those things; he'd authorized her to set up the details, and it had always come off beautifully. He felt another surge of irritation that she'd left him—her timing was atrocious.

"Let's just take a look at the rooms," he finally suggested to Ms. Bradshaw. "I can tell a lot more by looking at a real space."

She glanced impatiently at a thin silver wristwatch. "Both rooms we've discussed are in use right now. But let me see. If the Microsoft people have gone on their lunch break, we can step in and you can get a feel for the conference room."

"I think we're looking more at a ballroom of some type," he said, remembering the elegance of the great hall at The Breakers.

"This one is multi-purpose," she said. "It converts quite well. Or we have the King's Ballroom, which is currently being set up for a wedding reception tonight. Senator Willis's daughter. Very elegant."

"That sounds more my speed. Let's take a look in there."

She gathered her folder and pen and led the way. She was right—the ballroom was spectacular, especially done up for the wedding. Place settings of dazzling white china on gold chargers, sparkling crystal, and showy centerpieces of purple and gold flowers covered the tables. Huge sliding doors along one wall opened to a covered patio with views to the golf course and the sand-colored mountains in the distance.

"At night, the patio is beautifully lit and is available on the fourteenth, I believe. The lawns are also fairly well lit, but of course after dark you lose the view of the mountains."

"Yes, well for our purposes, we usually keep the guests seated during the presentation, then we will require a few side rooms where we meet individually."

He had noticed lettered rooms along the corridor leading to this one, and she confirmed that three of those were also available for the date he wanted. He supposed they would work. Another detail Abby would have known off the top of her head.

Ms. Bradshaw was making notes, sketching something on a blank room layout, as she led him back to the room beside her office, where they had started.

"I'll prepare the quote for you," she said. "Meal prices are based on a minimum of fifty attendees. I trust that isn't a problem?"

He nodded.

"We usually offer choices of a meat dish, a chicken dish, and a vegetarian option …"

Again, she looked to him for approval and he shrugged. Whatever.

"You'll go over the actual choices with our chef's department."

"Can't we just say everyone gets a steak or something?"

"Of course. If you're certain everyone eats beef. Sometimes it's best to offer choices."

He felt his toe starting to tap under the table. "I'll trust your judgment."

She didn't say it, but clearly she was wishing he'd brought a woman along. Men weren't supposed to be good at this stuff. But she didn't comment, simply promised again that she would have the quote ready within two days. He thanked her and headed for the bar.

Chapter 22

"Well, so much for our inside source in Rob Williams's office," Sandy told Pen.

The two had met for lunch at a favorite salad place. Amber had locked herself away with her computers, and no one liked too many questions about what little hacks she was experimenting with. Gracie and Mary were in California for another day, having delivered surprising news this morning by phone.

"At least Abby agreed to testify against him, if only we can persuade the law to go after him. It's rather a big *if* at this point. We don't know what Gracie and Mary will be told." Pen broke croutons into tiny chunks with her fork.

"It would be ideal if we could get another insider at his office on our side. Do we know who else works there?" Sandy asked. She proceeded to nibble the pieces of chicken in her mandarin salad.

"Mary only mentioned a receptionist having a desk there. It sounded as if the place operates on minimal staff, with helpers and interns hired on the spot for their events. How about if I call on some sort of pretense and see if I can get a feel for it?" Pen's eyes lit up at the prospect.

"Why not? We've already put Mary and Gracie in enough danger by going in there—I don't think it would be smart to send them again. But over the phone I imagine you could learn something. Hey, you could say you're researching a new book and you need to know how an important movie producer's office works."

"I like it. The perfect opportunity to ask any question I want."

"Just don't get Rob himself on the line. Novelist, asking about his operation. He might recognize your distinctive accent from when you met."

"Don't you worry, honey," Pen said in a cultured Southern voice. "Ah can fake my way through one little ol' phone call."

Sandy laughed. "Do it. You're great."

Pen pushed her plate aside and picked up her phone. "Ah think ah will." She batted her eyes and tapped in the number for Intrepid Dog Pictures.

A young-sounding female picked up. "Intrepid Dog Pictures, Aspen speaking."

"Is Mr. Robert Williams in, please? It's Lily Nightingale, the romance author. Ah'm researchin' a new book and would *love* some information from him."

Sandy could barely contain her laughter. Pen had to turn away and not look at her friend's face.

"Oh. Well, Mr. Williams is out of the office the rest of the week. May I take a message?"

"Oh dear. Perhaps someone else can help—who is next in charge there?"

"Abby—um, no. Sorry. Otherwise, there's just me right now, and I really only answer the phones."

"Is there somewhere Mr. Williams might be reached?"

"He's in Phoenix right now, checking out some meeting venues, and I'm afraid I can't give out his cell number. But if you'll leave a message—"

"That's all right, honey. Ah'll just call back next week." Pen clicked off the call before the girl could ask anything more.

"I heard that. Phoenix. He's right here." Sandy was practically squirming in her seat.

"Yes, well, right here among nearly four million people," Pen observed.

"How about this," Sandy said. "How about we infiltrate his business? He has no executive assistant right now, and I'll bet he's missing Abby, big time."

"Most likely." Pen was looking sideways at her.

"Think about it. There are only a handful of places here in the valley that are near the caliber of the place you described. Well, none quite *that* fancy, but a few he might choose from. My guess is that he's going to target a Scottsdale crowd, maybe some of those wealthy retirees who've settled in Pinetop or Paradise Valley. He'll choose a place nearby."

"What are you saying?" Pen asked.

"Let me do it! Please. I don't get that many chances to leap into the thick of things, and I could do this without having to schedule vacation days from the bank. I'll … well, I'm not sure, but I'll think of something."

"You're certain about this?"

"Yes. Think about it. I have years of management and

executive experience. Dealing with snooty people at the bank can't be that different from dealing with them in a resort or hotel or whatever sort of venue he has in mind. My entire job is details—and with Abby gone now, that's what Rob needs."

Pen thought about it as she picked up the check their server had left beside her plate. "Why not? You truly would be a perfect fit, it seems."

Sandy beamed. She grabbed her own check and the two went up front to pay.

Two hours later, back at her desk at the bank, she phoned Pen. "I've found him."

"That was quick. Where is he?"

"The Royale. It was so simple. I just called around, using the story that I was with Intrepid Dog Pictures and my boss, Robert Williams, had left his cell phone behind at the office. I knew he had to make a last-minute hotel change but he hadn't let me know where he'd checked in. I finally got the one where he is. They rang his room, but he didn't answer. I'm heading over there now. If he's not in his room when I get there, he'll have to walk through the lobby at some point and I'll catch him. Easy peasy."

Easy? Pen withheld comment. She only hoped the whole ruse would work.

Chapter 23

Argh ... I can't wait to get back home," Gracie muttered under her breath to Mary. "It's as if my mother's shadow is hanging over all of Southern California."

They were sitting in a waiting area in the main L.A.P.D. headquarters. The morning had begun with a trek to the nearest community station where they were told they needed to go higher up. The crime they described was grand larceny because of the amount of money lost and would be handled by the Major Crimes Division. Ninety minutes in traffic hadn't improved Gracie's mood a bit.

Mary patted her hand. "Don't stress. We have our luggage with us in the car, Southwest has flights all day long. All we need to do is turn over the evidence we have and explain the crime. The police will take it from there."

"Ya think?" Gracie's expression went from miserable

to skeptical.

Mary couldn't help it; she started chuckling, and Gracie couldn't resist. They were both laughing when a man approached.

"Mrs. Nelson? Ms. Holbrook? I'm detective Roy Mason—Major Crimes Division." He looked like a cop who hadn't chased down a bad guy in at least twenty years, one who had a dozen-donut-a-day habit. His smile was tired and his loafers run down at the heels. But his chinos were neatly pressed, the button-down shirt stain free, and his tie was only slightly crooked. He offered coffee—which both women declined—on the way to a cubicle at the end of a long, noisy hallway.

Gracie and Mary edged their way into the two chairs in front of his desk.

"Now. What can I help you with?" he propped his elbows on the desk in an imitation of someone who was truly interested.

Gracie, as designated spokesperson, began with the story of her mother's meeting and subsequently investing with Robert Williams of Intrepid Dog Pictures.

"Investment fraud really isn't normally our thing—just too hard to prove intent to defraud. Nearly all investments are risky, to some degree. Have you talked to an attorney, one who specializes in contracts and the language?"

"We have reason to believe—in fact, we *know*—that Mr. Williams's fraudulent activities go much farther than just my mother's case, farther than the state of California. Last week he was in Newport, Rhode Island, pulling the same scam, and right now he's planning another of his 'investment opportunities' in the Phoenix area."

Roy Mason sat up a little straighter. "What evidence do you have?"

Mary pulled out the rubber-banded stack of business cards, the copy of Pen's contract, and the copy Amber had made of the video from the night at The Breakers. Item by item, they explained to Mason the significance of each.

"We got Rob Williams's administrative assistant to admit that he's never actually made a movie with the money he collected from all these people."

Gracie pulled out her phone and played the conversation she'd recorded with Abby the previous afternoon. Unfortunately, the quality was terrible—too much background noise in the bar, and Abby's slurred speech didn't help either.

"Sorry, I should have listened to it before we came," she told the detective. She started to put the phone away.

"Not yet," he said. "Sometimes our lab can isolate parts of recordings, cut out the extra background noise and such. Let me have one of our guys make a copy, okay?"

Before she could respond, he'd picked up his phone and called someone elsewhere in the building. "Barry will be here in a second."

The sound technician took Gracie's phone away. While they waited for him to return it, Mason shuffled the documents around on his desk and reviewed everything the women told him—all they knew about Pen's and Janice's experiences, plus the calls they'd made to a few of the investors on the business cards.

"You understand that each of these victims would have to give his or her own statement? Out of state or not, they'd have to show up here to testify in court." He was scribbling notes on a yellow pad.

Gracie nodded. She felt sure Pen would be willing, had no idea what Janice would say or how she would present herself in court. It was one thing to nag the ear off your daughter, another to show up in a public place and admit to having been fleeced.

Barry came back after about ten minutes, his expression blank. "Not sure how much I can do with this one. It's pretty distorted." He saw the disappointment on Gracie's face. "But we'll do the best we can."

"Okay then," Mason said, after the young technician had left. "We'll look into it."

He stood, and it was clear the meeting was over. Gracie felt numb as she and Mary walked out to the parking lot.

"*Look into it?* I don't even know what that means," she said as she slid into the passenger seat of their rental. "Do you think we'll ever hear anything at all?"

Mary paused before starting the car. "I don't know, sweetie. All I can say is, I don't envy you having to tell your mother."

"Maybe I can stall her. Or maybe I'll just give *her* that cop's phone number. She can follow up."

Mary wished her luck with the plan and headed toward the airport.

Chapter 24

"What the f—" Rob felt his blood pressure rise as he took aim to throw his phone into the swimming pool. At the last second, he caught himself and turned the screen to face him so he could reread the text message. "This cannot be. There's no way I'm over my credit limit."

There were actually two messages, the automated text alert from the bank and, as he discovered when he noticed the voicemail, one from the hotel saying his dinner charges last night had been declined.

"Well, too bad about that," he said with a grin. "I already ate the food, and I'll bet you buzzards don't want me to return it."

Still, it was a problem. He'd only brought two cards with him; the rest were locked in his safe at home. His personal card was always near the limit. He only paid the minimum each month because somewhere in the back of his mind was a day in the future when he would bail, leave the States and to hell with MasterCard. His corporate card had a high limit and he knew he'd not come close to using all of it, even with the Newport and Scottsdale trips.

He tapped the phone screen and it dialed the number from the text message, the one that said 'If you believe this message is in error ...' There had to be a mistake—he would get it straightened out.

The female who answered was easy enough to charm for the first five minutes, and once he'd given all the security clues she wanted, she agreed to check the charges on the account.

"Yes, I do see some hotel charges in Rhode Island, airport purchases for food ... and I do see that the hotel in Scottsdale has placed a preliminary hold for what must be a few nights."

"Right. So what's put the whole thing over the limit?" His voice had lost its charisma.

"There are some charges yesterday and the day before in Beverly Hills. A Louis Vuitton, something at Prada ..."

She got no further.

"What the hell? I'm in Arizona—even *you* can see that. Who the shit's charging stuff in California?" The answer hit him. "Abby—that little bitch! She can't be doing this!"

"Are you saying there's fraud?"

"Hell yes, there's fraud! I'm going to—"

But she'd put him on hold. The bank's irritating non-stop blather about all their wonderful services played in his ear. *Shit.*

"Mr. Williams, thank you so much for holding."

Against my will.

"I've brought up copies of the charges in question, and

it appears those in California for the past two days were signed by an A. Singer. And, as I'm looking at your account record … there is an Abigail Singer shown as an authorized user for this card. Her position is stated as administrative assistant. Is that correct?"

"No! She quit. Walked out."

"I see, sir. In that case, her name should have been removed from the account."

"*Yeah*. So, do it."

"I can take care of that for you now, sir, although I cannot remove the charges currently on the account. What we'll need to do, since she is in possession of her card, is to close out this account and send you a new card. It will arrive in the mail, at your address of record, in seven to ten business days."

"NO! Not acceptable!" How the hell had this become so complicated? "Listen, you little—"

"Sir—sir! If you resort to profanity I will be forced to end this call."

"No way, bitch. No—" He stopped. The line was dead.

Dammit—taking care of details like this was exactly the sort of thing Abby did for him. He didn't have time for this b.s. This time he did throw the phone—just not toward the pool. It bounced once and landed at the feet of a blonde lady in the lounge chair next to his.

"Problem with the bank?" she asked, handing the phone back.

He looked at her for the first time. She was probably in her late forties, a little heavyset, good haircut and subdued makeup, wearing capris and a flowing top with a big straw hat and sunglasses. Corporate woman on vacation, he guessed.

"You heard, huh?" he felt a little sheepish comparing

his outburst to her calm demeanor.

She smiled with genuine humor. "I think everyone around the whole pool heard."

He almost got up to stalk away.

"I have some experience in banking. Believe me, you aren't the first guy to lose his cool over the rules and procedures the call center people have to follow." She stuck a finger in her magazine to hold her place. "Is there anything I can do to help?"

"Probably not, unless you just happen to work for Federal Trust Bank in California."

"Well, it's a thought, although I was hoping to find something other than banking for awhile. Kind of tired of that particular routine," she said. "I've recently left my management position, and I'm just looking around."

"Management, huh?" Hey, if she could manage a bank, she surely could manage the details of his life. "Would you consider becoming administrative assistant to a film producer? We get to rub some classy elbows in this business."

He flashed her the famous Rob Williams smile, but toned it down from the sexy version that had worked so well with Abby. On the spot, he decided he was done with hiring babes. They fell for him every time, and it just got too complicated. This one looked more like he imagined his older sister would be, solid and steady and knowledgeable.

"Let me think about it," she said with a glance at her watch. "I've got a spa appointment now but maybe we could discuss the job again later?"

"Sure. I'll spring for dinner," he said, belatedly remembering he wasn't sure how he would cover it. "What's your name?"

"Sandy. Sandy Werner." She gathered her belongings,

shook his hand, and walked into the women's dressing room.

Chapter 25

"It was all I could do not to shout 'yes' the minute he offered the job," Sandy told Pen on the phone that night. "But I'm glad I played it cool. He was practically begging me to help him, once we met over drinks. I adapted my expertise to fit exactly what Abby did, all based on what the rest of you have described about his operation. It was a great help, having those bits of the insider view."

"That's brilliant. When do you start?"

"First thing in the morning. Well, apparently, an early morning for Rob begins at ten. But I told him I would work on the banking mess with his corporate credit card early and have some answers for him when we get together to start the day. It's not a big deal at all. Federal Trust Bank has already cancelled his old card and issued a new one—I got that much by listening to his battle with the call center.

All I need to do is get the new card number, expiration—all the pertinent data—and he can begin using it. I speak banking lingo well enough to accomplish that much."

"Wonderful idea to impress the boss on your first day," Pen observed.

Sandy laughed. "The boss. How weird to think of Rob Williams that way. At least I do think he'll be relieved that he can cover his hotel bill and keep on with business as usual."

"Meanwhile, be sure to find out what he has in mind for this next investor party he's planning. If it's to be here in Arizona …"

"I'm on it, and I definitely plan to make sure Scottsdale is the choice. While he thought I was in the spa this afternoon I looked up the event planner here at the hotel, a Cicely Bradshaw. Nice lady. Very professional and she likes working with people who are quick and decisive, a comment she made when I told her I'd just come onboard with Rob Williams's company because of my event planning experience. Do you suppose organizing the bank's Christmas party counts? Oh well—she bought it."

"You weren't worried that Rob would check in with Ms. Bradshaw and realize you talked with her before you were actually hired?"

"A little … but once I met her I could see how she would intimidate a guy like Rob. She's completely no-nonsense, while he comes across as a spoiled little boy in comparison. This evening when he and I talked about the job, he was more than happy to let me handle everything with 'the little tyrant' as he described her."

"Woo—not much respect for women, has he?"

"Very little. So far, he's been very deferential with me, but I have a feeling it's because at this point he needs me more than I need him. I'm not kidding myself—the attitude could do a whole turnaround very quickly."

"Well, be careful. Abby saw a more ruthless side of him, apparently, and I witnessed his sparkling personality turn a tad sour during my meeting in his boiler-room. I wouldn't put anything past him."

Sandy went to bed with those words in her head.

* * *

Rob Williams sat at a patio table, a Bloody Mary and a plate of dry toast in front of him. Sandy took it all in, including his bed-tossed hair, puffy eyes, and the manila folder he'd set at the place directly across from his. She took the seat and laid her leather portfolio beside the folder, while he played for another minute on his cell phone.

"Morning, boss," she said, nodding to the server who offered coffee.

She had already been down the road for a breakfast that didn't cost fifty dollars, made her phone calls to the bank on behalf of Rob's credit card mess, and chosen an outfit similar to yesterday's but with long slacks and a jacket. At this point, she looked more professional than her hungover boss. She handed him a printed page, folded in quarters.

"Morning. What's this?" He stared at the paper.

"Your new corporate credit card. I figured for tax purposes you wouldn't want to be putting your travel expenses on a personal card. Now you can use your new one."

He opened the folds.

"It's not the actual plastic," she explained. "That's still coming in the mail, although I did convince their customer service supervisor to overnight it rather than using the standard method. It will be delivered to your California office tomorrow morning."

"Nice work." His eyes went back to the screen on his phone while he took a nibble from the toast.

She told herself not to expect effusive compliments from this guy.

"Sorry," he said. "I should've asked. Want some breakfast?"

"No, thanks." She turned to the manila folder. "Is this for me?"

"Yeah. It's all the stuff that events lady gave me yesterday. She promised a quote for our gala in two days, but if you can nudge her any faster on that, it'd be great." Again, his focus went to the phone.

"Certainly, Mr. Williams. I'd be glad to check on it." She didn't mention that she'd already met Cicely Bradshaw yesterday afternoon.

"Rob—just call me Rob. People say Mr. Williams and I think they're talking to my dad." He chuckled at his own humor.

"Okay, Rob. I'll follow through on all this. Am I correct in thinking you are only considering the Royale, or are there other venues in mind? Competing bids, or something like that?"

He stared out over the golf course for a few seconds. "Nah, this is good. I got things to take care of elsewhere. Don't want to run around all over the city looking at a dozen places."

"Very well. I'll bring you the figures and we can go over the line items."

"Yeah, whatever." He looked in her eyes for the first time this morning. "You know, you don't have to be so formal. We're a fun, casual organization, Sandy, not some stuffy old bank."

She sent a smile meant to assure him that she knew how to relax.

"Great. Got it."

"Okay, now the other thing we need to go over this morning is the guest list." He picked up a small notebook computer she hadn't noticed, from the seat of the chair beside him. "I've got names and contact info here. Once we've confirmed everything for the venue, we'll want to get invites printed up and mailed immediately. Go with first-class engraved stuff, thick paper, all that. And we'll follow up by email as well."

She nodded and took notes. "Do you have a way to get the names and addresses to me?"

"Yeah … do you have a computer with you? If not, no worries, just pop over to Best Buy or someplace like that and pick one up. Here, take the credit card number."

Sandy tried not to appear startled. Thinking fast, she decided it would be best to have a separate computer that would contain only the Rob Williams information. There was a good chance it would end up confiscated by the law.

"I'll get one this morning," she said.

"Perfect. I've got things to do right now, so you get your computer and we'll meet back here at the hotel … let's say at two?" He drained the Bloody Mary, shuddered slightly, and picked up his phone and laptop before walking away.

Okay. Sandy watched him walk through the restaurant and lost sight of him. She fingered the page with his credit card information, amazed at how cavalier he seemed with spending.

The rest of the morning went quickly. She had

wondered whether she would hit a snag in purchasing a computer with a brand new credit card, but the purchase went through easily once the clerk could be convinced to manually enter the numbers at her terminal.

She took the new machine home and set it up with a password and basic information to get it running. Amber came over to assist, assuring her if she used Intrepid Dog Pictures, the company address and contact information, her personal name wouldn't be shown in any capacity other than as a user. Their young computer whiz also performed a few programming tricks that Sandy didn't actually understand.

"Just in case," Amber said. "What I've done here is install some tracking applications in case the machine and you become separated, so we can figure out where it is. He'll have no way of knowing about it."

"He wants to transfer some files to me," Sandy said, "a guest list and such. I'm thinking that could be super valuable to a prosecutor."

"Absolutely. Okay, so here's your file-share software." Amber walked her through a little tutorial so Sandy wouldn't fumble anything in front of Rob.

"And make sure I can do video chats."

"Done. It's right here. And, you can tap into his phone calls—once he's within range with his phone, to sync them just do this—" Amber clicked a couple of icons. And you're not only limited to sharing or conversing with Rob. You can send anything you want to my computer, as well."

"Will the police find that suspicious?"

"Um, let's just say they won't necessarily know either."

"But, if this thing is taken into evidence, they have experts—"

"I can wipe the connection with one click, if it comes

to that. Meanwhile, think of it as additional backup. If Rob gets wise and decides to dump this computer, fire you, do whatever ... we'll have the guest list and other stuff in a place he can *never* get to." Amber shut down the computer. "I'd also recommend you get a separate phone to use for his calls. Just pop in at a Walmart and get something cheap, and buy some pay-as-you-go minutes for it."

Sandy smiled. "Great idea. We'll fill the throwaway phone with evidence on Rob, and I'll be happy to turn it over to the law." She noticed the time. "I'd better be getting back to the resort. A meeting with the new boss."

Forty minutes later, he met her in the lobby, waving from a quiet corner with cushy chairs and a small table. She showed him the new computer, and he immediately got out his own machine and began transferring files—the guest list, layout for the invitations to which she only had to insert the finalized date and time, the document for the investor contract. He instructed her which documents to print and how many copies. Sandy felt herself practically salivating at all the important data.

"Any questions on this?" he asked, once the documents had transferred to her machine and he'd described the purpose of each. He closed his computer, stuffed it into the front pocket of an airline bag, and they exchanged phone numbers.

"It all looks very straightforward," she said. "One thing I'll need to know when I see Ms. Bradshaw again tomorrow—what's our budget for the gala?"

He raised his eyes upward, thinking. "I'm guesstimating twenty thou should do it. If it goes a little higher—say, twenty-five—that's okay. Any higher bid, call me in California and we'll discuss."

"Right." In her head, math figures zipped along. Based

on rough math at the Newport event, she knew they would likely bring in several million. Not a bad investment return.

Too bad the innocents who *thought* they were investing in a winner didn't get the same assurances.

Chapter 26

Sandy set a plate of sandwiches on the coffee table, fluffed the sofa pillows, and was about to check the teakettle when the doorbell rang.

"Make yourselves at home," she told Amber and Pen, the first to arrive.

Mary had a midday self-defense class to teach, but Gracie should be along any minute. As if reading her mind, the doorbell rang again while she was in the kitchen. "Get that, someone? I'm making my special autumn cider."

It was always hard to get into the spirit of fall and winter in the Phoenix area. November typically was one of the mildest months of the year, and it wasn't uncommon to have Thanksgiving dinner outdoors under a full moon. People considered it 'cold' when the temperature hit sixty, and out would come the sweaters and shawls. Sandy liked to do a little pre-Thanksgiving treat, her own hot cider recipe. She could hear the Ladies gathering at her back sliding door, commenting on how well the oleander was still holding up.

"All right," she announced, carrying a thermal carafe. "A very simple lunch is served."

"So, you've been a week in the employ of Mr. Williams," Pen commented once they had all taken sandwiches and were seated around the living room. "How is it going?"

Sandy smiled and nodded toward Amber. "I think we're gathering some good evidence, wouldn't you say?"

Amber's wild curls bobbed as she nodded, her mouth full of egg salad.

"It's been a little challenging to keep Rob believing I'm working from home when I've actually been at the bank several days this week. Can't see using up all my vacation time just waiting for his calls, so I've taken them on my new throwaway cell phone. I'll warn you, though, I've been committed to a video chat with him at some point today."

"Is he suspicious?" Gracie asked.

"I don't think so—well, certainly not about what I'm doing with the data he's sent to my computer. He's been a little impatient about my not making the move to California yet."

"It's only been a week."

"Yes, and my stalling is working for now. I told him I'll have to rent or sell my house and it must be organized and packed. The details all of *us* understand, but a guy— well, he's just used to making a decision and moving on it immediately. Maybe it's a youth thing." She looked at Amber, who shrugged.

"Rob isn't that young," Pen said. "But I do get the impression he's accustomed to the quick-quick-quick lifestyle."

"I can put him off as long as I need to. What do we know from the police in Califor—?" An electronic tone interrupted. "Oops—the video chat signal. You all stay in here and keep quiet, okay?"

Sandy rushed to the kitchen counter where she'd left the new computer set up. Circling, she came face to face with Rob.

"Good morning, boss," she said, clicking the button to activate the audio.

"Sandy, hi." On the screen, he appeared freshly showered, goatee trimmed. "Okay, what's on our action list today?"

Behind her computer, Sandy saw Amber, Gracie, and Pen appear in the living room doorway. She started to raise a finger to her lips and remembered Rob could see her.

"Uh, well, all's on schedule, I think." She turned her eyes back to him. "The invitations are being printed and will go in the mail next week. Our events manager assures me the holiday decorations will be up all over the resort so our chosen date will be among the most festive of the season."

"Yeah, okay, that sounds good. Look, I haven't seen any charge on the credit card for this thing—weren't they going to bill us a fairly hefty deposit?"

"Actually, I was able to waive the requirement for an advance deposit. I admit it, I threw around some of the celebrity names you've told me about, and when they realized how important you are … she was somewhat wowed, I have to say."

He grinned. "The old bird was impressed, huh."

Amber almost laughed out loud and Sandy sent her a firm look.

"Somebody there with you?" Rob asked.

"The cats. One of them jumped up where I've got my glass figurines. I may need to go swat him or something." She aimed her gaze firmly back at the computer screen.

"You didn't tell me you had pets." His tone was somewhat accusing.

"Oh, yes, Heckle and Jeckle—two black cats. But I'm sure they'll adapt to life in California when it comes time for the move. Don't worry about it at all."

"Cats. No, I'm not worrying."

Gracie made a fist, as if she wanted to punch him. Sandy used every bit of will not to acknowledge the women.

"So, yeah, the deposit for the venue will be due two days before—I felt sure that would be okay with you—and the balance is billed on a net thirty-day invoice."

His mood went back to chipper. "That's great. Sandy, you're really good at this."

"Thank you." She matched his happy tone and asked if there was anything else she needed to attend to in the coming days.

"The venue, the food, and the invites. That's it for this stage of the game. I've got production tweaking the video trailer we'll show at the conclusion of the dinner. Just doll yourself up for a black-tie affair, as you'll essentially be acting as hostess, my second in command."

"Got it. I'm excited about it!"

"'K—bye."

The chat ended and she closed the computer screen. "Ohmygod, acting in front of an audience is *not* my forte. I couldn't have faked one more second of enthusiasm."

"You did a great job," Gracie said. "Amber's little laughing spasm didn't help."

"Sorry." A contrite Amber went back to her sandwich.

Pen spoke up. "The details about booking the Royale

and mailing invitations …"

"Are completely false, all for his benefit. I told the woman he'd changed his mind and decided to book another venue."

The Heist Ladies had decided, early on, not to let the event go through—Rob Williams would not get a chance to take money from any more unsuspecting victims.

"He won't call and check up on it?"

"Nah. He's not at all into details like this. Even if he did call, I learned the woman he had spoken with, Ms. Bradshaw, is out on medical leave through the first of the year. The resort has someone else filling in, and Rob doesn't even know who to ask for. At the first roadblock he'd call me and demand that I get it all straightened out."

"Still, I think we don't dare wait too long," Pen said.

Chapter 27

Rob stared at the photo of the villa. He'd made it the background on his computer's desktop and the temptation was to look at it for hours, imagining himself walking through the rooms, hosting lavish parties to which the entire Cannes crowd would come, bedding one sexy lady after another ...

He snapped himself back to reality. The villa wasn't his yet, nor had he ever actually visited it. One inquiry to the real estate agent in the area told him he'd better brush up on his French or take along a translator when it came to negotiating the deal. Still, he checked the online listings every few days to be sure the house of his dreams was still available. He sent a longing glance toward the photo, then went to his email.

A message from Sandy informed him that a hundred

guests were now confirmed for the Scottsdale presentation. He gave a satisfied sigh. In three weeks, Sandy Werner had accomplished amazing things—snagging the prestigious venue only weeks before Christmas, for one thing. The way she'd had the invitations printed and mailed in record time was another.

His only complaint was that she still hadn't moved out here. He missed the convenience of having an assistant right here in the office, someone he could shout for, who came running at his whim. Okay, face it, he missed the other services Abby had provided—his pulse rose a little at the thought—but that wouldn't be happening with Sandy, even if she were here. Frankly, her businesslike efficiency would have intimidated him a little in the bedroom.

He idly flipped through his contact list, looking to see which of his past young beauties might be available. He was ready for the kind of dinner that put a woman in the mood, followed by an evening of pleasure—his place or hers. It didn't matter, as long as she satisfied the increasing itch that had begun to build since Abby left.

He even thought of calling Abby herself, just to see if her mood had mellowed, but that was asking for trouble. She would want her job back, then she'd start with the 'When are we going to France?' crap, then it would come back around to whether they'd get married. He took a deep breath and deleted her from the contact list. On to other things—he spotted the number for that flight attendant who frequently overnighted in L.A. She'd been a lot of fun. Her phone immediately went to voicemail and he left a quick message.

Back to emails, a couple of bills had arrived and he paid each with a click or two, glad for the multiple credit cards in his various corporate entities. The Intrepid Dog

Pictures card would soon be filled with charges from the Scottsdale event, and this way he could rack up some social expenses during the holiday season, maybe even a little extra travel, without Sandy becoming aware. Since he'd given her access to the new card, she'd handled all the details without wasting his time.

He closed the browser, and there was the photo of the villa again. What if … He felt his pulse quicken.

The Scottsdale event was nicely filled. If history was any indicator, he would easily bring in enough to meet his goal. He could grab a business-class ticket to Paris, then into Cannes, go personally to check out the property and have the agent write it up. A grin spread across his face— he'd been scrimping and saving for a couple years now, and this was the big one, his dream.

If all went smoothly, he could be lounging beside that big indoor pool, a gorgeous hottie on each side of him, by the new year. He went to the Air France website and began searching flights.

Chapter 28

Gracie Nelson?" The man's voice on the phone was vaguely familiar; otherwise she would have taken him for a telemarketer and hung up.

"It's Detective Roy Mason, in Los Angeles."

Gracie quit chopping the pecans for her favorite cookie recipe and set the knife aside. "Yes, Detective Mason. Do you have some news for us?"

"Well, don't get your hopes up. We don't have Rob Williams in jail or anything. But I do think there's reason to be optimistic."

"That's great!"

"Let's call it semi-great," he said with a chuckle. "We've contacted some of the other names you gave us. Turns out one is a guy I know personally."

Grace felt a tingle of optimism.

"My partner—I don't think you met him—he's familiar with Rob Williams and he's eager to push this to the attorney general's office as quickly as possible."

"That's good news, right?"

"I think so. And we've got a contact named Jim Hesperson in the A.G.'s office who, by some weird stroke of luck—I'm guessing the holidays—has made the time to work on it. The courts typically have a long recess in late December and we might, just might, be able to get this case heard. At least as far as the arraignment phase. I think we can make a good enough argument for Rob Williams's ability and means of escaping jurisdiction that we can have him held in jail until his trial."

"Wow, I'd say that's great news," Gracie said, cookie batter completely forgotten.

"There's just one little fly in the ointment, so to speak," Mason said. "We're having a hard time locating Rob Williams."

Gracie gulped. What was he talking about?

"We don't want to tip him off by going to his office or home," Mason was saying. "He's got access to lots of money so we don't want him having advance warning. When we swoop in to pick him up, we want it to be a complete surprise. You do understand what I'm saying, right?"

"Of course. No one among my family or friends wants to see this guy get away with it."

"We're monitoring his personal credit cards but there is no unusual activity. I wish I had the manpower to park someone outside his house and his office 24-7, but I just don't."

"What are you saying?"

"Random calls to both locations and he's never there.

This has been going on for two days, and wouldn't you know, it's right when we were getting close to having a warrant issued for his arrest."

"Doesn't anyone answer at the office?"

"A receptionist who sounds about eighteen and just says she'd be happy to take a message. She won't say where he is or when he's expected back. You understand, I can't make too many of those calls without arousing suspicion."

Gracie came close to telling Mason about Sandy working for Rob, about their lying to him about having the Scottsdale gala all arranged. But since they'd not shared the information with the police right from the beginning, it could get tricky. Plus, of what relevance was it, really? She was fairly certain Sandy was still in daily contact with Rob and that he was calling from his California office.

"Okay, thanks, detective. It's great news that you've found enough witnesses to build the case against him. And I will definitely let you know if I hear of anything new." She hoped her voice didn't betray the deception. Cops could have uncanny instincts about that sort of thing.

The moment the detective hung up, Gracie dialed Sandy's number.

"The California cops say Rob Williams has disappeared," she blurted. "You're still talking with him every day or so, aren't you?"

There was a blank silent space before Sandy sputtered. "Yeah. I just spoke with him an hour ago. Well—backtrack that—I had a text from him and I responded and he answered back. We're definitely in touch."

"They're ready to issue an arrest warrant and they've been watching his house and office, calling both places. They haven't been able to spot him in several days. What are we going to do? If this falls through and my mom doesn't get her money back ..."

"Take a breath, Gracie." Sandy's voice stayed low and calm. "I'm actually at the bank right now. Hang on ..." There was the sound of a door closing. "Okay, let me think a minute."

She was being literal, Gracie realized. A long silence with only the sound of computer keys tapping, then Sandy spoke again.

"I've just emailed Amber and asked her if she knows any other way to track him down. I guess I'm a little worried what will happen if he's headed out here and starts looking for me. He could discover that the venue was never booked ... that I'm not working from home ... Our idea that he would be in police custody before he ever showed up here in his tuxedo could come crashing down on us. He absolutely cannot find out about our sham working relationship until the police are ready to act."

"And that's just it—they *are* ready to act. Where's Rob?"

"Hold on a sec ... a reply from Amber. She asks 'have you thought about the villa?' I don't know—have we?"

"She thinks Rob may have taken off for the villa in France? Really? This close to his big event out here?" Gracie was trying to wrap her mind around the implications.

Sandy went quiet again for a moment. "I suppose ... I mean, I've convinced him I'm working for his company. He could easily convince me he's still in California, as long as he doesn't slip up and mention the wrong time zone or something."

"Oh, god." Gracie was leaning against her kitchen counter, resting her head on her left palm. "We're going to have to admit to the cops that you've been working for Rob. We never told them."

"It wouldn't be the end of the world, although it really

could complicate things," Sandy said.

"What if they got an anonymous tip to check Rob's passport for any recent foreign travel? That would send them off in the right direction without our having to say anything."

"Good. And meanwhile, I'll get Amber on the trail to see if she can figure out where this villa is, exactly, and whether that's really where he went. And I'll put the word out to Pen and Mary that we should all get together tonight."

Gracie hung up and took a deep breath. Mason would surely recognize her voice since they'd just spoken a few minutes ago. She needed an anonymous tipster.

The little prayer was answered five minutes later when her teenage son waltzed into the kitchen and stuck his finger into the chocolate chip cookie dough in the mixing bowl.

"Uh-uh," she said. "Cookies will be ready in ten minutes. I'll give you the first three while they're warm and gooey if you'll do me a favor. Grab your cell phone."

Now, she could only hope his maturing voice wouldn't crack during the call.

Chapter 29

Rob lounged back in his business-class seat, legs up, a movie playing on the screen in front of him, but his mind wasn't on the film. After checking text messages from Sandy at the airport, he'd spent the first two hours of his flight working out the details for the villa.

At first, he'd thought he would walk in and plunk down the whole asking price—well, wire-transfer it—it would be a grand gesture to impress the French realtor. But he didn't have it all, not until after Scottsdale, and it would look really half-assed to say, 'I can only pay you three-quarters of it now.' That wouldn't do.

So he would give the minimum down payment. He had that much in good old American cash in the briefcase below his feet. On Tuesday he would fly back, prepare for the Scottsdale event Friday night, rake in the dough, and be on his way back to France by early next week.

It would be the first time he'd held one of his gala events so close to the holidays, but it made a lot of sense. People were in a giving mood this time of year; those who weren't philanthropic would be after the tax breaks. Investments made before the end of the year could be classified in a bunch of ways to save taxes—at least he thought they could.

He practically salivated at the idea of all that cash going into his account, then getting transferred to the hidden ones in other countries. He was so busy dreaming he almost didn't hear the flight attendant ask if she might refresh his drink.

"Sure, another Glenlivet," he said.

Something about the woman sparked a memory; a tall, classy blonde in her fifties—no, the other one was maybe ten years older. Yes, the novelist, the one whose payment never showed up. It had slipped his mind, with all the Abby drama and the Scottsdale plans. Another thing to add to his agenda while in France. Or maybe he'd dash off a quick message to Sandy and have her handle it. It wasn't one of his bigger proceeds, but every little bit helped. He'd already visually formed a picture of new furniture for the villa. He would hire a chichi decorator and really do it up right.

He pulled the photo of the villa out of his wallet. Silly, maybe, keeping the picture to himself, his little secret. At one time, he'd printed a larger full-sheet version of it, intending to stick it to the bathroom mirror at home. What had ever happened to that copy?

Oh well. He admired the picture and sipped his drink. It was a long flight and he began to feel drowsy. He set the drink on the little side table, pressed the photo to his chest, and closed his eyes.

Chapter 30

The Heist Ladies met at Sandy's house again. Gracie had put out the word, and the tone of her panicky message brought them all within the hour.

"Detective Mason just called me. His department enlisted the cooperation of the feds. Homeland Security told him Rob Williams has left the country. He checked in on an Air France flight for Paris."

"So, what does Mason say they'll do about it?" Amber asked.

"Nothing. A municipal police department doesn't have the means to extradite on this sort of case, he told me. They can barely catch murderers and drug lords. Apparently wiping out people's life savings doesn't qualify as important enough." Gracie was nearly in tears. "And then he asked me if I knew anything about this. I can't even remember what answer I gave, I was so shaken. Now he probably thinks I've tipped off Rob to the police investigation."

Sandy held out a plate of cookies. Sweets could solve so many problems. "Okay, let's take a breath and think about this. We had a feeling Rob might go to Europe. You saw the photo of that huge house, and we know he's stockpiling money for something—it must be that.

"I've been in touch with him by text and email very recently, although I have to admit there were no new messages the last few hours. His being on a plane could explain that ..." She picked up one of the cookies for herself. "But I do believe he's going to be here Friday for the gala. Nothing he's said indicates he's suspicious about the plans."

Was that correct? He had questioned her about the deposits that had not been charged to his card yet. She munched down the cookie and took another.

"The cop—Mason—he sounded pretty urgent about finding Rob and getting him to L.A. Apparently, the attorney general is pushing to get the case on the docket because only one judge is working through the holidays, and it's normally a slow time of year in the court system. After the first of the year, the calendar is full and it would take much longer to resolve this thing. Now would be the ideal time to arrest Rob and get him indicted for inaccurately representing the investment and taking money under false pretenses. They can't proceed with any of that unless they have their suspect in custody."

"So, we go get him," Amber said, a gleam in her eye. "We've dashed off to Europe on other missions. We can do this."

"We don't even know where in Europe this big villa is," Sandy pointed out, "other than it's probably somewhere in

France since that's where he went. In our business dealings, he's talked fondly of Cannes, but I assumed it was because of the big film festival."

Amber was tapping away at her tablet. "I'll just go through the real estate listings …"

Pen spoke up. "I believe we can narrow this matter down to a couple of possibilities. Rob is either going to show up here in Scottsdale by the end of the week, or he'll stay in Europe to elude the police. My vote is that he'll come back. Greed will win out."

"Plus, he doesn't have any reason to believe the police are after him, does he?" Mary asked. "I think he'll come back."

"Oh, gosh, I had another thought," Sandy said. Her face had gone a bit white. "What if he expects me to put on the show at the gala? Abby used to do it—get right up there on stage with him. I can't handle that. I have horrible stage fright."

"Sandy. Sandy—calm down," Pen said. "Remember, there *is* no gala in reality. We've faked him out, as they say."

Sandy grinned. "You're right. I'm getting rattled for no reason."

"Well, there's still reason. He could just decide to stay in Europe and blow off everything that's going on here," Mary pointed out. "I think we need to discuss a plan of some sort."

The room got quiet for a few minutes, each of the women lost in her own thoughts. Pen got up and began to pace the room.

Amber was the first to speak. "Found the villa!" She held up the image shown on her tablet. It was the same picture they'd found among Rob's papers.

"As I see it," Pen said, "we can't actually let him show

up, expecting all the guests to be at the gala. He'll have to be waylaid before he can get to the resort."

"I can handle that," Sandy said. "I'll offer to pick him up at the airport, and I'll just tell him not to bother with a rental car. Then what?"

"This may sound insane, but I say we grab him and deliver him directly to the police," Amber said.

Gracie's eyes were wide. "What? Kidnap him?"

The word reverberated around the room.

Chapter 31

Think about it. There are five of us and one of him," Amber said. "And we've got Mary, who bench-presses, like, a *ton* every day."

"Well, not quite." But Mary grinned and flexed a muscle anyway.

Gracie looked around the room. She couldn't picture Amber's tiny frame able to lift anything much heavier than a laptop computer; Pen was so tall and elegant, never breaking a sweat; Sandy—ambitious and hardworking, but a bit out of shape. As for herself, sure, she wrestled her living room furniture around at times, and she'd been known to tussle with her kids quite a bit, and once in awhile she even joined Mary at the gym for aerobics classes. Still, Mary was definitely their best bet when it came to pure strength.

"So, what's the plan?" she asked. "I don't like heading into things without specific details."

"I agree," Sandy said, looking a little nervous.

Gracie pulled out her ever-present day planner and turned to a blank page at the back.

"The simplest thing," Sandy said, "will be to grab him when he shows up here for the gala. It's the one fixed time and place we know about on his schedule."

"Could be a little tricky to get him into the building without his realizing the guests aren't there and his event isn't happening," said Mary.

"No, no, no. This has to happen in the parking lot." When Amber said it, they all realized she was right.

"Okay, so I'll be in touch with him, establishing contact from the moment his plane lands. I'll tell him everything is all set, but because we're short on time he should meet me in the parking lot and I'll walk him directly into the ballroom." Sandy chewed her lower lip for a moment. "And for that to happen, I'll need to book him on a flight that gets in at the right time for our purposes."

"He won't balk at that, try to argue, or worse … change his ticket?"

"I doubt it. He's really the type that just likes to show up and be the leader. Hates the details and paperwork stuff. But I'll keep him texting all day. That way, we'll know where he is each step of the way."

Pen nodded approval. "Excellent reasoning."

"Okay, so you've got him in the parking lot at the Royale on the night, and then what?" Mary asked.

"We all step out, wearing ninja black, and we grab him!" Amber said with a sparkle in her eyes.

Nervous giggles all around.

"Even five of us can hardly wrestle a man to the

ground in a public place without him putting up a lot of resistance, shouting, or something to draw attention. We need to incapacitate him without doing damage that the police will question when we turn him over."

"I know a little shoulder-pinch trick," Mary said. "It'll bring a guy to his knees, but he'll be back up, mad as a hornet, shortly after. I don't see that as a way to get him all the way to the Los Angeles police."

"What we need is …"

"A drug!" Amber said. "Anyone got Xanax or Valium? We slip it into a drink … I read where that's the kind of drug the date-rapists use."

Sandy's eyes became calculating. "I meet his car at the entrance, glasses of champagne in hand, tell him we should have a little toast to the success of the evening, and a glass of champagne will take the edge off so he's nice and relaxed for his presentation."

"Better yet—he'll be more likely to believe it if you pick him up at the airport in a limo with a bar in back. We can spring for the cost of a car and driver to get him out to the Royale," Pen said.

"Yes, excellent!" Gracie said, madly jotting notes.

"The limo drives the two of you to the venue, and you make certain Rob has a drink or two on the way. Before the limo can pull around to the grand front entrance, you say you've forgotten something in your own car and have him come around to another part of the parking lot, where the rest of us are waiting in Gracie's minivan." Pen was warming to the subject.

"This is the best plan yet, but won't the limo driver want to hang around and drive us to the front anyway?" Sandy asked.

Pen thought about it for a few seconds. "Not if you've

told him in advance that the whole thing is planned as a surprise for your friend, that his girlfriend is waiting in the other vehicle and she's got a birthday surprise for him."

"Wow—I see why you're good at plotting fictional stories," Amber said with a grin.

"By this time, Rob should be getting a little woozy, but we still need him to be on his feet until the limo driver leaves. We open the side door on the van and guide him over there …" Pen said.

"We'll have blankets in the back," Gracie said. "He can be nice and cozy on the floor."

"How long does it take to drive to Los Angeles?" Mary asked. "Will he stay unconscious that long?"

"I'm adding duct tape to the list, just in case."

"I'll bring some snacks," Amber said. "We'll be driving through the night and might get hungry."

Gracie read from her notes. "Okay, here's the checklist: Have minivan serviced and gassed up; put blankets and duct tape in back; pick up Mary, Pen, and Amber. That's my part. Amber brings snacks. Sandy gets the hired limo and goes to airport, brings dear old Rob to the parking lot. Does that cover it?"

"I'll get the Xanax," Mary said. "Women at my gym have all kinds of worries—someone's bound to have a prescription and be glad to share a couple of pills with me."

"Check the dosage and be sure we're not using too much or too little," Pen suggested.

"Got it."

"I'll study the road map," Gracie said, "and program my map thingy on the phone to give directions."

Amber was busily searching something on her tablet. "Looks like anywhere from six to eight hours for the drive.

If we're arriving in L.A. in the early morning, add some time for rush hour traffic and to get all the way downtown."

"We can take turns with the driving, and be sure to add potty breaks," Sandy said.

"I love traveling with women—we think of everything." Gracie grinned as she added notes to her checklist.

"What are we forgetting?" No one could think of a thing.

"Now the hard part—waiting three days."

Chapter 32

Rob Williams stood at the top of the hill, hands casually in his pockets, surveying the beautifully landscaped slope, imagining the twenty-acre property as his. Behind him, the estate agent patiently waited. They had toured the house, from the sweeping driveway which brought visitors to an impressive nine-foot-tall glass front door, through the seven bedrooms, home movie theater, and open living spaces with windows that showcased the astounding views. The amount of light was incredible, accustomed as he was to his small California bungalow wedged among neighbors on all sides.

"Ze present owner, she is an artist. Ze house is designed for maximum showing of the paintings," the agent had said. His grey-flecked eyebrows twitched as he extolled the features of the mansion.

It was true. One of the bedrooms with northern exposure was in use as an art studio. The rest of the home looked like a gallery, every wall hung with a modern art canvas done in colors that went with the rest of the room's scheme. The art itself was a little beyond his scope—he liked it, but had no clue what the swirls and swipes of paint were meant to depict. He just smiled at the agent when he said that the value of the art could be negotiated into the selling price of the home, if Rob wished to keep it.

He gave a final longing stare down the slope, imagining himself on the terrace below, floating in the infinity pool, which seemed to blend right into the sea in the distance. When he turned back toward the house, the agent was talking on his mobile phone.

The man's narrow mustache seemed stretched to the limit when he smiled at Rob.

"So, it seems you are falling in love with the property, *non*? Imagination shows you how it would be to live here?"

Rob rocked back on his heels, playing it cool. "Yeah. I mean, it's a nice place. As good as some of the others I've looked at."

"Ah, *oui*, I can see you here. *Certainement*." The agent put on a small look of distress. "We have only one, how do you say?—blockade?"

"Roadblock?" Rob's tone took a sharper turn.

"I have now received a call … My associate, another agent in my office, he tells me there is an offer for this property." He held up his phone as proof of the call. "A lady he show the home last week, she has come to the office with a full cash offer."

Rob's balloon began to wilt.

"I have explain to my associate that you are here, this very minute, considering the home very seriously. He tell his client he must have the time to receive your answer." The man dithered a little, seeming unsure. "Can you tell me, Monsieur Williams, would you be ready to make the offer to match the other? If so, I believe I can make the better deal—is that how you say it?"

"You're saying my offer would trump the other? That I could get the house?"

His wheels began to turn. He could do this. With the money he would rake in from the investors in Scottsdale, his dream could come true.

"I'll give two hundred thousand over the asking price, provided I can wire transfer the money on Monday." Rob watched the agent ponder the offer. "Of course, I will give a decent amount as earnest money. In cash."

A slight pause. "*Oui—oui*, I am certain my associate will accept." The man turned away, making the call, firing away in rapid French.

Rob pretended to be nonchalant, although his insides were in a twist. From the moment he'd seen the photos, he knew this was the house for him. He casually surveyed the shrubbery and outdoor furniture, wishing he could decipher what the agent was saying, wishing he could at least gather the outcome based on the tone. But none of it made sense, including the hand gestures and shrugs, done as if the agent was standing face to face with his associate.

He strolled the length of the terrace, down the steps to the edge of the infinity pool. The view grabbed at him, making him want the place even more. Lost in his reverie, he barely heard the footsteps behind him.

"Monsieur?"

Rob jumped.

"Very good news, monsieur. Your proposal is acceptable. We shall ride to my office and draw up the agreement. You have your cash deposit with you?"

Locked up. "I'll need to stop at my hotel. We can meet at your office in thirty minutes."

He was practically floating on a cloud when the agent dropped him at the Radisson Bleu. With a glance at the time, he calculated this would be a good time to catch Sandy. While he entered the digits on the safe's keypad in his room, he listened to the phone ring.

"Rob—how are things going?" She answered a little breathlessly.

"Did I catch you at a bad time? Well, anyway, just wanted to let you know I'm in Europe for a couple days, but I'll be back in time for our event Friday night."

"Europe? Oh my, you really do get around. Do you have your return flight booked already?"

"Yeah, but I need a slight change of plans. I was supposed to fly out of Paris tonight, but I'm delayed. Can you—?"

"Of course," she said, smooth as glass, no hint of frustration at the whims of a boss. Not the reaction he would have gotten from Abby, for sure.

"Let me see … how are the days going to work out …?"

"What would you think of flying directly into Phoenix, rather than going back to L.A. and turning right around to come here? I don't see why it wouldn't work, as long as you have the clothing you would want for the gala."

"I always pack my tux," he said. "You never know when it'll come in handy."

"I'll email your itinerary as soon as it's set. And, Rob— have a great trip."

He liked the new plan. It would give him an extra day in France. He'd said hello to a gorgeous woman this morning who'd been walking a tiny white dog down the street in front of his new place. Maybe he could time it so he would encounter her again, and maybe meet some other neighbors, just let them know an important man from Hollywood was moving in next door. He pulled the briefcase full of cash from the safe, checked his reflection in the mirror, and headed for his rental car and the real estate office.

Two hours later, he walked out with a signed purchase agreement in hand. The one clause that left him a little uneasy was the absolute requirement that the balance be wired no later than midnight Monday. His earnest money would be forfeited and the other buyer would swoop in if he failed to comply. He was cutting things close but, god, he wanted that house.

He was eyeing a small bistro across the street, thinking of a light dinner and a good bottle of wine, when he received the text from Sandy.

Only Air France flight on Friday arrives PHX at 5 p.m. Will have limo waiting at the curb. Suggest you change into tux on the plane or airport to save time. Need to be ready to walk into the ballroom at 7. Full itinerary attached.

He beamed. Loved how efficient and organized this new assistant was, not wasting his time flying all over the place. She was definitely a keeper.

Chapter 33

The limo rolled to a stop at the south curb at Sky Harbor, and there was Rob, wearing his tux. Sandy permitted herself a satisfied little grin when she saw how well he'd followed her instructions. She handed him the drink she'd already prepared while the driver stowed his luggage in the trunk.

The rest of the capture took place without a hitch, right up to the moment Rob spotted Pen standing at the back of the minivan as the limo drove away. A vague flicker of recognition crossed his face. He started to say something, but at that moment his knees buckled.

Sandy and Gracie dashed forward to drape his arms over their shoulders, and Mary took his feet. There were a couple minutes of awkward wrestling to get his limp body into the van.

"Hurry!" Pen whispered. "Someone's coming!"

The other car turned, one row south of them, apparently cruising for a parking space.

Mary swung Rob's legs into the van.

"He saw me," Pen fretted. "Do you think he'll remember?"

They could hear the sound of duct tape being pulled from the roll, as Mary neatly trussed their victim's wrists and ankles. "I'm not going to do his mouth unless he starts making noise, but I think it'll be good to blindfold him."

Sandy was climbing out, brushing lint off her black palazzo pants. Her gold-spangled top was slightly askew. "He's really out of it. I doubt he'll remember much of anything after getting in the limo at the airport." She looked down at her outfit. "I need to change into something more practical for the drive."

"Um, we were talking about that," Gracie said. "Wouldn't it be better if Rob isn't aware that you're in on this plot?"

Pen nodded. "Right. If, for some reason, the police don't take immediate charge of him, it would be smart of us to keep someone as an insider in Rob's office."

Sandy seemed a bit deflated. After all, she'd played the key role in getting him to this point, but she agreed. Rob's trust in giving her access to his business might still be needed. She acquiesced.

Pen peered into the van where Mary and Amber were sitting watch over the inert man. They gave two thumbs-up.

"Okay, then." Gracie closed the van door. "We'll be in touch along the route."

Pen and Sandy watched the van pull out of the parking lot.

* * *

The sun was rising behind them as the van reached the outskirts of Indio, and the fairly open stretch of Interstate 10 began to fill with early morning traffic. Mary was at the wheel now and she competently navigated the way into the downtown maze. It took longer than any of them had imagined, but she managed to get them to the police station as the morning shift was settling in. A call up to Roy Mason's desk brought him out to the main entrance.

Rob had slept through the long ride, apparently lulled by the van's motion and the soft music Gracie played on the radio. He woke to the sound of duct tape being peeled from his ankles and, a minute later, being stripped from his wrists.

"What's going on?" he mumbled. "Where am I?"

Detective Mason approached the van just then, greeting Mary and Gracie with surprise. "Ladies?"

"We told you we'd find him," Gracie said. She clicked the control on her key fob and the van's side door slid open.

He recognized Williams immediately. "We thought he was in Europe. How did you—? And what's with the tuxedo?"

Gracie gave an enigmatic smile. "We just need you to take it from here."

Mary and Amber teamed up to give Rob a push out the door. He stumbled to his feet, blinking in the sunlight and rubbing his wrists. "What happened?"

Mason stepped forward and pulled handcuffs from his belt. "Robert Williams, you are under arrest for fraud and grand larceny. You have the right to remain silent …"

Chapter 34

Well, of course he pleaded not guilty," Gracie told Pen on the phone. "And I'm sure he's filled his high-priced lawyer with all kinds of crazy stories. Can you imagine—he somehow thinks he was brought to California against his will."

They had a chuckle over that. The 'traveling group' as Gracie, Mary, and Amber called themselves, had stayed over to attend the arraignment Monday morning, accommodations provided at Janice's Pasadena home.

"Detective Mason is still pushing to get the early procedures done before the court's holiday break, so a preliminary hearing is set for Thursday afternoon. It's where the judge rules that there's enough evidence to schedule a trial. Mason thinks we should gather as many victims and witnesses as possible, just in case the judge would like to ask a few questions, although he does say that's not usually the case. Mom is up for it—she's really excited we caught Rob. So, I wonder if you also want to come, Pen. I mean, technically you're more a witness than a victim—you did attend a gala and sign one of the contracts, even though you weren't out any money."

"Absolutely," Pen said. "I'll fly out on Wednesday and I'll see if Sandy is able to get away as well."

"Mary's going to contact Abby Singer, too," Gracie said. "She'll be happy to know Rob is finally going to get what's coming to him."

* * *

The downtown courthouse was not exactly bustling on the Thursday before the Christmas break. As they'd been warned, aside from traffic court and a few small domestic cases, no major trials were scheduled until the first week of the new year. The Ladies had arrived together, bringing Janice along. They parked in an underground garage and rode the elevator to the third floor, where each had to pass through metal detectors and have her purse searched.

Gracie found herself scanning the faces outside Courtroom A. She spotted Detective Mason speaking with a tall man with pale ginger hair. Both wore off-the-rack business suits. She guessed the second man to be Jim Hesperson, the Attorney General for the county. Without making eye contact with the women, Mason and the other man turned and were admitted to the courtroom by a uniformed bailiff.

The gathering was small—essentially their group and a half dozen people whose purpose was unknown. No jurors were to be chosen today; if there had been, Gracie knew it would have been a much larger crowd. One young Asian man hung to the side, a notebook in hand, but showed no particular interest in anyone else. Another man came striding purposefully through their midst, charcoal suit and blue tie immaculately tailored, no-nonsense expression. He pulled a wheeled briefcase along, gave a nod to the bailiff, and was admitted to the courtroom. A guess told them it was likely Rob's defense attorney.

Abby Singer came rushing in just as the bailiff opened the door to admit them. Mary gave her a hug and introduced her to Amber, Pen, and Sandy. They found seats on a bench behind the prosecutor's table, with Sandy moving to the defense side to keep up the pretense of being on Rob's side.

Five minutes later, there was a stir in the room as Rob Williams was escorted in. He wore an orange jailhouse jumpsuit, but his hair and goatee were neat, his face clean, his manner one of easy friendliness as he greeted his attorney. No handcuffs or shackles. Obviously, no one was worried about Rob presenting a danger to the court. He sent Sandy a confident smile.

The bailiff announced the judge and everyone stood. The bald man in robes must have been as wide as he was tall—the black garment draped outward in front, as if covering a basketball, concealing what no ordinary street clothing could have. His gaze swept the room. Something about it satisfied him. With a nod toward each of the attorneys, he sat. Gracie wondered if he had a booster seat in his high-backed leather chair.

"Welcome to my courtroom. I'm Judge Alderston. We are not here today for a trial. This is a preliminary hearing in which I shall determine whether enough cause exists to warrant the cost of a trial to the State of California. I have received and reviewed the briefs presented by both the prosecution and the defense. Does either attorney have any additional evidence for my consideration?"

Hesperson for the prosecution stood. "If it please the Court, the victim of the theft is here today."

"Yes, yes," Alderston said. "Does this victim have any further evidence to present, beyond what I already know?"

"No, your honor, but—"

"Never mind, then. I've already read it."

Beside Gracie, her mother seemed relieved that she would not be called to speak.

The judge continued. "Anything else?"

The defense attorney seemed curiously quiet, yet in an anticipatory way. He gave a small shake of his head when the judge looked his way.

"All right, then," said Alderston. "I have read the statements by both sides and reviewed the statement by the so-called victim."

Gracie stiffened at his wording.

"A woman, Mrs. Janice Weaver …" He looked up. "Mrs. Weaver invested some money and lost it. The contract I was given in evidence is not the actual contract the victim signed, but was submitted as an example. Frankly, I do not see reason why this case is in my criminal court. I'm not even certain it's a case at all, but if it is, it's a matter for the civil courts."

"Your honor, we've submitted other evidence," Hesperson said.

"Some video and audio recordings? Nowhere in your brief does it state said recordings take place between the victim and the suspect."

"They don't—"

"Exactly." The judge banged his gavel. "And that's why

I'm dismissing this case."

Jaws dropped all over the courtroom. Janice gripped her daughter's arm; Gracie felt tears rise; Pen, Amber, and Mary were alternately sputtering and turning toward each other. Detective Mason seemed dumbfounded. Sandy and Abby were both stone-faced.

The word on everyone's lips was "What!" Everyone except Rob Williams. He turned to his attorney as the judge exited the room, and the two exchanged smug smiles. Gracie caught it and felt her teeth clench. She elbowed Pen and nodded toward the pair.

"They set this up," she muttered.

Chapter 35

Detective Mason looked as if he wanted to escape, but he stayed behind on the courthouse steps to speak with the Ladies.

"What happened in there?" Gracie demanded. "I thought at least a jury would get to hear about this crime. *They* would have surely been more sympathetic than mister roly-poly judge."

Mason gave a rueful smile, in spite of himself. "I'm as disappointed as you are. Jim and I thought we'd gathered enough evidence to make a good case. We really did."

No one said it, but the reality was that the women had gathered the evidence *and* had brought in the suspect. The police had done precious little. They probably wouldn't have pursued the case at all if they'd had to trek all over the country to track down Rob Williams and catch him in the act of presenting his movie investment scheme.

"Who's that guy?" Amber asked, with a nod toward the Asian man who'd been in the courtroom and was now lurking nearby, taking notes.

"That's Jason Chen. He works for one of the smaller newspapers here in the county," Abby told her, hanging back but listening to Mason's comments.

Mason ran a hand through his thinning hair. "In hindsight, I know we rushed the case to court, pushed the prosecution. We should have presented more of his victims, besides Mrs. Weaver, before we proceeded. Maybe the media can help locate them. Maybe you'll meet others—could press it as a civil suit."

He cleared his throat. "Please believe me—I've taken a personal interest in this and will do everything I can to rebuild it into a stronger case. If we get more victims to come forward ... We can even bring in federal assistance once we determine that they come from multiple jurisdictions. If I have to haul the file home with me every night ..."

The women's glances told how little effort they believed would go into the case, especially the minute a more urgent case came across Mason's desk. The cop walked away with one final, lame apology.

"I wish I could have been of more help," Abby said, "but I swear, the minute the money came into the bank account, Rob handled it. He had me fooled, too, believing he was in negotiations with actors and was scouting locations for the movie."

"Come on, girls," Janice said, with a steely glance at Abby. "Let's go."

Amber had moved away and approached the reporter, but he seemed to have all the material he wanted. He brushed her off with the excuse of a deadline and rushed away. The women moved as one deflated group, back to the van, for the drive to Pasadena.

"What did the reporter say?" Sandy asked Amber once they were on the road. Amber just shook her head.

"Maybe that should have been our tactic," Pen said. "If we'd gone to the media with the story, put more pressure on the police and the judge."

"You're probably right. I wish we'd thought of that," Gracie said.

"We still could," Mary offered. "And now it would be a bigger story because of the way the judge blew us off."

Pen nodded thoughtfully. "Perhaps. Let's think about it."

No one felt like eating the tamale casserole Maria had prepared when they got back to Janice's house. Hannah turned on the television, and Pen kept one ear tuned to it, on the chance their case might be mentioned with indignant commentary on the result, but a tragic shooting at a high school in a quiet Midwest town was the lead story and nothing else came on.

The women sat around the table, pushing bits of food around their plates, no one talking much—until Sandy's phone pinged with an incoming text message. She picked it up without much interest, but when she saw the message her eyes widened.

"It's from Rob." She read it aloud. "Saw you in the courtroom. Thanks for your support. Where'd you go after?"

She looked at the stunned, silent group around the table.

"It worked. He didn't realize I was with the rest of you."

Pen was the first to speak. "This could be a turn in our favor. He still thinks you are on his side."

Chapter 36

Rob Williams shed the horrific orange jumpsuit and, although it felt a little weird to be dressing in his wrinkled tuxedo, got into his own clothing with a heart full of joy. He was free!

The past ten days were a blur. He'd put on the tux in order to make it on time for his latest gala event, the one in Scottsdale. Somewhere around the time they'd arrived at the Royale, he lost track. He'd awakened with a splitting headache, in the back of a vehicle, and the next thing he knew the cops were slapping cuffs on his wrists. There were female voices but he had no idea whose. Fingerprinting and booking went by in a fog of nausea and throbbing head, which felt as if it could explode. He'd slept for two solid days and nights in a cell, and he only knew that because the creep in there with him told him he snored the whole time.

Tyler Chisholm had met with him once, when he was informed he needed to release twenty thousand dollars to cover the initial legal fees. At the time he'd pitched a small fit over the amount, but now he was glad he'd done it. His longtime lawyer had obviously steered him right.

He buttoned his shirt and stuffed his tie into the pants pocket. A knock on the dressing room cubicle and the guard came to let him out. Tyler was waiting at the end of the hall, not a thread of his custom-made charcoal suit or blue silk power tie out of place. The lawyer held out a plastic bag containing the rest of Rob's personal effects: slim leather wallet, passport, phone, keys, the boarding pass from his Air France flight, a half-full box of Tic-Tacs, and a comb. He took a quick peek at the cash in the wallet—it was still there.

"We need to talk," Chisolm said, taking Rob's elbow.

"Someplace away from here." Rob hoped to never see the judicial complex again in his life.

They got into the attorney's silver Lexus and drove to the building where Chisholm's offices filled a quarter of the sixth floor. He parked in his designated slot and they walked to the bar at the corner.

"I'm buying," Rob said when they settled in a dark corner booth. "Man, I owe you one."

"Actually, you owe me ten." Tyler pulled an envelope from inside his jacket. "My invoice. The twenty you already gave me went directly—well, you know where. I'll take a check or a wire transfer, and it's due before you leave town again."

Rob bit back a retort, swallowed hard, and nodded.

"Look, Rob, we've known each other since college. I don't know what you've got yourself into now, but this thing could've been real messy. You are *so* lucky—" He stopped mid-sentence while the cocktail waitress set down their two whiskeys and a basket of popcorn.

Rob smiled up at her and halfway wished she'd hang around so he didn't have to hear the rest of Tyler's lecture. It wasn't to be.

"*So* lucky they were only ready to present evidence for one plaintiff. The scuttlebutt is that there are probably dozens more like that lady, the one claiming fraud. If all of those should band together and push for a class-action type case … Well, let's just say all the money you have in the bank won't get you off as easy as you did today. One word of caution: Madoff."

Rob winced, willing his hand to hold still as he raised his glass. The famed hedge fund guy would spend his life in prison, and the feds had tied up every penny of the money he'd made, returning it piecemeal to the chumps as they began to recover it.

"It doesn't pay—"

"Okay, okay, I get it," Rob said, impatient to get out of the place.

"Fine. Enough said. Where's your car? You need a ride to pick it up someplace?"

"Nah, I'll get an Uber." He picked up a handful of the popcorn and stuffed it in his mouth, mainly to get out of talking anymore to Tyler Chisholm. His phone was dead, so he had to ask the lawyer to order the ride for him. Pile on one more humiliation.

They said goodbye at the sidewalk, Tyler handing Rob the invoice envelope he'd left behind on the table. His mood plummeted another notch as he got into the hired car.

At home, he stripped off his tux and threw it into the corner of his closet. No way he was putting it back on until it was thoroughly dry-cleaned. He stood under the shower until the water began to run cold, then spritzed himself with cologne and put on jeans and a Henley. Nothing seemed to take away the jailhouse stink.

He thought of the courtroom and something clicked. Sandy. She'd been there in the audience, or gallery, or whatever they called the crowd. Crowd—hardly. A dozen or so, come to watch his downfall. He'd plugged in his phone when he got home and it had enough charge now to send a text. Although he didn't really want to know, he wondered whether anything had come of the Scottsdale event, or if there was a possibility of scheduling another. He sent a brief message.

Tyler's words came to mind—*You are so lucky—It doesn't pay*— Well, who knew if Sandy would even respond.

His computer case was sitting on the dining table and he caught sight of one of the villa photos he'd printed before—before his life went to shit. He ripped up the picture, picked up the bottle of Glenlivet from his bar cart, and poured a glass.

He'd lost the villa. Even if he scooped up every penny from every hidden bank, it wasn't enough, and by now the other buyer was probably already moving his things into the palace on the hill. His throat felt tight. That house was the one thing he'd ever wanted. The home, the lifestyle, the women, the film festivals—the bubble burst right before his eyes.

The first drink went down in a gulp; a second followed, then a third. A picture of his father sitting at some Milwaukee dive, beers going down easy, popped into his head. Was that where he was headed? At least Pop had once had a good woman in his life. Rob couldn't even say that much.

He looked at his phone screen. No message from Sandy. No message from anyone. Truth be told, he missed Abby. He poured his glass a little fuller this time. He swallowed the last of the golden liquid and looked down, verifying the glass was empty. Two tears ran off his chin and plopped on the table.

His head pounded, with Tyler's words echoing around in there. *Don't be a Madoff,* he told himself. *Don't get caught. Don't get caught ... don't get ...* His head hit the table top with a thump and he barely noticed.

Chapter 37

They were beginning to feel grubby, having brought only one spare change of clothing, and no one's mood was exactly the best either. All five of the Heist Ladies had piled into Gracie's van at the crack of dawn, ready to be *done* with California. No one had slept much. An hour into the drive they decided breakfast would boost their energy and brighten their moods, so Gracie pulled off at a diner somewhere near Rancho Cucamonga.

The place looked like the type of mom-and-pop non-chain where the atmosphere would be relaxed, the prices reasonable, and the eggs would at least be freshly cracked. Amber trailed the rest of the group, and just outside the door her gaze fell to a metal newspaper vending machine where a headline screamed out at her.

Allegations of Movie Producer Scamming Rich People Falls Flat

She quickly fished in her purse for change to buy the paper. "No, no, no ..." she muttered as she scanned the opening lines.

Gracie had stood back, holding the door. She watched Amber with a puzzled look on her face. "What's that?"

"I can't believe it," Amber said. "I absolutely did not tell him any of this." She nearly crashed into the doorjamb as she held the paper in front of her.

Gracie led her to the large corner booth Pen had found. The others were watching Amber's stricken face.

"It's that Jason Chen, the reporter. This is what he wrote; 'The Los Angeles County Courthouse was quiet yesterday, with the upcoming holiday recess looming, but one interesting case came on the docket. A wealthy investor who put money into a picture to be made by producer Robert Williams of Intrepid Dog Pictures, was screaming 'no fair' and Williams found himself in the defense chair.' Wealthy investor—where'd he get that?"

Gracie seemed stunned. Her mother was about to lose her home over this deal. She obviously wasn't floating in *wealth*.

Amber continued: "There's background stuff we knew about Intrepid Dog Pictures, how Rob Williams started the company after having one big success, an Oscar nomination in the late '90s for a documentary ... blah, blah ... It says Williams was part of the sound effects department at the time."

"Exactly. Rob Williams really had very little to do with his one big claim to fame." Mary said.

A young waitress in black jeans and a black t-shirt with the diner's logo came up to the table, her face perky as she surveyed the troubled faces of her customers. They unanimously ordered coffee and she scooted away.

Pen provided the voice of reason. "First things first—we all need some food."

"I wonder how widespread this story is. Is all of America going to think my mother is some kind of rich bitch who doesn't deserve to get her money back?"

Sandy leaned over and patted Gracie's hand. "I don't think so. For one thing, look at the TV screen over there." She tilted her head toward the back wall, where a set was broadcasting one of the national networks, sound muted. The video showed coverage of the horrible shooting that had been the top headline last night. "The old saying in journalism apparently still holds true—'if it bleeds, it leads'—and no one gives a hoot about our case."

Gracie seemed somewhat mollified.

"If we're going to continue our search for more victims and look for a way to bring this thing back to court in a bigger way, it's good for us that it's not getting wider coverage," Sandy said.

"How so? Wouldn't more investors come forward if they heard about it?"

"Perhaps," Pen said as the coffee arrived, "but—well, let's order our breakfast first."

Keeping it simple, everyone ordered omelets and toast and their waitress scurried away again.

"As I was saying, it's possible more investors would come forward, but it's also possible Rob Williams would begin feeling the pressure and this time he might actually get away."

Sandy had been quiet and thoughtful. "Maybe I should stay in touch, continue to be our inside track and monitor his movements."

"That's right—we'd forgotten he sent you a text last evening." Clearly, Mary's wheels were turning.

"I answered him, just a quick, noncommittal reply. I've heard nothing more."

"Yet," Amber said.

"Yet," Sandy agreed, her smile widening.

Conversation lagged as their food arrived and the women gave the omelets their attention. Fifteen minutes went by with barely a word, until Gracie began to fret. "I'm still worried about taking this back to court. Do any of you believe Detective Mason will really give it top priority?"

"Maybe until the next murder case comes into the department," Mary said.

"Exactly. And in L.A. something bigger *will* come along."

"So, I'm thinking we go after him ourselves," Amber said. "Rob Williams, *and* the judge who pulled this crappy trick, and *that* reporter." She jabbed a buttery finger over Jason Chen's name on the front page byline.

The others laughed at her vehemence. "A slanted headline by a reporter isn't punishable, unfortunately," Pen said, "but I do agree with your assessment that the judge was also somehow in collusion. The whole courtroom presentation was just a bit too pat. It had a staged feeling. If we could track Rob's finances and find out money went to the judge—we'd have them both."

"Ooh, if only I had both my computers and my secure internet connection here …" Amber sent a crafty grin toward the rest of them.

"We'll be home by this evening," Gracie said. She drained the last of her coffee, then fished her keys from her purse. "The bus leaves in ten minutes."

Chapter 38

One eye opened. Rob couldn't comprehend the dark expanse. A groan. He closed the eye again, felt dampness beneath his cheek. He tried to raise his head from the dining table but it felt as if it weighed a hundred pounds. He managed to lift it with the help of both hands, then sat there with eyes squeezed shut, willing the blazing pain to go away.

When he peered out between his lashes, a glint of light beamed through the window across the room and struck the empty Glenlivet bottle. His heavy crystal glass stood nearby, coated with thick residue and smeary lip prints. He turned away and felt bile rise in his throat. Everything in his life had gone to shit. He felt pressure behind his eyes, the threat of emotion.

"Okay, this is ridiculous," he muttered.

He found his legs and stood shakily. Somewhere in the kitchen he'd had a packet of some purported hangover remedy. Maybe there was some of it left. The cupboard door squeaked, shooting another pain through his head, but eventually he found the package. One pill, and it was sealed inside a stupid blister-pack that would have taken a sober person ten minutes to get into. He fumbled about with it, cursed in frustration, and threw it across the room.

A shower. He could smell his own sour breath and slept-in clothes. He shed shirt and pants on the way to the bedroom, balling them up and tossing them in the laundry basket at the bottom of his closet. He swallowed three aspirins with tap water and stepped into the shower. The water never made it beyond lukewarm, but it was better than nothing.

With no hot steamy water to luxuriate in, he hurried through soaping and shampooing, rinsed off and grabbed his towel. His beard had grown out to nearly conceal his carefully trimmed goatee. It would take more effort than he wanted to spend today to shape it up. He took the electric razor to it and wiped out everything. It was the first time he'd seen his upper lip in a year, and the effect in the mirror was startling. Oh well, the stylish facial hair would grow back.

He dressed in clean jeans, a black turtleneck, and his favorite leather jacket, hoping his mood would improve with the fresh clothing. He tried to remember whether he'd eaten anything last night, but the strain of thinking brought the headache back.

He'd barely noticed his surroundings when he got home. Now, he saw the signs of his hasty packing for the trip to France. Had it really been two weeks ago? The villa, the real estate agent, the woman walking her small white dog—it all seemed ages away from the police, handcuffs, jail, and the courtroom. Everything in between was still a blur. Hell, last night was a blur. He needed food.

A neighborhood pub was an easy ten-minute walk from his bungalow, but Rob couldn't quite imagine putting one foot in front of the other enough times to cover the distance. He found his car keys on the table near the front door, his phone and wallet nearby. Even wasted, apparently some actions came automatically to him.

The Land Rover didn't want to start on the first try, but he nudged it gently and got it to turn over. The dashboard clock said it was after ten. He thought of his regular life and wondered if whatshername was at the office, answering phones. *If* the phones were even ringing. He glanced at his cell phone on the seat beside him and nearly missed a stop sign, earning a blare of horns from two other drivers.

"Okay, okay." He set the phone down and concentrated on getting himself to the pub.

He'd never been inside before, preferring the higher-toned establishments downtown where he was likely to spot a star and grab a selfie now and then, but this little joint had a banner, which he'd noticed in the past, announcing breakfast. He parked on the street and went inside.

This time of day, the clientele consisted of two elderly couples chatting in overly loud voices, comparing medical conditions. He got a table as far from them as possible and immediately asked the waitress for a Bloody Mary. When she brought the drink, he declined the menu.

"Just bring me a couple eggs, scrambled, a bunch of bacon and about four pieces of wheat toast. Oh, and coffee—biggest one you got." He set his phone on the table beside the napkin-wrapped flatware she'd placed in front of him.

She didn't write any of it down, but it was a simple enough order. He downed half his spicy drink as she walked away. He glanced at his phone again. Not a single text or missed call. What happened to the buzz, the busy thrill of his daily life?

He thumbed through his emails. Nothing personal, nothing exciting unless you called a twenty-percent-off sale at The Gap a biggie. He sighed and turned to his plate of eggs as the waitress set them down.

"Another of these," he told her, tapping his empty glass.

"Sure. Anything else?"

What else would I need? He hadn't taken a bite yet. But he kept the sarcasm to himself. Apparently, he had few friends anymore. He chomped down a slice of bacon and a big forkful of the eggs. Wiped his hands on the paper napkin and checked his phone again. Still nothing. There'd been that one quick text to Sandy yesterday. He barely remembered what she'd said. Something not informative, he knew that much.

His second drink showed up. It didn't taste as good as the first one had. He switched to the coffee and wolfed down more eggs. His mood went up a notch as his head stopped pounding. He should check in with Sandy. In fact … *what if* she had followed through and done the presentation at Scottsdale? There was a chance.

He typed a text to her: Scottsdale—how'd it go?

Chapter 39

Sandy heard the text message ping and looked at her phone. "Seriously? He's asking how the Scottsdale gala went?"

She was sitting at her desk at Desert Trust Bank where she'd been catching up after being in California for two days.

"Knock-knock," came Gracie's voice as the door swung open. "I just came in to make a deposit and saw you sitting here."

Sandy smiled and invited her in. "Want a good laugh?" She showed Gracie the text message from Rob Williams.

"What!"

"Yeah, obviously he doesn't remember anything at all about that night. We really put him out with that drink."

"Do you think he *really* doesn't remember what we did?

Maybe he's just testing you." Gracie dropped her purse on one of the chairs in front of Sandy's desk.

"One way to find out," Sandy said. She dialed his number.

"Rob, it's Sandy. Um, you are aware that the investor meeting here in Arizona never happened, right? I'm sorry—I thought you knew that." She put on the speaker and set the phone on her desk.

"Shit—yeah, I suppose. I was hoping you might have taken over for me and done the presentation yourself." He sounded dejected and she almost felt sorry for him.

"I wish I could have," Sandy said, rolling her eyes toward Gracie. "But it was my first time. I wouldn't have had any idea what to say."

"Were the people disappointed? Were you able to rebook anything? We could still do it, maybe right after the first of the year?"

Such grasping for straws. Gracie covered her laugh.

Sandy aimed to sound noncommittal. "Well, I suppose that might be a possibility."

Gracie had picked up a pen and scribbled on Sandy's notepad—*Get $$*. Sandy's brow wrinkled. Gracie wrote again—*Venue bill, he should pay*.

Sandy brightened at the idea. "You do know there's still the matter of the invoice from the Royale. Someone from the billing department handed it to me that night, and she didn't care one whit that you didn't show up. They'd prepared the food and decorated the ballroom. I didn't know what to tell her, other than I would get it to you." She strived to make herself sound worried at this last bit.

"Oh, god," he moaned. "I'd forgotten about that part of it. Didn't we put down hefty deposits ahead of time?"

"No ... remember they did us a favor on that part."

She mouthed to Gracie, *What if he calls them?*

"Rob, I'd be happy to handle it for you," Sandy said, putting strength back in her voice. "I can just draft the company checking account, and it'll be all taken care of."

"How much is it?"

Gracie was scribbling numbers on the notepad, turning it to face Sandy.

"Let's see … With the tax it comes to $25,486.51—that includes everything, as far as I can see." Sandy sent a puzzled look toward her companion, and Gracie shrugged. "Last time I balanced the account there was plenty to cover that."

"Wait until Monday," he said. "I've had some other expenses and I want to review it."

Rats! "Okay. Will do. Let me know if you need anything else, boss."

"Now what?" Sandy said, the moment she'd shut off her phone. "He'll try to worm out of this, I know he will."

"Well, it's kind of found money anyway, isn't it? But it'll be a great way to start reimbursing his victims."

"We shouldn't wait until Monday," Sandy said.

From her briefcase she pulled the folder of notes she'd been keeping on Intrepid Dog Pictures. The bank account information was right at her fingertips. She paused. "I can't do this from here. It's beyond iffy, and I *am* the manager of this bank."

Gracie reached for the page. "I need to get going now," she said coyly, "but I'll be seeing our friend Amber this afternoon. I think she can manage to handle this little item."

It took a good forty-five minutes to reach Amber's off-campus apartment and another ten for Amber to get home from her Pilates class, although she swore she'd left the moment she received Gracie's call.

"Here's the banking information Sandy had, the business account for Intrepid Dog Pictures. Her login info and password is here … And this is the amount she quoted Rob for the room at the Royale."

Amber's eyes widened at the dollar amount. "Nice dinner."

"It would have been."

They both laughed.

Amber sat at her keyboard and logged into her virtual private network, setting the location at Los Angeles. "Just in case there's a question about why the transaction would be happening in Arizona."

Gracie helped herself to a handful of M&Ms from the coffee table bowl while Amber keyed her way into Rob's business account.

"Nuh-uh, not going to work," Amber said. "Look at his balance."

"Ninety-seven dollars?" Gracie called Sandy at the bank and told her.

"He's beat us to it," she said. "I wasn't fudging when I said I knew he had enough. That account had more than thirty grand in it last time I looked."

Chapter 40

Close call, Rob thought as he watched his checking account balance transfer to another, secret account. He'd forgotten he'd given Sandy authorization to make payments from his account for the venue deposits. Lucky she hadn't actually done so. And really lucky she hadn't gotten to his last ten grand. Tyler Chisholm was pretty clear that he expected payment on Rob's legal bill *now*.

He pushed away his breakfast plate and swigged the last of the coffee. The conversation with Sandy had put him in a foul mood, despite the fact he'd saved the money. He slapped a twenty on the table and got up, preferring to leave the waitress a generous tip rather than have to smile and converse his way through receiving and paying the check.

Why did life have to be so damned unfair? Adrenaline

pumping, he started to walk home then remembered he'd driven to the pub. He strode back and got into the Land Rover. The Scottsdale event was a total bust, the villa in France was now gone and everything else in that region way out of his league. He squealed the tires leaving the parking lot. A cop on the corner gave him a look and he backed off the gas.

Keeping an eye on the police car and restraining himself at the wheel only served to darken his mood further. What he needed was to get to an open stretch of road and take the Rover up to a hundred—blow out the cobwebs, both in the car and in his head. But it seemed like too much effort to navigate the jam-packed freeways and get out to open space. He found himself cruising his neighborhood, hating the row after row of old houses like the rental he lived in, overpriced little pieces of crap where people thought by adding granite countertops and stainless steel appliances they had actually taken them out of the Depression Era. His landlord was a prime example.

Rob tried to think of somewhere to go, someone to call and make plans, but nothing came to mind. Abby was gone; the other office girl—well, he couldn't even remember her name; Sandy was in Arizona but he couldn't socialize with her anyway. She would soon discover his account couldn't cover the Scottsdale bill and she would have to bring that up.

He thought of all the celebrities he'd met over the years, the ones whose pictures graced his mantel and dotted the walls at the office. Not one of them would call him a friend; most wouldn't even recognize his name if he called and said, "Hey, this is Rob Williams."

It was pitiful. *He* was pitiful.

He missed his villa in France. Okay, the *idea* of his villa.

He found himself parked in the driveway at his house, staring at the skimpy front yard and cracked red tiles on the roof. Couldn't spend a day looking at that. He went inside and switched on his widescreen TV, drawing all the drapes shut. Maybe if he found a tennis match or football game he could get wrapped up in it, could find himself cheering for a team or a player. He needed something to cheer for, and at this moment it certainly wasn't himself. He stretched out on the couch and let the sports announcer's patter lull him to sleep.

He found himself standing on the courthouse steps beside Tyler Chisholm, knowing as their conversation took place that he was dreaming.

"Hey, man, you got lucky in there," Tyler said. "You got away with it."

"I did, didn't I? I got away with it. Fat chance of any of those other dupes putting together enough of a case to come after me, right?" His heart soared and he felt light as a feather.

Tyler held out his hand and Rob put a stack of banded hundred-dollar bills in it. The lawyer thanked him and walked away. Rob watched him go and felt his mouth form a huge grin. Ha ha! The judge had done him a huge favor and no one was after him. No more running scared!

You know you can't keep this up. His lawyer's voice came back to him. *You can't keep taking money or someone will hunt you down.*

Rob's eyes popped open. The sports announcer was in a frenzy over some fantastic play. But the words from the dream echoed through his head. *Someone will hunt you down.*

He sat up, fighting off a dizzy spell. The dream held a warning and Rob knew he'd better heed it.

Chapter 41

S o," Gracie said, looking around the small space in Amber's apartment at the others, "what are we going to do now?"

Mary had paced the length of the short living room at least six times. "I'm so angry I could just shoot the guy's balls off."

Sandy laughed. "Tempting—but not very practical."

Gracie piped up. "Yeah, guns are dangerous. I could bake some poisoned cookies."

"Yeah ... no. That just *has* to backfire somehow."

"I believe we're on the right track with the money," Pen said. She was looking over Amber's shoulder, where the details of Rob's bank account showed on the computer screen. "Look at the amounts of money he moved in recent weeks."

"Twenty thousand two weeks ago, ten thousand today," Amber said. "But that's not even close to the amount we know he's brought in. He took a couple hundred thousand from Gracie's mother alone. And that doesn't even count all those people we saw in Newport, signing up for his scheme right and left."

"There must be other accounts," Sandy said. "If we can get details about where some of these transfers went, I can help you decipher them."

"Let's also consider who else Rob might have paid money to," Pen said. "His lawyer most likely got paid—they always do. That could account for those two transactions you just mentioned. What about prior to those? Do you suppose he actually did sign contracts with a few film stars? He might have paid handsomely to associate their names with his projects."

"How we would ever find out?" Sandy wondered.

Pen was quiet, thinking. "The book I had optioned for film … nothing ever came of it, but I still have contact information for the agent who represented me on the contract. He's a chum of my literary agent. Perhaps one of them would know what's churning in the Hollywood rumor mill. I'll give a call when I get home."

"That sounds good," Sandy said. "Meanwhile, Amber and I can see what we come up with on the banking angle. Gracie, I heard your phone ding at least three times, so I'm guessing your kids need something—go to them. And Mary, you most likely need to get back to the gym and find a punching bag in need of a good beating."

Mary stopped pacing and grinned. "I think you're right. Call me when you've got something for me to do."

Once the others had left, Sandy pulled up a chair beside Amber's and watched as their youngest member scrolled through the pages of transactions.

"Okay, money, money, money … Where did you go?" Amber stared at the skimpy balance in the Intrepid Dog Pictures account.

"Click that transfer," Sandy said, "the one where the twenty thousand left the account."

A smaller box appeared, three lines of gibberish text and numbers.

"Those are codes for the type of transfer it was and the bank it went to," Sandy explained.

"I think I recognize some of those digits. I was in Rob's personal account earlier." Amber opened a new window and backtracked through a few screens of information, consulted her notes and entered a password.

"Okay, here it shows the twenty thousand coming from his business account. But now here …" She pointed to the screen. "Here it shows the twenty thousand being drawn out in cash at a branch bank near his office."

"How did he do that?" Amber asked. "Wasn't that the day we turned him over to the police?"

"Yeah, it was …" Sandy studied the transaction and asked Amber to click a small link. "Okay, it looks like he did a teller authorization to pay the cash to someone. Most likely he knows someone at the branch bank well enough that he could do this over the phone. Looks like the money went to a Tyler Chisholm. Do we know—?"

"His lawyer! The guy who got his case dismissed."

"Ah, yes. That's who it is. Funny, I can't imagine a lawyer requiring payment in cash."

Amber sat back in her chair, quietly staring at the computer screen. "Who would Rob need to get that much cash to, right at that moment? You don't suppose—I mean, it would be crazy—but what if he bribed the judge?"

Sandy turned toward her, her face drained of color. "That's a serious allegation."

Amber held both hands up. "I'm not alleging anything. Not yet. Just wondering …"

"My god, it could explain so much. The push to get the case heard right before the holiday break, the fact it would certainly go to Judge Alderston, the way he barely listened to any of the evidence before blatantly dismissing it …"

"The way neither Rob nor his attorney seemed very surprised at the outcome …"

"How would we ever prove it? All we know is that the attorney received the money. He'll just claim it was for his fee." Sandy couldn't sit still. She was up, pacing the same track Mary had done earlier. "There's no way to go back now and catch pictures of the lawyer and the judge in some secret conversation. It's done."

"We'll have to set a trap." Amber had that familiar gleam in her eye.

"Right, and how do we do that?"

Amber's fingers drummed lightly on her keyboard. "I'll think of something."

Chapter 42

Gracie called the next meeting, and it came sooner than anyone had anticipated—four hours after they'd been at Amber's place. They met in Gracie's kitchen. Scott had taken the kids to a pizza place because, as Gracie put it, "I'll kill the first person who crosses me tonight."

"I can't handle it," she said, once the group had assembled. "All those texts this afternoon—my mother. She's been given thirty days to get her loans up to date or leave her house, and guess where she's planning to come."

"Here?" Amber's voice squeaked as she said it. Everyone else's eyes were wide.

"Four more people. Shifting bedrooms, we might figure out, but it's also taking on all their problems and their drama. Mom will lose the social life and shopping that makes up her day. She'll be joining me to do *everything*.

Hannah's kids were quiet enough when you saw them, but that's not the real story. They pick at each other and fight all day, and they aren't in school yet—they need *constant* entertainment. I tell you, I'll go insane."

She'd heated the kettle for tea, but her hand shook so badly she had to set it down.

"And you know what Scott said when I told him? 'You're having a real crisis moment, aren't you, honey?' Well, *yeah*. Aside from something dire happening to my kids, I can't think of much worse. Mom and I, we come from different planets. Half a day is our max time together."

Pen took over the teakettle. "All right, we must keep our heads. How much money was it?"

Gracie named a figure that put Mary, Amber, and Sandy completely out of the running as far as offering some help. "Scott and I have already borrowed to help her once. We just can't do it again. Things are tight."

Pen looked thoughtful. "I don't have it in ready cash, of course, but dipping into my retirement funds is certainly an option."

"Pen! You will not. This is my mother's problem—and okay, it may soon be mine too—but it's not up to you to bail her out."

Sandy put an arm around Gracie's shoulders. "Let's take this a step at a time. We're still working on getting the money back from Rob Williams. Trying to be logical about this, I'm thinking he's hoarded it somewhere. He was about to purchase a villa in France, and we don't think that happened. So it means the money is still in his name."

"And we'll find it," Amber said, her chipper, upbeat voice trying to lighten the mood.

"That's right." Sandy went on to tell the others about the banking codes she and Amber had discovered on

Rob's fund transfers. "I haven't had time to track them down yet, but I will get on it first thing tomorrow. The basic information will be easy to gather from our internal system at the bank. Once we know which banks he's using, it should be easier for Amber to work her magic."

Amber preened a little.

"I can't believe I'm saying this." Sandy put a hand to her forehead. "It can never, *never* be known at the bank that I have anything to do with hacking someone's account."

"Trust me," Amber said. "Your name will never show up on anything. How can it? I'm the one performing the searches. And we haven't actually talked about taking any money from these accounts of his. We just want to know where it is, turn the knowledge over to the law, right?"

And look how well that worked out last time. No one said it, but they all had the same thought.

"Along those lines, Amber and I did discover something interesting this afternoon." Sandy told the others about the twenty thousand dollar transfer and cash payment to Rob's attorney, along with her reasons for believing the judge might have been the one to end up with it.

"How will we ever prove it?" Pen asked.

"Amber suggested setting a trap. Clever, but I can't imagine how."

"I've had some other thoughts," Amber said. "Let me work on it a bit."

Mary spoke up. "Meanwhile, I think we need to find someone higher up within the law. Even *if* we managed to get money back for the victims—by whatever means— Rob Williams needs to answer for his actions, and if a judge was bribed to let him off, well, we really want to be sure that comes out."

"Working another bit of the puzzle," Pen said, "I

called my Hollywood agent to ask about Rob's contacts with the famous actors he claimed to star in his films. The agent has never heard of Rob Williams. She offered to look up Intrepid Dog Pictures, in case Rob is merely a silent partner, and said she would get back to me with any news. We shouldn't hold our breaths. I got the distinct impression this agent would have known if Brad Pitt or George Clooney had worked for him."

The lines around Gracie's mouth had relaxed. "Okay, so Amber's tracking money movement, Mary will look into the judge's actions, and Pen is checking Rob's Hollywood connections. I think I also mentioned that before I turned over all those business cards with various investors' names to the California police, I photocopied them. I could be compiling the list, calling some of the people ... it might lead somewhere."

"Great idea," Sandy said. She looked closely at Gracie. "I hope this helps. I feel certain that we'll come up with the answers and be able to get your mother's money back. Do you feel a little less like killing someone now?"

Gracie laughed. "Yeah, I guess it's safe for Scott and the kids to come home tonight."

The women finished their tea and said goodnight. Having definite plans, and Sandy's words of encouragement, had helped. But, could they wrap it up and get the money in a short thirty days?

Chapter 43

He hadn't been out of his house in three days. The dream, in which Tyler warned him, had kept him awake that night. Midway through the next day he dozed on the couch again, and another dream caused him to thrash around so badly he fell off and hit his head on the coffee table. Same song, second verse—someone would hunt him down.

Sandy had texted him twice and left three voice messages. Where was the money for the Royale? They were hounding her and Rob needed to pay the balance he owed. Was this what the dreams were telling him, or was it someone else tracking him down?

In his dreams that night, bad guys were lurking outside his office. One approached and asked where the money was, shoving a gun into Rob's gut as he uttered the threat.

Rob woke from that one in a sweat and couldn't fall back to sleep the rest of the night.

Maybe it was the booze.

He quit drinking but still had the dreams. His eyes would close in exhaustion, but the moment he drifted to sleep someone would be chasing him down the street, or they would corner him in an alley, or he would catch a guy trying to plant a bomb in his vehicle. He let his phone's battery die so he couldn't receive messages. One of the days that passed in a blur—he wasn't sure which—was Christmas Day. He didn't remember a single detail about it.

He started drinking again.

On the fourth day he considered getting a gun but discarded the idea when he considered the background check and mandatory ten-day waiting period. On the fifth day he was glad he didn't own a gun because he would have drawn it when the doorbell rang. Peeking out the window he saw it was the FedEx driver with a flat envelope in hand. He opened the door a crack and the driver informed him the delivery required a signature.

The guy gave him a funny look when he reached one hand out to sign for it and to snatch the package. Rob didn't care. He knew what he looked like—unshaven, greasy hair, wearing sweats that hadn't been laundered in a week. There were probably homeless people in the city who looked better than he did. He snarled at the driver and closed the door, turning the deadbolt with a click.

The package had a return address he didn't recognize and contained two sheets of paper, an invoice from the Royale and a letter. Sandy had tracked him down.

He wadded up the invoice without looking at it and tossed it into the trash. No way was he paying that thing— let them come find him. The letter nearly followed, but he glanced at it.

Dear Rob, I hope everything is all right. I've been so worried because my messages aren't going through and I haven't been able to reach you by phone …

The kind words were the last thing he'd expected to hear. He sank to a stool at the bar and started crying.

Chapter 44

I think I'm wearing him down," Sandy said.

The weather had turned cloudy and rainy—Phoenix's version of winter—and people all over the city had taken to wearing sweaters, hats, and mittens even though it was fifty degrees outside. The Heist Ladies had spent Christmas day together, except for Gracie (for whom the holiday was sacred time with her kids) and Amber (who had flown to Santa Fe to be with her parents).

Now, a few days later, it was time to get the group together officially for updates. They were seated at a corner table at their favorite lunch place, where soups had been the choice for the chilly day.

Over her tomato-basil soup and toasted cheese sandwich, Sandy told the group about the FedEx letter she'd sent to Rob in hopes he would reveal some other bank account and authorize her to pay the invoice she'd enclosed. "I put the return mailing address as that of the bank's post office box, since I'm the one who checks it each day."

"And?" Gracie was especially eager.

"Rob finally called and he sounded awful on the phone. He must have had a terrible head cold, stuffy sinuses and the whole bit. But, long story short, it didn't work. No money forthcoming."

"Did he say anything else?" Mary asked. She ripped a corner from the garlic bread that had come with her minestrone.

"I asked if he was planning another gala, acted very chipper and eager to help with the planning." Sandy shook her head. "He's got nothing on the horizon. I tried to pry information, but he sounded so listless, as if he doesn't care about anything in the world. I almost felt sorry for him."

"Yeah, well, just remember my mother is moving in with me in three weeks if we can't get that money back. Don't start feeling too sorry for Rob Williams." Gracie waved her spoon in the air for emphasis.

"Sorry," Sandy said. "I mean … you know what I mean. I certainly don't pity the man. I just wonder what's going on with him."

"And I *do* think you should stay in touch with him," Pen suggested. "We still need information."

"Yeah, I've hit roadblocks on the banking situation," Amber said. "I managed to track some of the transfers to other banks, but none of them contain large balances either. It's as if he's got the money hidden under the mattress or something."

They all exchanged glances. It was true—while inside

Rob's house, no one had thought to literally check under the mattress.

"Nah—surely not," Mary finally said.

"Besides, we were interrupted, if you recall," Gracie said.

From the depths of a purse, a cell phone rang. Pen reached for hers, pulled out the phone, and looked at the screen. "Nice—it's my agent."

She took the call, her expression brightened, and she reached into the purse again for pen and paper. A number of short responses, some jotted notes, a profuse thank-you, and she turned back to her friends.

"This might actually be useful," she said, dropping the phone back into her bag. "Remember, she previously told me she'd never heard of Robert Williams, but it turns out a few people in the business have got wind of Intrepid Dog Pictures. She took an interest and did a bit of further research. Intrepid has been associated with a Valiant Flame Films, which in turn was listed in an industry directory with one called Gallant Man Films."

"Let me see," Amber said, abandoning her bowl of chili and reaching for Pen's tiny notebook. She scowled at the written words, trying to remember whether any of them had come up in her research.

"Wait a second," Sandy said. "Intrepid, Gallant, Valiant ... don't all those words mean the same thing?"

"Or nearly so. I hadn't caught that during the call," Pen said.

"What do you think the odds are of three unrelated companies choosing such names?" Mary asked.

"And the fact that they essentially indicate being fearless, bold, courageous ... Doesn't that sound like *such* a Rob Williams thing? He really does think those words describe him, doesn't he?" Sandy was nearly beside herself with excitement. "It's got to be—all those companies must be related, and Rob Williams has to be behind them all."

Amber had picked up the small notebook and was tapping it on the table thoughtfully. "Now, the question is whether we can find the money through those."

Sandy appeared the most lost in her thoughts. "I wonder what I can say or do to get the information."

"I'd be very cautious. We can't afford to spook him," Pen said. The others nodded. "He's left the country once. He could easily do it again."

Chapter 45

Rob stepped out of the shower, kicking his grubby sweats aside. He found a clean pair in the closet and put those on. His dark suits were already showing a layer of dust on the shoulders. How long since he'd dressed and gone to the office? He couldn't remember.

When he'd charged his phone, one of the messages was from the receptionist—Aspen, she said her name was—who whined about not getting a paycheck in two weeks and what did he think she was living on anyway? He deleted the call without waiting for the end. No doubt some kind of deadline for a check or she was quitting. Fine. Let her quit.

Then he remembered the phone call he'd made to Sandy the day after Christmas. The conversation was kind of a blur—she being all solicitous, he in some kind of mood he'd not felt since his mother died. He hoped he hadn't become too maudlin. How embarrassing.

Sandy's two themes were: when would he pay the invoice for that Scottsdale thing that didn't happen. Answer: never. And then she wondered if he had another gala in the works and did he need help with the planning. No and no.

He'd already been thinking about dumping Sandy. She was a lot smarter than Abby had been, even though she lacked the showmanship to handle the crowds and rake in the investors; and there was certainly no question of sex with her. She was like a big sister who showed a guy up with her efficiency.

Other things bothered him about Sandy—how she knew what Air France flight plans to change, how she got his home address for FedEx, and—strangest of all—why did she come to the courtroom and barely wave hello? He liked efficiency in a PA, but one who practically read his mind and made it her business to check up on him? It kind of creeped him out. On the other hand … he had to admit she'd aced the planning for Scottsdale, and if he ever wanted to hold another event, it would be real handy to have her around.

His hand lingered over the screen on his phone as he debated calling to fire her. From his contacts list, it was only a click away to the app where his movie trailers were available. He sat on the edge of his bed and went through them. He remembered the thrill of piecing the footage together, taking A-listers and putting their website clips together with stock backgrounds and flashy fonts. So simple with a basic video editing program, and he'd even gotten the 'announcer voice' down pretty well too.

It *would* be fun to do another.

It would be a lot of work, and no guarantee the returns would be lucrative. Things could go wrong. Again.

Tempting, but dangerous. He sighed and shut off the video, went into the bathroom.

Yeah, the movie investor jig was up. Tyler Chisholm had made it pretty clear, and Rob's heart wasn't really in it anymore. He'd been so focused on that villa, on getting away to a place where he could live the lifestyle of the rich and famous without having to work for it.

The bubble had burst; he'd spent a week feeling sorry for himself. Now it was time to think of his future. He still had a *lot* of money. The idea improved his mood. A completely fresh start, a beach somewhere, maybe a quiet little town where he could change his name and live anonymously. It was beginning to feel like too many people knew too much about Rob Williams.

He looked at himself in the mirror, stroking the dark facial hair that was nearly long enough to be trimmed into a decent beard. This could be the perfect time to change his appearance. With his dark hair, he could blend in somewhere to the south. There were places you could cross into Mexico without showing your passport, weren't there? The law was only looking for dark-haired people sneaking *out* of Mexico.

From there, a whole continent awaited. He ran his fingers through his hair and smiled at himself.

Chapter 46

Gracie hung up the phone and gripped both sides of her head. "Mom's packing. What am I going to do?"

Sandy looked up from her notes. The two of them had been at Gracie's dining table all morning, calling those on the list of investors Gracie had compiled from the stolen business cards. So far, the results hadn't netted much more than anger at Rob Williams and quite a few promises to join in if a lawsuit was filed. Many had broken down in emotional tirades over their personal circumstances, tears over the fact that they could not afford to lose the investment. She wondered if others were in the same position as Janice, moving in with family members as a solution.

"You could move in with me and let Scott handle your mother?" Sandy suggested it with a wry smile.

"Tempting as that sounds, I really don't want to end up divorced. Of course, with Mom in the house, after a week or two that's still a possibility. I tell you, I'll go nuts."

"Oh, Gracie … I wish I knew what to say." Sandy indicated the names she'd checked off. "I can't believe the personal grief this man has caused so many people. Did he truly think everybody who fell for his scheme was only giving away 'spare' money? People like him—I believe they only think of themselves."

They both remembered Mary's experience with her ex-husband last year, another example of a man's single-minded selfishness.

"Do we have *anything* to go on?" Gracie asked. She set her phone aside and went to the kitchen to top off her tea mug.

"I'm waiting for a callback from one woman. She remembered a lot of details about the night she went to one of Rob's investor meetings. She paid by check and is fairly certain she can get a copy of it."

"Which gets us to Rob—how?"

"I made sure the woman understood I needed to see both front and back of the cancelled check. From that, I hope to get numbers that will tell me the account it was deposited to, and *that* may lead us to the money."

"Sounds like a roundabout method."

"It is. The good news is she wrote the check to an entity called Fearless Filmmaking."

"A new one!"

"Yes, and this was only a few months ago."

"So it's likely the account still exists." Gracie was so excited she nearly tipped over her mug.

"We shall hope so. At least all these new names are ones Rob never shared with me, so I have a feeling he thinks no one knows about them."

Sandy's phone rang just then, startling both women. Gracie crossed her fingers.

"Yes? Yes, Mrs. Peabody. Oh, that's great news. Both sides of it, yes please. Can you take the photos with your phone? Oh. Well, that's okay. Get a photocopy and put it in the mail for me." Sandy gave her home address and reiterated how important it was to send the copies immediately. "Keep your original in a safe place. We're hoping to bring the case to court and it could be evidence."

She ended the call and turned to Gracie, whose mood had quieted again.

"It's only a couple of days. She promised to mail it today. Hang in there."

She walked over and gave Gracie a hug.

"Meanwhile, let's keep calling the folks on our lists. If nothing else, touching base will give them some reassurance, and we may even come across more information that will help us track the money."

Gracie perked up. "Whatever it takes to keep Mom in her own home."

Chapter 47

Amber set Mary up with her spare computer at the breakfast bar and showed her the basics of exploring social media.

"It's always a good place to start when you want to know what people are doing, thinking about, or bragging about. Remember how I located Abby Singer that way?" Amber said. "Have fun with it—I'll be over at my desk digging into that information Pen gave me."

Mary began with the most popular site for those over fifty, since that was their judge's age range. Facebook showed a slew of Alderstons, but only two in southern California. One was younger, but the one that caught her eye was a Lois Alderston of Glendale. Her most recent post began with 'Look what Layton got me for Christmas!'

"Amber, that judge's first name ... is it Layton?"

"Yeah." Amber didn't take her eyes from her own screen.

"Bingo. I found his wife." Mary looked at the posts. Only a few showed. Apparently you had to 'friend' someone to see everything they wrote, but in this case she might have come up with what she really needed without revealing herself. She read the most recent two entries:

Luxury owner's suite on the SS Wellington! Woo-hoo!! First time I've ever been treated so royally.

The post accompanied a photo of a huge fruit basket alongside a box of chocolates and bottle of champagne. Three other photos showed a large shipboard suite with stunning aqua seas in the background.

The next post showed an extremely rotund man in baggy trunks on a lounger by the pool. On a table beside him were two beer glasses and a plate heaped with nachos. He held out one hand, as if to say, *Don't take my picture*, but his face showed clearly.

"Yep, it's our man," she told Amber. "Looks like he sprang for quite the Christmas gift."

"Price it—see what that trip costs," Amber suggested.

Mary felt slightly out of her depth—martial art classes were more her speed than internet searches—but she got the knack of Google pretty quickly.

"What do I put—Caribbean cruises?"

"Get more specific," Amber advised. "Put the name of the ship and something like 'luxury owner's suite pricing.' No point in dallying with a hundred million useless search results."

Mary followed instructions and up popped a link to the cruise line's official website. It didn't take but a few clicks to get to Accommodations and Pricing. And sure enough, there was the owner's suite photo, all decorated up in the same scheme she'd just seen on Lois Alderston's Facebook page. "Got it. Whoa, that baby's pricey. They're getting ten days for what I paid for my car."

Amber got up and looked over her shoulder. "And isn't it interesting … it's about the same amount Rob took out of his account right before the arraignment."

"Now, if we just had a way to find out whether Judge Alderston paid in cash," Mary mused.

"Maybe we can. For now, let's just get screenshots of these Facebook posts and the cruise line's price list." She instructed Mary on which keys to press, and immediately emailed the shots to Sandy, Gracie, and Pen.

Within two minutes Mary's phone rang. Gracie. "I bet I can tell you the travel agent who booked this trip," she said, her voice shaky with excitement. "Her name's Tonya Bridwell, and she advertises herself as California's cruise specialist. 'We'll get you there in style.' And last-minute bookings are welcome. Mom used her a couple of times, but she says Tonya is only friendly to people who want the high-end cruise packages, the ones who spend the most."

"Sounds feasible," Mary said. "I'll give her a call."

She turned to Amber when the call was done. "So, how am I going to get the travel agent to admit whether the judge showed up with cash in his chubby hands?"

"Pretend to be a friend of Lois's?"

"That'll work." She found Bridwell Travel online and got the number, insisting on speaking directly with Tonya.

After gushing about what a great time her friend Lois was having on the cruise and telling the agent she wanted to do the very same one, she found Tonya warming up. Tonya verified the pricing and that the owner's suite would next be available in four weeks.

"Lois hinted that maybe Layton got a discount by

paying cash—is that true?"

"We are sometimes able to negotiate cash discounts," Tonya said, being a bit cagey.

"That Layton, I'll just bet he did. The man loves to walk in and flash some money. I remember a time we were all— Oh, never mind that. For a man who loves to spend money, he also loves to get a deal. So did he? Get a discount by paying cash?"

"If what you're really asking is whether you could get the same deal … yes. Twenty thousand even, and the owner's suite is yours for the cruise. When can you come into my office?"

Mary almost flubbed her next lines, but managed to pretend she was setting up a real appointment while remembering to give a fictitious name, address, and phone number. Her hands were shaking as she ended the call and pressed the button to stop recording the conversation.

"We've got him," she said.

Chapter 48

Amber smiled at Mary's good news, pleased she'd thought to show her less-techie friend how to record the conversation before dialing the travel agent. Meanwhile, Amber had been delving deep into the locked areas of three different banks.

Rob Williams was no dummy when it came to moving money around and disguising transactions—she had to give him that much, although why he hadn't closed the various accounts after taking out the money still puzzled her. The fact that the near-empty accounts still existed was definitely making her current efforts easier, and it would have been such a simple matter for him to close the accounts, knowing after a year or so they would virtually vanish.

She'd found connections between his personal account

and that of Intrepid Dog Pictures—that had been simple right from the start. Less straightforward were the links between the other business entities Pen's agent had divulged. Valiant Flame Films appeared to be completely separate from Gallant Man Films, banking wise, but when she entered both names into a Google search, at least two websites linked them to shared film projects.

Reading the articles attached to the links, though, was when it really got interesting. A partner in Gallant Man Films had registered a complaint that expenses had greatly exceeded projections and he'd not been able to recoup his investment. This had happened ten years ago. Although a separate search showed this person to be well acquainted with film production and Hollywood's ways, in other aspects his story sounded eerily similar to what had been happening recently.

She followed a link to the movie in question, discovered it was now way down in the backlist of titles on Netflix, and brought up a page with the film description. Rob Williams was nowhere to be found among the producers, executive producers, or director. In fact, a search of the entire Netflix website came up with no results matching the Rob Williams they knew. Where was his supposed Oscar winner? Why didn't his name come up alongside all the big stars he'd claimed to have worked with?

There was one person she could ask, knowing she would get straight answers—her father. Edward Zeckis had a bunch of colorful and varied past experiences, and in one of those past lives he'd been a film editor, valued as part of Santa Fe's movie industry because he not only had a talent for putting scenes together in memorable ways, but also because of his business sense. The latter was one reason he and Amber had exchanged words over her choice to leave college, but their close relationship since her childhood overrode what he saw as her youthful folly. He had to admit there'd been plenty of folly in his own youth.

"Hey, Dad," Amber said when he picked up. "I know I probably caught you and Mom either finishing meditation or about to start your pre-dinner glass of wine …"

"We're right between. What's up?"

Cutting to the chase was a trait shared by both father and daughter, and Amber wasted no time formulating her questions about why someone in the movie industry would have so many bank accounts and such a variety of business entities.

"You want the long answer or the short one?" he asked.

"Short."

"Taxes. Run money through enough different shell corporations, drum up enough expenses, you can shelter almost all the income from taxes."

"What about investors? Can you shelter it from them too? Make it so they never see a penny of profit on their investment?"

"Wow—how did I raise such a smart little girl?" He chuckled.

"I'm guessing, actually, but is that true?"

"It is. It's why it's critical in a contract whether the language states gross, adjusted gross, or net profits. Why is this coming up, honey? Have you invested in something?"

"Not me. A relative of a friend, and it's a little complicated."

"I'm guessing it's a *lot* complicated, since you're calling me. Anyway, tell your friend to read the fine print. The wording is everything."

"Is there ever a way to find out the real story—what

was really earned?" Amber wasn't sure why she was asking. They had every reason to believe at this point Rob Williams had simply pocketed the money.

"Whew—I don't know. Find a lawyer or accountant who's been burned and see if they'll cross the line and turn over evidence? Maybe? It won't be easy. Those are usually the ones who actually *do* get paid, and paid very well, to not let go of secrets."

"Thanks, Dad."

"Hey, sweetie? Be careful." There was indistinct conversation in the background. "Oh, and Mom sends her love."

"Love you guys too." Amber put her phone down, pondering what he'd said.

Was there a whole tangle of corporations set up by Rob Williams to hide the true nature of his dealings? It seemed likely. Could five women peel away enough layers of the onion to get to the heart of the matter? That part felt scary, getting into the tax records and delving deep. She knew she should talk it over with the rest of the group before proceeding. But her fingers lingered over the keyboard, itching to begin the search.

Chapter 49

Sandy placed another glass ornament into its compartment in the storage box and closed the lid, just as Amber arrived.

"I don't know why I put up a tree every year. It's just for me and, I suppose, the cats. They get a kick out of knocking all the little danglies off so they can watch me put them back." As if to prove the point, Heckle and Jeckle wandered through the room, brushing their backs against the lowest of the branches.

Amber laughed and called the two black cats over to her. "I liked your tree this year. My apartment is so small, I can barely handle one of those little table-top ones. By the day after Christmas, it's back in the box for another year."

"Well, with everything else going on, I'm more than a week late in getting this organized. At least the ornaments are off. I'll work on getting the tree back into its box and the whole thing out to the garage later. When did the others say they would be here?"

"Mary can't make it. She's got classes at the gym all day. Gracie was making waffles for the family and says she'll come as soon as they're off to their other activities."

"Ooh, we should have gone to her house. Waffles never happen around here, unless I toss a box of frozen ones into my grocery cart now and then. What about Pen?"

The ringing doorbell answered her question. Pen was decked out in wool winter-white slacks and jacket, with a lavender silk blouse.

"Wow, you dressed for the occasion," Amber teased, indicating her own leggings and baggy tunic sweater.

"I've a book signing downtown later, an indie shop where the owner likes to do it up with tea and crumpets. They think it goes with my English accent, although personally I don't care at all for crumpets." She set her bag on a chair in the living room. "At least I've dressed the part."

Sandy stacked the Christmas decoration boxes in one corner and fluffed the pillows on the sofa. "Sorry about being so disorganized."

"You should be," Amber teased. "After all, we're accustomed to yours being the haven of order, while my place is ... I'm not sure what you'd call it."

"Early American Dorm," Sandy offered with a laugh.

The sound of Gracie's minivan out front got their attention. She bustled in, bringing a hint of the chilly day and a whiff of bacon. "Okay, girls. Scott took the kids for a Saturday at the mall. I'm free for awhile."

Amber started the conversation by passing along what her father had told her about the various layers production companies could form, ostensibly for tax purposes but also a convenient way to assure no one made a profit on the film.

"I'm pretty sure it's exactly what Rob Williams has done. None of the accounts I located had much money in them at all."

"But why bother with the elaborate setup if he never intended to make the movie at all?" Gracie asked.

"Good question. My guess is that he had delusions of grandeur, thinking he actually *would* become a huge Hollywood mogul. Maybe he saw himself as the next Stephen Spielberg, but even with the money he gathered he never got the backing of a studio, or never managed to sign the actors he wanted." Amber shrugged. Her dad hadn't known the answers to those questions either.

"Dad did seem to think there would be some sort of written records somewhere. Unless Rob wanted to find himself in deep trouble with the IRS, he must have filed tax returns."

"Banks do report money movement," Sandy said, "and with the amounts Rob was collecting, I'd bet the government knew about it. I agree with your dad—surely, tax returns were filed."

"We could try to get copies," Gracie suggested. "If it's possible to match figures from those with the amounts we estimate he collected from his investors …"

"There must be an accountant or lawyer with those documents," Sandy told them. "We would need some official reason to request them. Or … it isn't as if we haven't broken in and retrieved documents before."

"Another thought. I could pose as a messenger," Amber said. "Tell the accountant Rob asked me to go pick up his records."

Pen looked a bit antsy. "It all sounds horribly complicated. And then what do we do with the information? We would have to be forensic accountants to decipher it all. And do we all want to run the risk of crossing paths with the IRS and having them question how we came by these private records pertaining to the claims we're making?"

"Or we turn it over to the law and they put their actual forensic accountants on the case," Sandy said.

The room went quiet. The law had not served them well.

Gracie broke the silence. "My mother is heading this way in a little over two weeks. I don't have time to wait for the slow process of the law. Can't we just—?"

"She's right," Amber said. "Our true goal is to get justice for the victims."

"A lot of the people we talked to gave almost everything they had to Rob Williams," Sandy said. "They can't afford the legal costs to pursue this in court."

"And don't forget, we're going after that crooked judge, too. Rob's business records won't necessarily get him."

In the pause that followed, Sandy noticed the mail truck stop at her mailbox. She got up and went out to meet it. When she came back inside, she had a triumphant look.

"I was hoping this would arrive today," she said, ripping into one of the envelopes. "The photocopy of Mrs. Peabody's check to Fearless Filmmaking."

"Another one?" Amber was puzzled.

"Yes. I didn't bring it up yet, thinking we could get more information from the check. And here it is." Sandy studied the back of the cancelled check. "I recognize the bank's routing number. The deposit went to New York Commercial Bank."

Amber already had her tablet out. "Account number?"

Sandy read it aloud and Amber began her search.

"I've got information on the bank," she said, "but I can't actually access an account without my special—"

"Don't tell me. The less I know, the better," Sandy said, handing Amber the cancelled check copy.

"I'll work on it from home later." She tucked the envelope into her messenger bag. "I was thinking about all his money movements yesterday and had to ask myself why he wouldn't have closed these accounts once he moved the money out. I mean, without this trail we'd be having a harder time than we are. But then last night it came to me—this could be evidence that he intends to keep doing the same thing. Maybe he's just lying low for awhile."

"I wondered that, too," Sandy said. "Could be that you're right, Amber. With new laws on money laundering and all, it's getting tougher to set up a new account. There are lots of questions. Rob could be counting on his collection of existing accounts. You know, he's still in touch with me at times. I'll see if I can figure out a way to ferret out the information."

Amber gathered her things. "I'm going home right now to start working on this. And I'm going to set alerts on as many of his accounts as I can. That way, the banks will notify me whenever a deposit is made."

"You can do that? On his accounts?" Pen asked.

"Let's just say, I have my ways."

No one questioned her.

Chapter 50

Rob Williams paced his living room, a dilemma on his mind. Half of him wanted to just get away, forget films and become a beach bum; the other half remembered the thrill of the conquest, setting up the show, wowing the people, getting the money. Maybe he'd been hasty when he'd vowed never to do another. He still had the bank accounts that enabled him to channel the money; he could always whip up another trailer.

A few days ago, he'd been one click away from phoning Sandy and calling it quits. Now he was thinking how handy it would be to keep her around to set up another gig—this one would be his last, he promised himself. He stared at the celebrity photos on his mantle, remembering the days when he'd bluff his way into a club or party, seek out the biggest-name stars in the place and greet them familiarly, then snap a selfie with Angelina or J-Lo or Brad as if they were best of buddies.

The reminder made him smile and he went into the kitchen for another cappuccino, which he carried to the sofa to enjoy while he stared some more at the photos.

He needed to think about this, but in the meantime he could string Sandy along with hints at doing another gala. Or maybe he'd tell her he was going on location to start a new film. He sipped the creamy vanilla coffee.

Yeah, maybe that was his best idea yet. Pretend to Sandy that he was heading out to a film location but have her work on setting up another investor gala. While out of the country, he could target the exact property he wanted to buy. If it went over the current budget, he'd come back and rake in some more bucks. If the plans for the gala started to head downhill, he could simply stay away.

This time he would look for something remote and private. No more grand plans of living in the midst of the celebrity community—he was sick of them. Sorry, Brad. Rob sent a wry smile toward the row of mantle photos. And no more of this huge city with its traffic and pollution and noise. The idea pleased him immensely.

His eyelids began to droop as he settled into his dream scenario. He lowered his cup to the floor and put his legs up on the sofa. The beat of mariachi music began to play in his head, and he went along with the whole scene: a pitcher of margaritas, a beach full of bikini-clad girls on spring break, just wanting to get wild with him. Oh yeah.

Chapter 51

Monday morning Sandy received a text from Rob. She was in a meeting when it came, so an hour went by before she was able to get back to him. In the meantime, two more messages came. So, Mr. Incommunicado was now wanting to talk again. She went into the restroom to read them.

Need to talk about plans. Call me.

Got some great ideas for a new plan. Call me.

Not speaking? What's this?

Sheesh. It's one hour out of your life—you can wait while I pee. She finished and went back to her desk, closing her office door behind her.

"Sorry, Rob, but I'm at my other job. I had to keep it since I don't hear from you for weeks, much less get paid ..."

"That's fine. I just needed to get your attention. I've

got some big plans in the works."

It was as if nothing she'd just said registered. As always, the world revolved around him. Sandy had to will herself to stop making it personal and tune her ears to pick up useful data.

"I'm thinking we can still do this in Scottsdale," he was saying, "but a different guest list and venue. No reminders of the one that didn't work out."

She almost laughed. If she had actually booked the venue and invited the guests from his list, *didn't work out* hardly covered the fiasco. She noticed he made no mention of the huge bill he supposedly owed. She supposed that ship had sailed, forgotten forever in his mind.

"So, what I'm thinking is that you'll get the gala all arranged and set up. I'm off to a location shoot, but we'll keep in touch. Once you've got everything ready to go, I'll buzz down for the evening and handle the real stuff."

The real stuff? Buzz in for one evening? If she'd been a real employee, actually working to pull the event together, she'd be royally pissed at his cavalier attitude. No wonder Abby Singer had bailed. This guy was a case.

Focus, Sandy. Try to learn something useful.

"Wow, Rob, that sounds fantastic. What's the new film about?"

"Oh, you know … There's this guy who's gone through a terrible setback, so he drops out, gets away from society to 'find himself.' That kind of thing." There was a pause. "We've got Denzel Washington for it."

"Nice." She put as much enthusiasm into it as she could muster. "I like the sound of the getaway. Where will you be? Is it like a rustic place in the mountains, a grass shack on the beach …?"

"More like the latter, but I haven't decided yet. I'm

heading out in the morning, going to scout locations. You know, it's tricky to get just the right feel for every scene. Sometimes we move around a lot. You know, the cantina's in one town, the hotel in another, just however it works best."

Hadn't he just said he was going to this location to begin filming? Now it was just to scout around for the perfect bar?

"Well, I guess not every palm tree looks great for the camera," she said.

"Start checking out venues for another gala. I'll have the office send the guest list—but feel free to add names if you know people who want in on a great opportunity—and I'll be in touch once I'm somewhere with a decent phone signal."

As if I would put my worst enemy on your guest list. "Okay, I'll have some information for you in a day or two." She ended the call and immediately dialed Pen.

"He's making his move." Sandy's heart raced as she realized it was true. Their quarry could easily get away.

"I'll gather everyone. We now need a plan."

Chapter 52

They met for a quick lunch, as Sandy and Mary both needed to limit the meeting to an hour.

"I have a feeling it's Mexico," Sandy said. "He avoided answering when I asked where, just gave little clues, such as, he can get back here within a day for an evening gala. He used the word 'cantina' instead of 'bar' and there was a reference to a beach."

Amber hadn't touched her burger yet. "I've seen some money movement from the Fearless Filmmaking account."

"You can get data from his computer, right?" Mary asked. "Didn't you add some little tracker?"

"Basically, I can only monitor his email and there hasn't been much lately that isn't junk. But I'll keep checking. If he's traveling, something is bound to show up." She picked up a fry and nibbled at it.

"The main thing is to be sure he doesn't move all the money in one big swoop. That will surely be our sign that he plans to disappear for good," Pen said. "Not to mention, we'll never get hold of it then."

"I've got some good ideas for the next fake venue for the gala he thinks I'm planning, so I'll keep in frequent contact with him. As long as we dangle the carrot of another possibly big event's revenue, he won't go too far away."

"Even so, we cannot become complacent. Even if it appears he's going to Mexico, it's a fairly large country to start hunting for him, plus it can be the gateway to all places south." Pen appeared concerned. "He could be targeting Brazil, Panama, Costa Rica, Columbia ..."

Sandy's phone pinged with an incoming email. "It's from Rob."

Everyone went quiet, as if he could hear their chatter, even through email.

"Ah ha, he's saying the guest list for the party is attached. Interesting. He told me he would have the office send it, but this message is definitely from him."

"He's shut down the office—I'll bet on it," Gracie said. "Why keep it open when he only had a receptionist sitting at a desk, right?"

Another sign he was getting ready to skip out. They all knew it.

"We'll have to act quickly," Mary said. "If we don't basically move right alongside him, he'll get away forever."

Amber reached over and touched her hand. "Forever's a long time, and don't forget—I have my ways."

As if in answer to Amber's promise, when she looked at her iPad again, one of Rob's emails had showed up in her browser. "Well, look at this, ladies. A vacation rental service confirms his reservation for a beachside condo in Puerto Peñasco, Mexico."

"Where is that?" Pen asked.

"Also known as Rocky Point. It's *the* hot spring break haven for every college kid in Arizona, *and* it's only four hours' drive from here." Amber blushed a little. "Well, okay, I did the spring break thing once with friends. Didn't do much for me—the bars and strip clubs are just too rowdy, and there wasn't a decent wi-fi connection to be found."

The others laughed at her assessment.

"But that was a few years ago—there's probably a decent internet provider down there now. The place does stay popular."

"When does his reservation begin?" Sandy asked.

"Friday night. And he's booked the place for a week."

"Friday is tomorrow—he's heading out!" Gracie seemed somewhat panicky.

Pen was more thoughtful. "If he's staying a week, my guess is he'll use the time to scout other places. He would want to be near enough to come rushing back once Sandy says she has the gala put together, yet he won't likely permanently relocate this close to the border. I'd think he would want to be farther away."

"Like deep in the jungle somewhere," Mary said.

"Hmm, maybe. But I sense our Rob is a man who wants his creature comforts. Remember the size of that place in France he was looking at."

"I wonder why he didn't go back there?"

"My guess—money," Amber said. "Remember the price tag on that place? Without the take from the Scottsdale gig that never happened, he couldn't do the deal."

"So … he's counting on me to arrange another one, he'll swoop in to grab the money, and then he'll be off to

France again."

"We'd best be watching all the exits," Pen said. "Right now, it appears Mexico is the place, but I don't think we should count on its being his final destination."

"You're right," Mary said. "He might have figured a fake booking down south was an easy way to throw us off the scent while he heads for Europe again."

"Anything's possible," Amber told them, "but I'm going to keep a close watch."

"I don't think he's onto us." Sandy sat back against the padded banquette. "But just to be sure, I'll make certain my responses to his messages make me look completely wide-eyed innocent." She batted her eyes a few times, and to make her point she answered his email, reading aloud as she typed. "Hi Rob, thanks for the guest list. I have two wonderful venues to consider. Do you want to come out and take a look, or shall I go with the best bid?"

Almost immediately came his response. I trust your judgment completely. Go with the better place—cost is no object.

"Wow, he's good at this," Mary said. "He gives no clue he doesn't plan to be right there."

"Well, maybe he does."

Chapter 53

The office had an abandoned look to it. Rob hadn't shown up there in a week, a fact that shouldn't have made much difference, he thought. Through the sidelight window, he could see envelopes on the floor under the mail slot. Even the doorknob felt disused. Inside, dust coated everything like a fine trace of snow.

Clearly, the girl Aspen had not been back since her ranting phone message. Her personal things were gone, the top of her desk bare. He felt a pang of guilt. He should have at least returned her call and paid the two weeks' wages. One of the items in the mail was an envelope from the state employment office. Trouble.

Another fat envelope from the IRS. Quarterly taxes would have been due more than two months ago. Employment reports, workers comp forms, and three charities wanted money. He hated the first of the year. Every agency had its hand out. He tossed the envelopes on the empty desktop and wandered back to his private office.

His executive chair felt cold and stiff, unused to having his backside parked there. He looked through the desk drawers, but nothing inspired him these days. Aside from Sandy's enthusiasm for planning another of his *gala* investor events, he'd lost all zeal for his business. It was time to get out, but he needed to plan correctly unless he wanted the authorities from every stupid government office in the country to come looking for him.

Someone had sent him a day planner for the new year; he stared at it, tapping his pen against the desktop. He needed to make his exit look unremarkable, as if everything was business as usual. He opened the little notebook's crisp pages and began writing. With different pens and pencils, he made notes of upcoming engagements, filling the pages with everything from dental appointments to important-sounding phone calls to meetings with well-known names at major movie studios. He blocked out the upcoming two weeks with one notation: **Scout locations for "Whizzbang."** The made-up movie name sounded generic enough; no one would guess whether it was a thriller or a rom-com.

Within ten minutes, he'd filled all of January and February with busyness, and jotted in random appointments throughout the first six months of the year. Even birthdays received attention. He noted when to send flowers to actresses he'd claimed to work with and a case of whiskey to certain A-list men. Hopefully, the fact that he was making up these dates would never get checked. Did cops actually know when Julia Roberts' birthday was? He was betting they didn't. He left the book in the center drawer of the desk.

That task complete, he scouted all the desk drawers and pulled out the few important items: the first Montblanc pen he'd ever bought himself, half a bottle of Courvoisier liqueur he'd rather keep than let some cop take home, a collectible postage stamp in a tiny glassine envelope. He'd bought the thing on a greedy whim when he was told it was nearly priceless. Turned out it wasn't, but you never knew when someone else down the line wouldn't know that.

All the ordinary office supplies stayed in place to make it look as if he would be back anytime to resume business. All except one large brown envelope. He hand addressed it to his accountant, went back to the reception desk, and dropped all the official-looking mail into it. Alice would assume he wanted her to take care of the taxes and employment forms, and she would simply fill them out and file everything without question. She'd been with him long enough she had his signature down pat.

He sealed the big envelope and set it beside the other 'keepers' on his desk. Now, to make it look as if he was actually heading out to scout those locations he'd noted in the appointment book. He walked through the offices, studying, making a plan.

In the art director's office were some old storyboards he'd designed back when there was a possibility he might actually make a movie. Same with a couple of good cameras. They'd been secondhand at the time, but were far from new technology today. He'd even had a Director chair made with his name stenciled on the back. He debated taking them along with him, but aside from sentimental value, they would merely be useless extra baggage. He shook his head and decided against hauling them along.

For the sake of show, he stacked the items near the door so it would seem he planned to come right back for them. Let the landlord keep them as souvenirs if he wanted—the old guy was a pain in the ass anyway, nagging him relentlessly the last couple months for rent. Let him sell the expensive furniture; it would more than compensate.

What do I need with office furniture where I'm going? Rob justified to himself. Even if the villa had worked out, it made far more sense to buy everything new over there rather than ship his old stuff.

The villa. What an embarrassing phone call that had been the evening he got out of jail, asking—practically begging—the realtor to say it was still available. Of course, it wasn't. Even though the man tried to put the best face on it and talk him into looking at other properties in the area, Rob found he'd lost his taste for the French Riviera. He'd rather spend his efforts brushing up on his Spanish anyway. His sights were now set to the south. Acapulco, Mazatlán or Puerto Vallarta … he could practically hear the mariachis already.

He looked at the small pile of items on the desk. Nah, there was nothing much worth keeping from this place. He slipped the expensive pen into his pocket, the postage stamp into his wallet, took a slug from the whiskey bottle, and jammed it into his briefcase. He would drop off the packet for the accountant at the post office on his way home. It wouldn't take but a few minutes to pack up his clothes and a few personal mementos. The crappy rental house could go the same way as the office, back to its landlord.

The Rover could hold everything he needed and he'd be on the road by nightfall. *Ai Chihuahua*, here I come!

Chapter 54

Rob threw the last of his belongings into the Land Rover, stopped at the post office to get rid of his tax obligations, then called for directions from the woman whose condo he had rented in Puerto Peñasco.

"You're heading out from where?" she asked.

"Los Angeles. Thought I'd drive down to San Diego and cross the border at Tijuana. I just need to know the way to your place from there."

She seemed hesitant. "Well, it's pretty far, the route you're describing. You'd be driving through the desert at night. I really don't advise that. We always go west and south out of Tucson."

"So, what should I do?"

"I'd take I-8 through Yuma, cut south at Gila Bend, and cross the border at Lukeville. Just be aware the border closes at midnight there. I'd at least stay the night in the States so you're crossing the border and navigating the Mexican roads in daylight. They don't have many signs and … well, it's just safer by day." She didn't seem inclined to say more.

Where the hell was this Lukeville? He stared at the map again. Next to the post office, Rob had spotted a bookstore where he'd purchased the road map in case his cell phone maps wouldn't work at his destination. He'd also picked up a CD set called "Learn Spanish in a Week."

The crossing at Tijuana was a lot closer, and surely it was a busy enough place it didn't close halfway through the night. What the heck, he decided. I've got hours to spend in the car, no matter how I go at it. I'll learn the language along the way.

The stretch of urban sprawl between greater L.A. and San Diego went on, basically non-stop, making a person feel as if the world was one huge, gigantic city. He almost didn't realize he was about to cross into Mexico until he was already in one of the eight traffic lanes for the huge port of entry at Tijuana. The border guards were bored and ready for a shift change, he could tell, and all they wanted to do was keep traffic moving. They waved him through with barely a glance.

Immediately, all the signage became Spanish. Women with children, beggars with missing limbs, and slick types shouting about timeshare deals crowded toward the cars, many risking their lives in hopes of selling tortillas or getting a handout. Rob felt a jolt of culture shock. He guessed the meaning of certain signs by the context— *cerveza* over a familiar Tecate can, *mercado* above the door of a small grocery—but, added to the intensity of the crowds and lights, most of it was a blur.

Ahead, he spotted a green and white road sign indicating Highway 20 and the city of Mexicali. For that particular stretch, the highway paralleled the US border. He imagined if he changed his mind he could somehow turn north again, but knew he would need to go south and follow the shoreline of the Sea of Cortez before he got to his destination. He took a deep breath for courage and proceeded.

The highway was of decent quality and as he left the bustling city of Tijuana behind he began to feel a bit more confident. He quickly figured out the speed limits were posted in kilometers per hour, when he found himself passing several cars in a row. He'd better be careful—he'd heard about encounters with the Mexican police.

Mostly, other drivers were simply minding their own business, going home after a long day at work or whatever they did around here. Delivery trucks with pictures of potato chips and loaves of bread poked along, but they willingly edged to the shoulder when others wanted to pass. Once he came upon a heavy-duty truck with no lights. It was full of big boulders and could barely drag itself down the highway at twenty miles an hour. He hit his brakes, looked ahead, and had enough room to swerve around the hulking behemoth. After that, he drove with his bright lights on.

Within a short time traffic had thinned and he settled into the trip, still keeping an eye for unlighted vehicles after the truck scare. The CD in his player had cycled through the first set of lessons, but he let it start over. He hadn't retained a thing.

"Good day," it said to him. "*Buenos dias*."

He repeated the greeting.

"How are you? *Como esta?*"

He kept up the rote recital and saw the lights of Mexicali after about an hour. His next turn would take him south to Golfo de Santa Clara. He hadn't spotted one single turn back to the north. The night became blacker and blacker.

Only one other vehicle made the southbound turn ahead of him. Obviously it was someone who knew the route. The car zoomed ahead and the taillights were out of sight within minutes.

"Now let's combine what we know so far," the recording told him. "*Buenos dias, como esta?*"

He kept his brights on and settled in with the lesson.

"Now let's learn the response. Say '*Muy bien, y usted?*'"

Rob copied what he thought he heard, although he had no clue what it meant, and the words were blurring together in a rapid flow. His upper-Midwest upbringing was not serving him well. He should have paid more attention during his years in southern California. Maybe he was just tired. He ejected the CD, deciding maybe some talk radio would keep his attention.

He was reaching for the Scan button on the radio when he saw the bright lights behind him. Someone was coming up on him—fast. He gripped the wheel.

The other driver didn't slow until he was right on Rob's back bumper, blinding him with the lights.

What is this? Am I about to be run off the road—hijacked?

His fingers gripped the wheel so hard he heard it creak. He concentrated on watching the center yellow line on the road. His instinct was to speed up, try to leave the other driver behind. But he couldn't see ahead well at all. He dared not touch his brake pedal. All he could do was keep his eyes on the road and pray.

Chapter 55

The Heist Ladies had decided to take two vehicles for the jaunt into Mexico, just in case some of them needed to stay longer. Sandy had taken a week's vacation; as manager of the bank she didn't answer to anyone within the branch, but management higher up had already looked askance at some of her absences. Mary's partner in the gym had told her it was no problem—stay as long as she liked—but she led classes certain days of the week and her women martial arts students liked it better when she was there. She'd told Billy she would do her best to be back within one week.

As for Gracie, she was still on the edge of panic about her mother, sister, and two nieces invading her home. Of the group, she was pushing hardest for a quick resolution to the case. Pen was treating it as a research trip—who knew when a Mexico location could come in handy in one of her novels? Amber would act as tour guide, being the only one who'd ever visited the small beachside town before.

They'd purchased their Mexico car insurance, packed their bags to include a number of special items, and hit the road early Friday morning. Rob's vacation rental began tonight, and they wanted to be in place before he arrived. One of Sandy's clients had offered the use of her three-bedroom condo and, fortunately, it was in a different complex than the one Rob rented, although the woman told Sandy it was only two or three buildings away from the other place. It seemed like an ideal setup.

Amber recommended a lunch place called Pollo Lucas, which turned out to be an open air grill with a palm frond roof and dirt floors where, once they placed their order, they watched a man grab a split chicken off the hot grill with tongs. Three or four whacks with a cleaver and the meat went onto a serving plate. Containers of beans, rice, and salsa plus garnishes of pickled red onion and cabbage, and the meal was served. The women carried the bounty to one of the picnic tables beneath the palapa, mouths watering at the heavenly, charred meaty scent.

"If we get to keep eating like this, I'm staying forever," Sandy commented, partway through her second tortilla-wrapped piece of chicken.

Nods all around, although no one stopped chewing long enough to answer.

Amber eventually spoke. "I'm sure our condo will have a kitchen, so we can always get more of this and eat at home. But you're going to find there are so many great restaurants in town, we could eat somewhere different every meal and not have time to come back."

As always, Pen was the voice of reason. "We may

not have time for restaurant meals, girls. Remember our purpose is to follow Rob Williams and figure out what he's up to."

That put a damper on the vacation-like mood until Mary suggested they get a couple more orders of the fantastic grilled chicken to go. "You know, in case there isn't time to eat out. We'll make tacos and carry them along on surveillance."

No one could disagree.

Thirty minutes later, completely sated, Amber cleared the disposable plates and plastic forks. "Ready to head to the beach?"

She rode in Sandy's car, while the others followed in Gracie's van. Amber knew the general direction to the stretch of beach that had blossomed with high-rise buildings in the late '90s, but she only had a sketchy map of where the various developments fit in. They cruised along, watching for the name of their building, turning and stopping at a closed iron gate where a security guard stepped out of his little hut and asked where they were going. Sandy handed over the authorization letter from her client, and the guard courteously indicated which of the three buildings they would be in and where they should park.

"Nice digs," Amber commented as they drove over a cobbled path, past palm trees and flowering hibiscus.

They had caught glimpses of the sea, but it wasn't until they rode the elevator to their third floor unit and walked inside that the majesty of the place really hit.

"Oh, my god," Mary said as she stepped over to the sliding glass doors which entirely made up the western walls.

The glass opened to a spacious terrace with cushioned

chairs and a couple of cocktail tables; beyond, the sea spread out below in brilliant, glorious blue. Amber had scouted the various doorways opening off the central greatroom, and she reported that all three bedrooms managed to face the same direction with views of the sea, the boat harbor, and the hill in the distance from which the town got the nickname Rocky Point.

"Okay, I could easily just kick back here for the rest of my life. I say we forget about Rob Williams."

Gracie gave her a light punch on the arm. "I say we don't. But, we could still kick back and enjoy the place for several hours until he gets here."

"We passed the development where he'll be staying," Sandy said. "I noticed it—the white building with dark blue trim. There was a gate and security guard there, as well. We'll have to figure out how to access it."

"The beach," Amber said. "I remember that from my last trip. It's easy to walk down the beach, go through the bar or pool area of any complex, and go inside. As long as we know which condo he's staying in, we can figure it out."

"I'd be happy to spy on his balcony from the beach," Gracie said. "I brought two bathing suits, but I'm surprised it's not warmer. I may be down there in sweatpants and a windbreaker."

Amber laughed. "It is January, silly. We may be slightly south of Phoenix, but it's also a lot more humid here. Humidity intensifies the chill, or the heat."

However, out on their balcony, midday, with the sun casting golden beams across the tiles, the temperature was perfect. They claimed rooms and set their bags inside, then voted that all strategy meetings should take place on the terrace and margaritas would be allowed, at least after lunch. Gracie reached into the coolers and bags they'd brought with a few basic grocery items and proceeded to blend the refreshments for their first afternoon.

Mary, ever practical, had brought binoculars and was scanning the beachside face of the white and blue condo unit. "Can't tell how to figure out which is his," she said.

"I have a solution for that," Amber told her. "When I get in there, I'll mark it for us."

Chapter 56

The rude driver with the bright lights had roared past Rob, the black pickup truck evil and frightening in the dark night. The woman's words kept coming back to him. *Well, I sure wouldn't drive that road at night. Cross the border in the daytime—it's much safer.* He'd talked to himself for hours, looking for assurance that the darkness wasn't filled with drug lords and highway robbers. He didn't even allow himself to consider coyotes and rattlesnakes.

Rob's heartrate only slowed down when he reached the outskirts of Peñasco as the sun was coming up over the desert. The Land Rover was low on fuel and he pulled into the first Pemex station he saw. When he got out and reached for the fuel nozzle, an attendant in a dark khaki green uniform called out to him in rapid Spanish. Apparently, they pumped gas for you here.

"You speak English?" Rob asked. Somehow he didn't think *buenos dias* was going to get the job done.

The man shook his head and proceeded to lift the nozzle on the gas pump.

"Just fill it up," Rob said, loudly, in case that would make the guy understand him better. He needed to learn some more phrases, and quickly.

He'd had the foresight to convert some dollars to pesos before leaving California, but he was astounded at how quickly the price was clicking upward on the gas pump. When it finally came to a stop, he owed more than six hundred pesos. He reached into a pocket and pulled out a fistful of cash, Mexican and American currencies mixed.

The attendant gave the money a long stare and Rob realized what a stupid move that had been. He found a 500-peso note but it wasn't enough. He gave the attendant a stupid smile and shrug.

The man smiled and said, *"Dolares okay."*

Rob held out a twenty but the man shook his head. He reached into his hip pocket and pulled out a smart phone. With a couple of taps, he came up with a currency converter app and showed Rob on the screen how much he owed. It came to eight dollars.

Hmm, Rob thought. Maybe it's not such a backward place after all. "Thanks, *amigo. Muchas gracias.*"

The attendant rewarded him with a wide smile.

Okay, good, Rob said to himself when he got back in the Rover and started the engine. I've already made a friend. And I need to get that app.

He'd been told he could check into his condo at any time. But first he wanted some breakfast. He started looking around. Should have asked the guy at the station where was a good place to eat, but that idea seemed a little iffy. He might get sent to a taco stand where the special included parts of the pig you didn't even want to ask about.

He drove a few blocks, noticing many of the signs here were in English. The benefit of settling in a popular tourist destination, he supposed. He saw signs indicating the way toward Sandy Beach, the area the rental lady had said where the condo was. What he saw in front of him was a packed row of high-rise buildings. That must be it.

He aimed toward the buildings, keeping his eyes open for indications of a breakfast place that would include some eggs over-easy and lots of coffee. Finally, it was a photo that caught his eye, a plateful of the exact food he had in mind, with the word *desayuno* hand lettered boldly in red. He parked next to a battered pickup truck that had probably once been white. Huge patches of rust left both rear quarter panels dangerously ragged. The rest of the cars in the lot were newer, but nothing as stand-out shiny as his. If he hoped to blend in, he'd better pay attention to little details like this, get himself less-obvious wheels.

When he walked into the little café, conversation came to a momentary halt and two dozen dark eyes raised to look at him. He gave a wary smile and looked for a hostess. In a couple of seconds the other patrons went back to their meals, and a waitress with a friendly smile greeted him in halting English, telling him to sit wherever he would like.

He picked up a newspaper someone had left on an empty chair near the door and carried it to a corner booth. After a little back-and-forth with the waitress, during which he pointed at pictures on the menu rather than trusting his limited Spanish, he picked up the paper again and looked at the front page.

The largest item on the page was a lurid picture of two dead bodies, complete with blood dripping down the sides of the faces, bulging eyes, and arms that showed the hands had been roughly chopped off. He concentrated instead on the headline, trying to translate.

Resultado de las drogas y narcos durante la noche

The references to drugs were fairly clear. Rob tried to piece together some of the sentences in the article, but it was way over his head. A twenty-something guy at the next table must have noticed.

"A terrible thing," the guy said in accented English, "those *narcos*. They give all of Mexico a bad reputation."

"Yeah. We hear a lot about it in the States," Rob said. He glanced uneasily at the picture again.

"This one, it is not here in Peñasco. It happen in Sinaloa."

"Is that nearby?"

"Oh, no. Sinaloa, she is much south. The only problems never happens near here—it's always out in the desert, late in the night. Most the people here, we love *la paz*. Um, the peace, and the quiet."

Rob nodded. His eggs arrived, and the other man turned back to his own coffee. He drained his cup as Rob was buttering his toast and said goodbye. Rob watched him get into a newer model Jeep with only two long cracks across the windshield.

The only problems happen out in the desert, late at night. Bright headlights, the black truck—the panicky feeling came back, and Rob had to set down his toast and the knife to hide the way his hands were shaking. Apparently, he'd gotten very lucky.

Chapter 57

Amber walked along the beach in shorts and a t-shirt. She'd slicked back her wild curls and tamed the whole mass into a bun in the style favored by the young local women. With her creamy-coffee skin, she fit right in. A couple of young locals addressed her in Spanish and she responded in kind.

When she came to the blue-trimmed white building, she strolled across the pool area and into the lobby. She knew exactly where she was heading. Rob Williams had rented unit 410B. The elevator carried her to the third floor, where she found the maintenance closet.

Maids wore a sack-like dress in the same blue as the building's trim, belted in white. She found one of the uniforms hanging on a nail behind the closet door, closed the door behind her, and slipped the uniform on over her clothes. A bottle of spray cleaner and a white rag completed the outfit.

When she emerged, she took the stairs to the fourth floor and let herself into 410B with the passkey she'd snagged off a maid's cart she passed in the hall. A furtive look through the rooms let her know Williams hadn't checked in yet. She opened the sliding door to his terrace and looked toward the Ladies' lodging, where Mary stood on the balcony, binoculars to her eyes.

The prearranged signal was that Amber would carry some brightly colored object out to the terrace. When she spotted it, Mary would send a text to Amber's phone, which would give a little buzz down inside her pocket. If Rob was present, he'd never realize a thing.

Amber looked around the condo. The bath towels were red—perfect. She carried one out and flapped it up and down, as if she was shaking it free of lint or something. Down in her pocket, her phone buzzed. She smiled.

For good measure, since she couldn't very well leave a bath towel outside, she found a brilliant red, yellow, and blue talavera flowerpot near the sliding door. A sprig of lush magenta bougainvillea grew out of it. She took the pot from the floor and set it on an outdoor table. Rob was unlikely to rearrange the patio furniture and plants, so they would have a more or less permanent way to locate his place. Her phone buzzed again. Fleetingly, she wondered what text messages in a foreign country were costing, then decided not to worry about it.

All at once, she heard the doorknob rattle. Quick as a fox, she picked up the bath towel, stepped inside, and closed the slider behind her.

Don't stress—you belong here, she reminded herself. She strolled casually to the bathroom where she rehung the towel.

The door opened and she heard a masculine grunt as his suitcase hit the tile floor. She ran her cleaning rag over the surface of the bedroom dresser and emerged into the living room. His appearance had changed somewhat—the goatee had become a full beard, the conservative haircut had grown out a couple of inches and had a bit of curl to it.

"*Buenos dias, Señor.*" She picked up her spray bottle and ducked her head slightly as she passed him on the way out the door.

"*Buenos dias*, miss," she heard behind her.

The door closed and she fast-walked to the stairs. Down to the third floor. No one in sight. She slipped back into the maintenance closet and replaced all the borrowed items, removed the pins and band from her hair and shook her curls free.

Strolling through the lobby, the dark-skinned girl with wild hair looked like any other guest as she went out back toward the pool and beach. A casual glance upward showed Rob Williams standing on his balcony, hands on hips, gazing toward the sea.

"He's here," Amber announced as she walked back into the condo.

Mary stepped in from the balcony. "I spotted him. Just to be sure, I counted—four floors up, sixth window from the left. Even if he moves the flowerpot—which was a great touch, by the way—we can watch."

"Too bad we don't have a way to watch the parking lot. What if he leaves? How will we know where he's going?"

The five of them exchanged a look. "I suppose we shall deal with that as it happens. Wing it, would you say?" Pen said.

Chapter 58

The sun felt warm on his bare stomach and he shifted slightly on his lounge chair to get a better look at the group of women who were obviously on a 'girl's weekend out.' They wore too much makeup and too-skimpy bikinis for their ages, in his opinion. All were over forty and their bodies showed the signs of childbearing and an American diet focused on crispy fried foods and diet soft drinks. No sign any of them had run a mile or lifted a barbell in at least twenty years. He liked that age—it marked a woman of experience and savvy—he just liked them better if they looked like Jennifer Anniston.

For some reason, his mind switched to Abby. She looked nothing like Jennifer but she was a hell of a lot prettier than most of the pickings around here. Maybe he should have taken her hints about commitment more seriously.

On the other hand, it was still his first day in Mexico and the weekend hadn't fully arrived yet. He could take his time. When he found the right one, or ones, his movie-producer line would fit right in.

"Sir, you want something to drink?" A slender young man in the uniform of the condo complex stood beside him, holding a brown tray. His hair was thick and glossy, his shoulders and arms showed evidence of regular workouts. "We have margarita … piña colada … mojito … cerveza …"

"Which is the best?" Normally he would have ordered a beer or a whiskey, but why not go a little local for a change?

"People love the margaritas. And it is our *especial* today. Two for the price of one."

"Okay, bring me that."

"*Dos?*" The waiter held up two fingers in a V.

"Sure—*dos.*"

See? He was getting the hang of the language. When he looked up, the group of women had picked up their towels and headed toward the beach, twenty yards away. They looked better at a distance so he watched as they dabbled their toes in the water and bent to pick up shells.

The waiter was back with his drinks within five minutes. They seemed a little on the skimpy side in small glasses. Where were those huge ones you always saw in pictures advertising the goodtime life in Mexico?

"Our bartender he make them very strong. You get you money worth."

"Great." He fished some cash from the pocket of his trunks. "Say, what is there to do around here?"

The guy waved an arm toward the beach.

"Well, yeah, but like for shopping or restaurants or just to watch the people. Where do the locals go?"

"Everyone go to the *malecon*. Is many shops there, very

good prices. On Sundays, everybody there, *everybody*. The fish market, the vendors with the candy and churros. Go to my brother's shop and tell him Jose send you. You get more discount." He tore a corner off his order pad and wrote on it. Chuey's Souvenirs. "You will see his name above his shop, and he have the best glass ... what do you say ... glassware?"

Rob nodded. He couldn't figure out why he would be interested in glassware, but the tip about the *malecon* sounded okay. He could settle in at the condo for a day or so and then give it a try.

"Do the pretty girls hang out there?" he asked as he handed Jose a little extra tip.

"Oh, the girls—for the prettiest girls you want *Guau-Guau*. They dance with the pole, they have the little outfits—" He stopped suddenly. "So sorry, maybe that is not what you mean. Maybe the girls at church are more you like."

Rob smiled and assured him it was okay. Jose thanked him for the most generous tip and backed away to check on one of his tables. Rob snickered as he picked up his drink. A tittie bar called Wow-Wow. Okay.

He sipped his first drink, pleased to see that Jose had not been mistaken about the amount of tequila in it. He drank some more. It was already midafternoon, and the air was cooling. If he downed two margaritas he'd better be thinking about what he would do for dinner. He'd driven around town a bit before coming to the condo and was pretty sure he could find his way to this *malecon* area, but that might wait until Sunday when it sounded like there was more action.

It seemed like a nice little town, kind of on the quiet side, but that might be all right too. He remembered the graphic picture on the newspaper's front page—murder and violence related to the drug trade. But wasn't that everywhere these days? There were certainly parts of L.A. he'd never dared drive through, especially at night.

Again, his memory flashed back to the big vehicle that had nearly run him off the road last night. Yeah, if he had any ideas about settling in this country, he'd better learn more about it, about which areas were safe and which were not. Maybe the guy at the breakfast place was right—most of the people minded their own business and wanted a peaceful life. Maybe the violence truly did take place among the *narcos*.

His first glass was empty and he picked up the second, after slipping his sweatshirt on. The air had definitely become chillier, and the sun was low in the sky, developing into a magnificent sunset. Yeah, not a bad little town at all.

It seemed like minutes later when someone jostled his chair and he realized the sun was gone and the vivid turquoise sky was fading quickly. He'd only closed his eyes for a moment to rest them. He didn't even remember finishing the second margarita or setting the glass down, but he must have. His empties had been cleared away, and most of the pool crowd had vanished.

He sat up a little too quickly and had to take a few deep breaths to steady himself. It had been an intense night and a long day. Maybe he would just go to the room and get a good night's sleep.

He barely remembered walking up to his condo.

Chapter 59

Pen and Amber entered their condo, pulling off the wigs they'd worn down to the beach—Pen's a froth of blond curls and Amber's a shaggy orange with pink tips. If Rob had noticed them at all, the vividness of Amber's hair would likely be the only thing he remembered. But he had never turned around to see the two women in the lounge chairs directly behind his.

"Tomorrow or the next day he'll be down by the port, cruising the *malecon*, I'd bet," Amber told them as she unpinned her own voluminous hair and let it free. "His waiter made it seem like the place to be."

Mary was out on the balcony. "I can see him in his living room … now the kitchen. He's got lights on but didn't bother to pull any curtains. He's standing in front of the fridge. Oops, he must have forgotten to buy food—he slammed the door."

"I wonder if he's going out for dinner," Gracie said with a yawn. "I don't know that I'm much in the mood to chase after him again."

"He's digging into a bag of chips he had with the cooler he brought with him. And a beer. Settling on the couch with the TV remote in his hand."

"Personally, I would bet the two margaritas he chugged down at the pool will have taken away his energy," Pen said. "Did you see how quickly he went through those?"

Amber laughed. "Yeah, and how he was snoring in about five minutes."

"As far as chasing after him, how much do you think we need to follow his every move?" Sandy asked. "I do still have the means of contacting him on the pretense of the new gala plans."

"Sandy is right. Our goal is to make sure he doesn't disappear into the jungles of South America somewhere," Pen said. "But as long as he seems comfy and happy here, this is most likely where he'll stay."

"Mainly, while he's distracted by women on the beaches and consuming strong drink, I'm going to be working on figuring out how to get our hands on the millions he took from his victims and how to get it back to them. Luckily, there's a good wi-fi connection here, and I've already got my VPN in place." Amber had parked herself at one end of the comfy sofa and was tapping away at her computer keys.

"Enjoy yourself," Gracie said. "I'm heading for bed." She went into the room she and Sandy would share and claimed one of the double beds as her own.

Sandy was busy with her phone. "I'm texting him as if I believe he's still in L.A. Telling him about this great venue

I've discovered and sending a few pictures. It's supposedly a country club on the west side of the valley, but I grabbed the photos from an online stock artwork site."

"He's taking a look," Mary said when she saw Rob reach to the end table and pick up his phone. "Seems interested. Oops—he tossed the phone down. Ah, nature call—he's heading to another room."

"Well, this is all very fascinating," Pen said, "but I agree with Gracie. It's been a long day. I'll be fresher and ready for more adventure in the morning." She'd drawn the straw for the single bedroom and bade the other ladies good night at the door.

By the next day, it became apparent Rob wasn't on a fast track to another destination. He hung around the pool some more, walked a short stretch of the beach and back. It was warmer today with more people out in bathing suits, which seemed to be Rob's central focus.

"What's he up to?" Pen and Gracie mused, watching from above. "I expected he would be much more on the move, meeting someone or traveling through."

Sunday morning he was seen gathering his wallet, sunglasses, and car keys. The Ladies did likewise, piling into Gracie's van in time to follow him out of the parking lot. It couldn't have been more than a couple of miles, but Rob took a meandering path toward the Old Port area, past the fish market, and finally parked in one of the cramped slots at the *malecon*. Gracie had no choice but to drive past and go another block—parking was at a premium.

"Keep an eye on him," she told the others. "I won't be able to get very close."

"I know where he's going," Amber said. "We just passed it, Chuey's Souvenirs."

Gracie spotted a curbside spot on one of the small side

streets and quickly whipped into it. Sandy tucked her hair up inside a large sunhat she'd brought and put on a pair of dark glasses. She was the most likely to be recognized.

"Don't worry," Amber said. "He's convinced you're in Phoenix." She had pulled her own hair up to the top of her head with a stretchy band, making a fluffy whale spout, and wore huge round sunglasses with orange frames.

Pen, the only other of the group Rob had ever met, had put on baggy sweats, a dark wig, and red lipstick. The others laughed at how unlike herself she looked in the new guise. As long as Rob was fooled, that was the main thing.

They got out of the van, a motley group.

"Maybe we should split up," Pen suggested. "A group is more memorable than one or two. Plus, we can maintain better coverage that way."

Amber and Mary volunteered to move in close and find out what he was doing at Chuey's Souvenirs. The fact he'd gone there right away, and the place had been recommended by the waiter at the pool, made them wonder if he'd asked for something specific and this was where he would find it. They edged along the crowded sidewalk where every shop's stock had exploded outward, taking over the space with t-shirts, ball caps, beach bags, brightly colored toys and more. Mexican vanilla and garishly painted shot glasses abounded in nearly every shop, and the wares began to look very much alike after half a block.

When they spotted Rob, Amber had to laugh. The 'glassware' the waiter had mentioned turned out to be a huge selection of water-pipes, bongs and similar drug paraphernalia. He was chatting with the proprietor, a short man with his black hair combed back from his forehead and a ready smile of gleaming white teeth, but Rob didn't seem to be buying.

The two women meandered past without catching
either man's attention. They weren't so fortunate at the
next shop down the line, where a dark guy with a crewcut
and gold front tooth called out. "You want something?
Some vanilla? Some new shirt? We got best prices—
cheap—almost free." His wheedling tone was cute and
they laughed as they shook their heads.

The next shop owner took up the call, as did the next,
and finally the women crossed the street where they had
spotted Sandy and Pen.

"Your turn. These guys'll wear you out with the patter.
We'll keep an eye on Rob from here."

Rob wandered in and out of a half-dozen places,
although the women never saw him buy anything. At
one place he came out with a couple sheets of paper
in his hands. He rolled them and stuck them in his hip
pocket, crossed the street, and strolled among the small
carts where vendors sold fried pork skins, foil wrapped
burritos, tamales in their cornhusks sealed in plastic bags,
and gumdrops and a variety of other candies by the scoop.
He shook his head at all the offerings, even though the
vendors called out just as pleadingly as those in the shops
across the street.

The wide concrete promenade was nice, bordered by
a railing along the shoreline where the gentle surf sent
waves splashing against the black rocks below. Palm trees
grew out of the sand at intervals where the walkway had
been poured around them. Halfway down stood a huge
monument of a shrimp fisherman with a tribute of some
sort in Spanish. Flanking the statue were purposely rusted
metal plaques, one for each of the American border
states—California, Arizona, New Mexico, and Texas. Pen
remembered when the governors of these states, from

both sides of the border, had attended a ceremony of friendship and solidarity between the two countries.

As it got closer to noon, the crowds thickened. The Ladies pretended to browse while keeping an eye ahead. As long as Rob wasn't walking toward his vehicle, they figured they had time. He eventually ended up at the end of the long promenade and aimed toward a restaurant with a sombrero-wearing frog emblem out front and frond-shaded tables in the sand facing the beach.

Rob walked inside and took a seat at the big, U-shaped bar.

"So, lunch?" Sandy suggested. They got one of the outdoor tables.

"How long do you suppose he'll stay?" Gracie asked.

"Let's see if I can find out." Sandy typed a quick text: **Did I catch you in the middle of lunch? What did you think of the venue pix I sent?**

A reply came back in less than a minute. **Liked them. Great place. Just having a sandwich at my desk.**

"Well, aside from the part about the desk, it seems true," Sandy said, noticing that the bartender had set some kind of basket in front of Rob.

They explained to the waitress who came outside that they were in a bit of a hurry. They settled on quesadillas, guacamole and chips, hoping to become mobile if Rob suddenly made a move.

It didn't happen.

He leisurely ate his sandwich, nursed a second beer at the bar, and strolled back to his vehicle. No side excursions, and by three o'clock he was again lying in the sun at the pool.

"I can't stand this," Gracie said. "What's the purpose of his trip, anyway? And how many hours do we have to watch as his lily-white body turns all glowy pink in the sun?"

Amber, too, had been pacing the room with impatience. "I agree. Gracie, come with me. I'm going back in his room. I need you to waylay him on the ground floor level if he starts to go up." She tamed her hair back into a bun and headed for the door.

Chapter 60

Rob let the sun bake his body for the third day in a row. He'd discovered that finding a place in the sunshine and out of the breeze was the secret to comfort here, even in January. Jose, the guy who'd begun to think of himself as Rob's own waiter, kept bringing the drinks.

Interesting morning at the *malecon*. He'd discovered Jose's brother to be quite the dealer in "glassware" and even though Chuey verbally denied selling any drugs through his shop, the look was in his eye. He would hook Rob up with anything he wanted. Rob shook his head. No thanks. He was likely one of the few in the Hollywood scene who didn't regularly use the stronger stuff, but he didn't care for most of it. Booze was fine with him.

Conversation with the bar owner where he'd eaten lunch had been interesting, too. The guy was an American expat who claimed he'd settled in Peñasco more than twenty years ago. He had the sandy, shaggy look of a beach bum—weathered brown skin, fried gray hair that hadn't had a real haircut in years, baggy shorts, and an oversized t-shirt with the restaurant's logo front and back. Rob remembered the conversation.

"How long you here for?"

"At least a week, maybe more. Thinking of moving to Mexico but I was looking farther south—maybe Mazatlán or Acapulco."

The guy—Butch, he'd said his name was—shook his head. "Nah, don't get yourself in the middle of the Sinaloa cartel. Bad shit goes down around those guys."

"They don't operate around here? I saw the newspaper headline—"

"Nah, you know, Sonora's pretty safe, as the Mexican states go. Keep out of Caborca at night, don't take that road unless you really have to … Otherwise, you know, it's a really nice place to live."

"I was hoping to find something with some privacy. All I've seen in town are condos and blocky little plain places with an occasional nice one thrown in."

"You speak Spanish? Didn't think so. Stick with the beach communities where it's mostly Americans and Canadians. You don't wanna be in town. Next door neighbor sees you got a nice place, next thing you know, you're gettin' ripped off." Butch eyed Rob up and down. "Nah, you'd have a hard time living in town."

He handed Rob a little touristy newspaper. "Lots of real estate listings in there. But if you really want to look at the good stuff … I'm talking how there's some million dollar homes around here … call my friend." A business card landed next to Rob's basket of fries.

"Thanks—good advice." He'd finished his meal and left a generous tip, stuck the card into the same back pocket with the other printed listings he'd picked up outside Chuey's shop.

Rolling over onto his stomach to let the sun have a chance at his back, he thought about his plans. It didn't sound like going farther south was a good idea, although he had to admit maybe Butch was only looking out for his real estate friend here in town. He thought of what awaited back home.

They'll catch up with you someday, Tyler Chisholm had warned.

That prosecutor in court had looked pretty angry over the judge's decision. Tyler had avoided commenting when Rob asked whether they could get more evidence and arrest him again. Plus, he'd now walked out owing rent on the office and his house, and there was a disgruntled employee who might come looking for her back pay.

But those things were small potatoes compared to the millions he'd collected from investors. A twinge of almost-guilt stabbed at him. Pop would be full of disdain for his son's actions; Mom would be rolling in her grave. He forced those thoughts aside, dampening them with another long swig of his mojito.

Hell, no one in the U.S. even knew he was gone yet.

Okay, worst case scenario—the authorities did decide to come after him. It would take them a long time to put a case together over the unpaid bills, even longer to come up with the names of all his investors. Then they'd have to figure out where he'd gone. So far, his only tracks led to Europe. As slow and ineffective as government worked, it would take years for them to get him.

He needed more cash to live outside of the electronic

network. Tomorrow, he'd better transfer money from one of the business accounts no one knew was connected to him. He'd see about opening an account here in Mexico. He could use a business name for that, too.

Chapter 61

Amber raided the maintenance closet once again and let herself into Rob's condo. This time, she decided, she would keep the uniform and passkey. One of these trips, she might find the closet locked, and then what would she do?

She peered over the balcony railing to be sure he was still on his lounger below. Good. She had a few minutes, so she did a cursory search of the whole place. Rob's personal stuff was strewn about this time—an open suitcase on the bedroom floor spilled shirts and boxer shorts like colorful scraps in the bargain bin at the fabric store. Toiletries all over the tiled bathroom vanity showed his taste ran to Ralph Lauren and musky scents.

She didn't spot anything of interest among the scattered mess. In the other room, bags of chips lying open on the kitchen counter had already attracted ants. Ants—on the fourth floor. She marveled at their ingenuity.

His computer sat on the living room coffee table, tempting her to check his recent browsing history. She sat on the sofa, and her fingers practically itched as she raised the lid of the laptop. Then she noticed the papers nearby. She reached for those instead.

Each of the four sheets was a printout of a real estate listing with a couple of photos, data on the property, and prices. She remembered the rolled up papers in his back pocket when he'd walked down the *malecon*. And after he left the restaurant, he'd been carrying a tabloid style newspaper. It lay on one of the sofa cushions, open to a full page of real estate ads.

So, he's thinking of relocating here … She took the single sheets, folded them twice and stuck them in the front of her uniform. A plan was beginning to hatch.

She got up and headed for the door, eager to share her idea with the gang.

Had she actually turned the computer on? She turned back to check, closed the cover, and a small white square on the floor caught her eye. A business card. She picked it up and looked at it, smiled, and stuck it in her pocket. Back at the maintenance closet, she took off the uniform and tucked her collection of papers into the waistband of her shorts. Folding the uniform so the logo didn't show, she casually walked into the lobby.

"Paydirt," Amber said to Gracie when she caught up with her. "We now know the purpose of his trip."

Back at their own condo, the five women gathered in the open living area. Sandy had offered to make her so-called 'famous chicken enchiladas' and Mary had produced a pitcher of margaritas. While Sandy stirred the sauce,

Amber told them what she had discovered in Rob's rooms.

"He's definitely looking at real estate to purchase," she said, smoothing out the flyers and setting them on the counter. "I don't see anything in the price range of that villa in France, but these are all definitely high-end properties. And," presenting the business card, "he may have already spoken with someone. A Lisa Fineman-Cardoza."

"American, or a local?" Sandy asked.

Amber looked at the card again and shrugged. "Maybe an American married to a Mexican? Anyway, here's what I thought we could do. It'll take some research …"

Chapter 62

Rob walked into the branch office of Banorte, the bank on Fremont Street, and approached the customer service desk. A cute young lady smiled up at him.

"Hola, buenos dias, señor."

He returned the greeting, hearing his own spin on the accent and knowing she immediately pegged him as American. "Do you speak English?"

"Some."

He started to explain what he wanted, to open an account with money he would transfer from his bank in Europe, but the girl's expression froze in a polite smile. She wasn't getting it. He tried shorter, less complicated sentences. Still, the smile. Then she pulled out a pamphlet and pushed it across the desk to him.

"The policy of the bank," she said.

The document was a six-page folder, in densely packed type, all in Spanish. "Is there someone else who could explain …?" He glanced around the lobby toward the three other desks in the room.

"*No hablo español,*" he tried, adding a shrug.

A twenty-something man rose from his chair at another desk and walked over. The girl sped through an explanation so rapidly that Rob didn't catch a single word.

"I want to open an account," he said to the man.

"Are you a Mexican citizen?"

"No."

"Do you have permanent resident status?"

Another negative.

The man gave a faint smile and shrugged his shoulders. "Then, I am sorry. You cannot open an account." He glanced at the brochure in Rob's hand. "It is due to the strict new money laundering laws."

"I'm not laun—" Although in a way, he was.

"I am sorry, sir. It is the law."

Rob walked out, feet dragging a little. What was he going to do for money? If he used the ATM beside the bank to draw money from his personal accounts, the US authorities would instantly know where he was. His only hope had been the Fearless Filmmaking account, which had his name nowhere on it. Hidden away in Switzerland, it couldn't be traced by American agencies.

He walked the half-block to his vehicle, silently cursing the stupid bank for not having adequate parking. Right behind his car, a woman with spiky short hair got out of a blue Mazda. She smiled and he immediately knew she was another American. The blond hair, trendy style, plus she looked like she worked out. She was looking intently at his Land Rover.

"Are you Rob, by any chance?"

"Um, yeah. How—?"

She held out her hand. "Mary. Mary Fineman. I'm Lisa's sister … Beachside Realty. Our friend at the restaurant on the *malecon* said he'd given you Lisa's card yesterday. Isn't that just the greatest location, cute bar and all?"

"Oh, Butch? Yeah he's a character. He said he had a friend in real estate."

"He mentioned you're looking for a place down here," Mary said, stepping in close as a car came down the street. "Look, Lisa's out for a couple weeks, did something to her back … but we work out of the same office and I'd be happy to show you around. Could we talk about your plans over lunch?"

Rob thought about the few pesos he had left in his pocket and how he didn't really want to use his credit cards.

"My treat, of course," Mary said. "You can ride with me if you want."

"My car will be okay here?"

"Sure. And we're not going far."

He got into the small sedan. She was right about the distance. She drove about two blocks, made a left turn and a quick right, and they arrived at a squat cinderblock building with a dirt parking lot with about a dozen cars in it. The sign had a picture of a mermaid, and brilliantly blooming bougainvillea covered the porch and filled two raised flowerbeds.

They stepped into a low-ceilinged room with stained acoustic tiles above and garish linoleum on the floor. The tables and chairs were a curious mixture of Formica and wood, modern and rustic styles, and the crowd seemed a mix of Mexicans and Americans. A stocky waiter invited them to sit wherever they wanted and immediately asked if he could bring margaritas or the house special drink. Mary asked for water and Rob followed suit.

"So, Rob, tell me what sort of house you have in mind. How many bedrooms? I'm assuming beachfront—everyone wants beachfront here."

"Yeah, well, if the price is right. I was in Europe recently, looking at properties in the south of France." He preened a little. "I'm still considering one, but the asking price of thirty-three million seemed out of line for what it was." *No way I'll admit I would have given my eye teeth for that villa.*

Mary actually laughed. "You're joking about that price, aren't you? Seriously? I can show you some gorgeous places around here, right on the beach, huge floorplans, and they'll be worth every penny."

"I saw some brochures," he said. "The best one listed was only about three mil. It has to be a fixer-upper for that, right?"

Mary paused to gauge her answer. "There are all types around here. Just tell me—is something around thirty million what you want to spend?"

"Mexico's a lot cheaper than France," he said. "Let's say twenty. What can you show me for twenty million?"

Mary smiled. "I've got just the place in mind. It's an exclusive listing that I haven't even shared details with anyone else in the office. It's in an exclusive gated community, a little way out of town, very private, *very* elegant."

"Can I see it today?"

"Let me make a call," she said. "Oh, here comes our waiter. Order me the seafood enchiladas—they are fantastic."

She pulled out her cell phone and stepped outside the noisy room to make the call.

Chapter 63

"Help!" Mary said. "I've got Rob on the hook and he wants to see a twenty million dollar property *today*. What shall I do?"

Sandy had to think fast. "Gracie and Pen went out to scout around. Last call from them, they'd found a great beach community. Touch base with them and see if there's a house they can get you into, and make sure you tell them it needs to look like it's worth the money. Meanwhile, Amber's online researching Mexican real estate laws to find out what kind of story to tell our 'customer.' I'll be in touch and update you on that."

"Okay, but hurry. I can only stretch out the lunch hour just so long."

Mary hung up, immediately called Gracie's number, and repeated her plight. Pen, ever the voice of calm, took over.

"Gracie is driving at the moment. I think we can come up with something. But twenty million, you say? Doesn't he realize nothing in this area sells for that kind of money?"

"I know. But who am I to argue—we want him to part with as much money as possible, right? Otherwise, how do we reimburse all his victims?"

"Oh, absolutely. The key will be to keep him isolated so he can't do any comparison shopping."

Gracie's voice gave a little squeal in the background.

"Oh, yes—that really is a nice one," Pen said. "All right, Mary, we have our eye on something. I'll send you a photo so you can describe it to Rob. Meanwhile, we shall figure out if it's possible to get inside. Linger over your lunch, and I shall call you once we have an answer."

Mary walked back into the restaurant where Rob was munching at a platter of tortilla chips covered in a creamy looking sauce.

"You know, I've changed my mind about having a drink," she said. "It's a warm afternoon. I'm debating between the margaritas, which are fabulous here, or just a beer. What would you like?"

Apparently, he'd heard people at the next table raving about the margaritas because that's what he chose. Mary had a Dos Equis, figuring it was easier to disguise how slowly she was consuming it.

Steaming plates arrived with their seafood enchiladas. Mary breathed deeply. She'd had the same dish at dinner Saturday night, the main reason she knew of the restaurant and the recommendation. The recipe truly was addictive.

"I love to savor this in small bites so I can relish every morsel," she told Rob. "Listen to me—I sound like a commercial, don't I?"

He laughed a little louder than necessary—the strong

margarita was already having its effect. But he agreed with her; the enchiladas were delicious.

Down in her pocket, her phone buzzed. She took a look at the message and picture Pen had sent. "Oh, good. My office. Apparently, we can go out to the house I had in mind. I think you'll love this one. Five thousand square feet, and it's on three hundred feet of beachfront property. I can't tell you how rare that is out here. Most of these beaches, the houses are jammed together. Well, you'll see."

Pen had said they could get into the house. Mary wondered how they'd managed, but knew better than to raise questions at this point. Instead, she offered to buy Rob another margarita. By the time they walked out to the car, he was slightly unsteady and had a huge grin on his face.

"I *love* this place!" he announced to a Mexican family walking toward the front door. They gave him a funny look and put protective arms around each of the children.

"Come on, Rob, let's get going." Mary had used the opportunity while Rob went into the men's room a few minutes earlier to phone Pen and get directions to the house they were to view.

"Hurry," Pen urged, "we don't know when the owners might turn up. Gracie and I are sitting on the beach in front, keeping an eye."

Mary pulled away from the restaurant and made two or three extra turns before heading south out of town. The goal was to keep Rob confused about where they were going, and judging by the fact he was practically dozing in his seat, she thought she'd succeeded.

He roused when she turned off the paved two-lane highway onto a dirt road that looked as if it had been recently graded.

"Wow, this is really taking us away from town," he said.

"Yes, a *very* exclusive area. You said you wanted to have space, privacy, and a luxury home. This is *the* area where you want to be."

He perked up, looking around a little skeptically at the miles of dunes covered with short green bushes. Mary hoped to hell the place she was taking him wasn't in the midst of this stuff, but Pen had said it was beachfront. From this angle, no glimpse of the sea had yet showed itself.

"I drove to town in the dark," he said conversationally. "I suppose the countryside is like this all around?"

"Mostly." Mary guessed at her answer. "That's why, as I mentioned, beachfront is the *only* place to be."

"It's not a bunch of condos around there, though, right? I'm feeling a little surrounded in the place I'm staying."

"Lots of space out here." She followed as the road curved and then she saw the guard gate ahead. A polite young man with a smile greeted them and asked where they were going. "We're meeting someone at the Smith place." *Oh god, hopefully that answer worked.*

It must have. The guard raised the barrier gate and waved them through.

Pen had told Mary to take the second left turn she came to, then a quick right. She'd memorized the look of the house—pale apricot stucco with white trim and balcony railings shaped like seahorses. And there it was.

She sent up a silent thanks to the ladies; the house was definitely huge and magnificent. She parked on the road and saw Gracie approaching from the left hand side of the house.

"Take a look around," Mary told Rob. "Notice the gorgeous landscaping, the courtyard with mature palm trees and multiple shades of bougainvillea in bloom."

While he gazed, openmouthed, she took Gracie aside.

"We found a door on the beach side open. The owners must be nearby, or maybe they went to town. It seems like the kind of area where you could go away and leave your doors unlocked. Take him through, but make it quick. They could come home any minute."

Mary looked around. "This place isn't really for sale, is it? What's our story?"

"Pen and I will watch for anyone returning, and we'll come up with something to keep them from going in. You just tell Rob the owners are here but have allowed you to show the place. As long as we keep them from seeing each other, it'll work." She had her fingers crossed, Mary noticed.

Heart pounding, Mary joined Rob in the courtyard. "Let's go around front," she said, taking his arm and steering him toward the beach. "Around here, people call the side facing the road the back of the house, the beach is the front. And here … we are!"

She had to admit the view took her own breath away. The tide was in, so the water came within twenty yards of the patio.

"You'll notice the deck affords incomparable views. You can literally dash right out here with your boogie board and be in the water in one minute. You'll want to see the view from the upper balcony as well," she said, ushering him toward the sliding door Gracie had left unlocked for them.

She pushed to get him through the rooms as quickly as possible, although personally she would have loved to linger and take in the details. "Here we have a spacious great room, open plan, with dining space for all your friends, a gourmet kitchen. If you love to cook, here's your ideal space."

"Well, I don't," he muttered, "but I suppose hiring a maid and a cook must come pretty cheap around here?"

"Oh, absolutely. You did notice the casita on the north side? Perfect for maid's quarters, or for visiting relatives." She hoped it was true. "Now, upstairs, we have the bedrooms …"

She counted them off as they peeked into each one. Luckily, only a couple of them seemed occupied, with suitcases and toiletries in evidence. All were beautifully decorated. "And, *here* is that fantastic view of the sea, right here from your master bedroom. Did I mention that all furnishings come with the house? Of course, if you don't like them, I know a wonderful interior decorator who can help you do the whole place over."

She heard Rob's gasp. "Wow," he said. "What can I say?—wow!"

"The seller is motivated to sell quickly, but I must tell you there have been two other offers, one of them at full asking price."

"Which is?"

"Twenty-one point six million." She looked him in the eye and managed not to stammer or blink.

"Tell them I'll give twenty-five. Cash. Immediately."

Mary smiled and took his arm. "Let's go write up the offer."

Chapter 64

Rob was beaming like a satisfied cat, Mary thought, as they drove back down the long dirt road toward town. Her mind raced. Where could she take him? She had no office, not even a 'pretend' one where she could write up this offer.

She had texted Amber while Rob took a last, long gaze at *his* beach. Now, a ping told her the answer had come through. She came to a stop and asked Rob's indulgence while she read it.

"Oh, wow," she said. "Looks like the pest control company came to the office this afternoon and my secretary says it smells pretty bad. She'll meet me somewhere and bring my computer. You want to see one of the best views in town?"

"We just did, didn't we?"

"Oh, yours is the *very* best at beach level, but let me show you what it looks like from above." Amber's detailed message gave directions to a restaurant and bar at the top of the rocky hill that towered above the port area. "You'll love this place." She hoped it was true.

Underway again, Rob asked how the purchase would work. "Can I do the whole thing with a wire transfer?"

"I'm sure you can. We work with an attorney here in town—wonderful lady, smart as they come—and she handles all the details and paperwork. You may have noticed, showing and talking about houses is my passion. I leave the money matters to a different set of experts."

Luckily, her answer stalled any further questions. He kept glancing back toward the beach they'd just left.

Oh, yeah, he's hooked, Mary thought.

She found the way up a rather steep road to the hilltop Amber had described. At the top were two restaurants with miniscule parking lots, which were quickly filling with the happy hour crowd. Gracie's minivan sat at the end of the lot, and Mary chose a spot as far from it as she could. No doubt Pen and Gracie had raced back to pick up Amber at the condo and were now hiding out until she could get Rob inside.

Mary spotted Amber at a window-side table, the computer in front of her. She stood when they entered the room and passed Mary.

"Just bring up the document I've got on the screen," Amber muttered in Mary's ear while Rob stared out at the shrimping boats in the harbor below. "It's a pretty self-explanatory Purchase Offer. You can ask him a few questions and fill in his personal info, then say you're emailing it to the seller for approval. If he questions anything at all, just say that's how we do it here in Mexico.

He'll never know the difference."

"We need to keep him in our sights," Mary said. "Once I take him back to his vehicle at Banorte Bank, you guys follow to see where he goes. If it's anywhere other than the condo where he's staying, we'll have to think fast."

Rob had turned around, so Amber scooted out of sight quickly.

"So, my secretary says she's got the document all ready to submit as soon as I get some basic information," Mary said, ushering him to the table. "We can take care of that, then I say we celebrate with a drink."

Rob eagerly complied, giving his old home address in California, but explaining that once he had the house on the beach he planned to live here full time. Mary typed everything into the provided spaces, had Rob add his electronic signature, then she saved the document and emailed it to Gracie.

"Okay, the seller should have it, and I imagine we'll have an answer fairly quickly."

Rob had already signaled the waiter and asked for a margarita. Sheesh, Mary thought, two at lunch and another midafternoon. How does he do it? She asked for another Dos Equis and nursed it along slowly while he went through a basket of chips with guacamole. How he kept his trim figure was another mystery.

He took out his phone, stared at the screen and frowned.

"Something the matter?"

"Oh, my assistant back home is coordinating an event I'm supposed to attend in a week or so. I haven't heard anything from her today."

"Ah. Well, I've noticed there's sometimes a delay in messages from the States. We really do live on *mañana* time down here."

Eventually, he excused himself to go to the restroom and Mary checked her own messages. How long would she need to babysit him? His company was wearing on her, but the Ladies didn't dare leave him on his own until the money was transferred. If he discovered what a rip-off price he'd offered for a house that was probably worth one-tenth what he was paying, he would go running back where he came from.

She looked at his phone, sitting on the table beside his half-empty margarita glass. Glanced toward the men's room door. Should she …?

She drew her hand back. He would remember he'd left it there. But later—they needed to get his phone away from him so he couldn't contact anyone and discover his blunder. She texted Amber. **Got any more of that wonder knockout drug?** Then she remembered how quickly it had worked last time. She'd better get him situated in his own rooms before she tried to disable him. He appeared at the table so quietly it startled her. Had he seen the message she'd just sent?

"Well," he said with a yawn, "I think I'm about ready for a nap. Can you give me a lift back to my car?"

"Certainly. Are you okay to drive?"

"Oh, yeah. I'm only going as far as Sandy Beach. I'm at the El Mirage."

Through a lot of narrow streets and traffic, she thought. But the contingency plan was in place, and the rest of the Ladies should be on surveillance near Rob's Land Rover. Mary gathered her things and Amber's computer and walked beside Rob out to the parking lot. When he got into her car and set his phone on the console between them, she casually set her purse on top of it.

At the bank she spotted the minivan. In one move, she

slid her purse along with Rob's cell phone, until it fell onto the floor of the back seat. He never noticed. She watched while he fished keys out of his pocket, got into the Rover, and drove away. The gray minivan followed.

Chapter 65

I thought he'd never call it a night," Amber complained. "I watched him in the lobby bar for more than an hour. That man can put away the booze."

"But you're definitely sure he went to his room and plans to stay put?" Sandy asked.

Amber nodded tiredly. "I followed him and saw him go inside. By then he was practically stumbling. I'd thought about dropping a pill into his last drink at the bar, but I didn't want to have to manhandle him into the elevator. He's out of it."

"And I have his phone," Mary said, "so I doubt he's going anywhere or contacting anyone."

"Okay, so what's the plan for tomorrow?" Gracie looked equally tired.

"All right," Amber said, sitting up straighter at the

dining table. "Here's what I found out, and I think it all works in our favor. I called the real Lisa Fineman and pretended I was interested in buying property and asked how the process goes."

The others gathered around to listen.

"Foreigners can't buy property outright within a certain distance of the waterfront. So, purchases by Americans have to be done through a bank trust. Apparently, it's a horrendously huge and complicated document and it takes months to complete one."

"Then how—?"

"The buyer has to pay the money up front, and there are some very skimpy closing documents, then the whole thing goes into the legal system down here, something that involves multiple government agencies and officials, and this hefty document gets sent all over—to the state capital, the federal capital, and then some."

"A realtor told you all this?"

"Well, I took what she told me and filled in the rest from stuff I learned online. Anyway, the point is, Rob would pay all the money upfront. So we—our 'lawyer' here—" A nod toward Gracie, "—will explain this, the parts we want him to know. Then we get him to wire the money."

Sandy spoke up. "I will go back to Phoenix, first thing in the morning, and get an account set up at my bank. We'll call it the victim's settlement account or something."

"Meanwhile, Gracie will have told him it will take a little time for the paperwork to come through, so he can either hang around in his condo here or go back to the States, whatever he wants to do until everything is finalized."

Pen brightened. "But the truth is, everything never will be finalized. He's given up the money and gets nothing. And there's no way to trace it to us …"

"Because by the time he begins to get a clue, we will have disbursed all the money out to the victims," Sandy said.

Smiles all around. Except Mary. "There's still more. Other than losing the money he took, he's not really being punished. And what about that judge in California? No justice there."

"Be patient, my dear," Pen said. "I do think there's a happy ending in sight."

"Let's just stay on script a bit longer," she continued. "Tomorrow, Amber will slip Rob's phone into his room just in time for Mary to call and let him know his offer was accepted. She'll pick him up and take him to the attorney meeting. Back in your role, Mary, you'll have to act excited about his getting the property he wants."

Mary gave a pretend growl but agreed to follow the plan.

"Do we have an office where our lawyer can conduct this meeting?" Sandy asked.

Gracie looked a little worried. "I've been working on it."

By morning, moods were better. Sandy had gotten up at the crack of dawn and headed north, planning to be in her office at the bank by noon. The others ate a leisurely breakfast on their balcony, spying on Rob's quiet condo.

When they began to see movement inside, Amber knew it was time to make her move. Back in uniform, she tapped at his door and walked in. The scent of shower gel assured her he was busy, and she tucked his cell phone partway beneath a cushion on the sofa. Out again, back to join the group.

Thirty minutes later, Mary called. "Hey Rob, I have some wonderful news for you. Your offer was accepted! I bet you hardly slept all night."

"Well, actually—"

"So, anyway, I've got it set up with our attorney to meet at noon at her office. I'll pick you up in front of your building."

* * *

The law offices of Menendez and Archer were normally closed on Wednesdays. Gracie had learned this by browsing ads in the newspaper, and the Ladies confirmed it by driving by this morning to check it out. Sure enough, the sign on the door showed office hours, and the shadowy interior appeared unoccupied.

Mary used a little trick she'd gleaned when breaking back into her old business offices, the one her ex had stolen from her, and used a thin plastic card to open the door. Gracie, Pen, and Amber went inside, while Mary turned back toward the condos to pick up Rob. It was the only time since they arrived on Friday that he'd been left unwatched. She worried, mulling the possibilities, until she saw his vehicle in the lot and spotted him standing near the main entrance waiting for her.

By the time Mary and Rob returned, the legal office was a bustling place—other than the front door being locked. Lights were on, the smell of coffee brewing, a petite dark-skinned girl let them in, then took her place behind the reception desk. She picked up the phone and began speaking rapidly in Spanish.

She smiled and directed them back to a private office where the statuesque, dark haired lawyer who wore perfect makeup and her hair slicked back in a bun at the nape of her neck greeted them and introduced herself as Graciela

Menendez. She looked over the top of her heavy-rimmed glasses at Rob, then referred to a sheaf of papers in her hands.

He commented on how perfect her English was and tried mildly to flirt, but she shut him down. The lady was all business as she explained the system in Mexico. The wire transfer would need to take place today—did he have his banking information with him? Good. Did he understand that it would take some time for the bank trust paperwork to be completed, but that he could have occupancy of the home he'd purchased once the sellers had moved their personal things out? They had asked for a period of thirty days to do this—was this agreeable with Mr. Williams?

Graciela added a nice touch by having him sign a paper stipulating to all the questions she had asked. She worked efficiently on the laptop computer in front of her, entering his bank's routing number and the account number, and confirming the dollar amount. Twenty-five million US dollars, yes?

He nodded, looking very excited about his new property.

The petite receptionist came to the door to tell the attorney she had received a call from the partner bank in Arizona. Everything was set up, and please let them know the moment the wire transfer cleared.

A tall, grey-haired older woman with purple glasses and a pencil sticking through her upswept hair came in and picked up the documents. A moment later a copy machine began whirring out the pages. Such an efficiently run office.

While they waited, Rob's cell phone buzzed with an incoming text message: **Gala all set for Saturday night. Almost 100% positive RSVPs. You'll be back by then?** Rob typed an affirmative response.

Everything, it seemed, was a go.

Chapter 66

Sandy looked at Rob's text response and smiled. All set. She watched the new account she had set up this morning. A nail-biting hour went by but then the balance jumped from zero to nearly twenty-five million dollars. The small service charge had been worth it for immediate balance update service.

She turned to the other program on her computer, the one where she'd uploaded Amber's spreadsheet of the victims' names. The Heist Ladies' devotion to weeks of phone calls had paid off. Every entry showed the name of the person Rob Williams had ripped off, the amount he'd taken, and the victim's bank and account number. With a couple of clicks, numbers began to tick across the boxes on her screen. As each account was credited with the amount due it, the balance in the new Victim's Settlement account dropped accordingly. A notation automatically went with each deposit: **Robin Hood thanks you for your patience**.

It had come out nearly to the penny, leaving a balance of only fifty cents in the settlement account. She smiled and sent a text to Mary: **All done**.

Then she picked up the phone and dialed a number she'd only told Pen about.

"Agent Daniels," said the voice of the man Sandy had spoken to a week ago. Before they knew they'd caught Rob Williams and returned the stolen money to his victims, Sandy had hoped this agency could help them. Now she had a different story to tell.

"Yes, Agent Daniels," she said. "It's about Robert Williams, the person of interest we talked about before. I'm sending you a list of contacts. I'm afraid it's not as lengthy as I'd first believed. It turns out he only walked out on a few thousand dollars in rent from his home and office, but I do believe several of his credit cards were up to the max and have accumulated quite a lot of unpaid interest. It seems Mr. Williams tried to escape to Mexico to avoid paying." She listened a moment. "Well, yes, I figured leaving the country would add some degree of severity to the charges. The amount? Well, we've tallied at least sixty-thousand dollars' worth."

The agent at the other end hedged a bit.

"I do understand that's probably not really enough money to justify tracking him to a foreign country, but what if I could get him to come to you?"

She named the date, time and place of the supposed gala.

Chapter 67

Rob dashed up to his condo as soon as Mary dropped him off. During the ride, she'd talked nonstop about how wonderful it was he'd found exactly the home he wanted. It was the most gratifying part of her job, matching people and properties. Rob's thoughts drifted to the text he'd received from Sandy.

The next investor gala was all set, so although he'd spent nearly all his money on the beach house, now he would have a handsome fund for living expenses. If this one brought in close to the amounts of previous events, he could retire comfortably in Mexico for the rest of his life. One of the points which had been raised during the real estate closing was that now, as a homeowner here, he could open a bank account. A nice account out of reach of the American authorities.

He set up his laptop at the breakfast bar and went through his files. For Saturday night's presentation, he would use the same movie trailer he'd shown in Newport. He refreshed his memory as to which major actors were supposedly signed to star in it. Picturing himself in a tuxedo at the front of the room, he mentally went through his presentation to refresh his technique and be sure he wouldn't forget anything.

Maybe he should shave off the beard and get a haircut. In the bathroom mirror he studied his face. Or not. The tousled hair and scruffy face went along with many people's image of Hollywood. He turned away. He had a couple days to think about it.

Meanwhile, he wanted to drive out and take another look at his new home. If he saw the owners around, he would play it by ear—maybe they wouldn't mind if he went in and looked over the furnishings. His tour with Mary had gone so quickly, he couldn't exactly remember everything. He might make a list of things to bring back the next time he came down from Phoenix.

He picked up his keys and phone and strolled down to the parking lot. First, some lunch. He realized he'd skipped breakfast and Mary hadn't offered lunch today. He pulled onto the road, hoping to find the same place they'd gone yesterday. The margaritas had been excellent and she was right about those enchiladas—he'd been thinking about them ever since.

At the next intersection, he looked both directions, unsure. Which way had they turned? He made a left but it didn't seem the same. He saw some restaurants but they sat among the ranks of the high-rise condos. The other place had been somewhat out in the open with a large parking lot. Ahead, the view opened up a bit and he spotted a place.

It wasn't the same one, he knew. This one sat close to the sea, but he pulled in anyway. His stomach growled when he read the sign bragging about the best burgers on the beach.

What the hell—all he wanted right now was something to eat. A heavyset man greeted him at the door, ushering him through with a smile.

"Come, *señor*, have a seat anywhere you like. Maybe something outside? You can watch the dolphins. They very active this morning."

Why not? Rob walked through the bar area and took a seat at one of the small cement tables which sat in the sand outside. Little palm frond palapas shaded each one.

The man handed him a menu and offered drinks. "Our margaritas are the best ones in town."

It was becoming obvious everyone said the same thing. Rob smiled but decided he owed it to himself to try one for comparison. When the foamy drink arrived, he let himself get talked into one of the famous burgers. A sip of the drink led to several long slurps—this one definitely might be a contender for the best.

"You are visiting from Arizona?" the man asked when he brought the burger.

"This time, I am. But I just bought a house. I'm moving here."

"Ah, congratulations! Welcome. Where is you house?"

"Down the beach." Rob waved vaguely. *Where, exactly, was it anyway?*

The man congratulated him again and left him to eat. Rob picked up the burger and wolfed down half of it immediately. Food would help. No wonder he felt a little confused. But the burger and fries disappeared and he still couldn't remember exactly which way Mary had driven him out to the gated community and his new house.

It would be a little embarrassing, but he would just have to call her back and ask for directions. He couldn't even remember the name of the development. Probably shouldn't have had all those drinks at lunch. He pushed his empty glass aside and refused another when the waiter offered.

A breeze wafted in under the shady palapa, a chill reminder that it was still January. He stuck money under the edge of the empty glass and walked out into the sunshine. In the distance, he saw how the shoreline curved toward the port area. It was lined with buildings, but he couldn't tell whether there were many individual homes, such as the area where Mary had taken him yesterday.

No problem, he told himself. He pulled out his phone and found her number in his recent calls from this morning. The phone rang without answer and without going to voicemail. Hmm. Maybe somehow things worked differently down here.

Well, perhaps he could catch her at the office. What had it been called? Beachfront ... no, Beach something ... Beachside. Beachside Realty. He walked back to the restaurant and asked if they had a phone directory.

The same man who'd acted as host and waiter shrugged and gave him a funny look.

"You know, a phone book." Rob watched the blank stare. "I need the number for a real estate office called Beachside Realty."

A bit of recognition. The guy walked over to a rack near the door and picked up a copy of the same touristy newspaper Rob had gotten his first day in town. "It could be in here," he said.

Rob took the paper to an indoor table and paged through it until he came to a page with the heading

Advertiser Listings. There was a number for Beachside Realty and he dialed it.

"Yes, I need to speak to Mary, please."

"Um, I'm afraid there's no one named Mary in this office." The female voice sounded young and American.

"Maybe her sister. She said her sister works there but was out sick this week or something?"

"All of our agents have been in this week, and none of them has a sister who also works here. But any of our other agents would be happy to help you."

"No, it's Mary I need to talk to." He felt his voice rise in irritation.

"Sir, you probably just have the wrong agency. This Mary must be with another company. Sorry." The line went dead.

How certain was he about the name of the agency? He rummaged in his wallet. No business card. He would have sworn he got a business card. His closing papers for the sale were back at the condo, but he didn't recall the name of the agency being there, only the names of the buyer and seller and the law firm. He couldn't precisely remember the route to the law office either. This was such a confusing town to drive around in.

He could go back to the condo and look through the paperwork, just to be sure. And he could always try calling Mary on her cell phone later. She was just busy right now.

The waiter came back. "Another margarita, señor? It seems you do not have appointment after all."

Rob nodded. He needed something to do before he called Mary again.

Chapter 68

The lights of Phoenix and the huge seventy-mile-wide metropolis glowed on the horizon well before the minivan reached the outskirts, the end of a triumphant journey for the Heist Ladies.

They'd spent the four hours on the road talking about their week, laughing over what Rob Williams must be doing right now. Mary had ignored seven calls from his number already. The law office had been cleared of all traces of their short occupancy within five minutes after Rob left, so even if he found his way back there, no one from the regular staff would have a clue who he was or what he was talking about.

"It must be quite the surprise for our mister Robert, being the one who is left penniless and confused," Pen said.

"Sandy said the money transfers went smoothly as a calm sea."

"Too bad none of the victims will know exactly what happened," Amber said, "but I understand the need for secrecy. I'm just glad they got their initial investment back, although I'm sure they might be disappointed there was no huge profit, as they'd been promised."

"Mom and Hannah are happy," Gracie said. "I got a call right away. As for me, I am *thrilled*, as will my loving husband be when I tell him about it."

"The only thing that still irks me," Mary said, "is that the judge never got punished for his role in the whole court debacle."

"We aren't finished yet," Pen reminded. "Sandy has a surprise waiting, concerning the greeting committee that will be awaiting Rob when he shows up for his next big gala on Saturday night. Perhaps we can think of a way to involve Judge Alderston and bring his crime to light as well."

"We're all tired," Gracie said with a yawn as she pulled off the 101 freeway and entered Amber's neighborhood. "I'll get you all home, then we can sleep on it. In a day or two, I'm sure we'll come up with something."

They had three days before the gala. If nothing went wrong, Rob Williams would be in custody by Saturday night.

If.

* * *

Mary spent a restless night and woke early. Lying in bed in the dark was no use. She got up and made coffee, pacing her small apartment while it brewed. The earliest edition of the morning news was on, but everything was negative—murders throughout the night, a brazen robbery in broad daylight yesterday, and no suspect in custody. She switched to a national news channel where it was all about bashing the president and corruption in politics.

The answer came in a flash. Of course—why hadn't she thought of it earlier?

She poured her coffee and went to the dresser, where she pulled out her small mini recorder. After recording the conversation in which the travel agent admitted accepting cash payment from Judge Layton Alderston, Mary had run into a wall as far as how to use the information. She could play the tape for the judge, but he would instantly deny it. Playing it for his wife would probably not mean anything either—the woman was most likely clueless about her husband's finances and would think nothing of it. And the man seemed immune from legal repercussions in his own jurisdiction.

But, another idea began to form. She played the tape, making certain the voice quality was clear and that the travel agent actually had admitted the cash payment. It sounded good. She phoned Amber, who at six a.m. wasn't at her perkiest.

"We still have the banking records that showed Rob Williams taking out the exact amount the judge received, right?" Mary asked, already feeling the effects of her second cup of coffee.

"I … I'm sure we do. Can I look it up later?"

But when Mary told her younger colleague what she had in mind, Amber woke right up.

"Is it too early for me to call Gracie?" Mary asked, after Amber said she was already booting up her computer.

"She's got kids in school—they have to be up by now," Amber said.

And Sandy would be preparing for a routine day at the

bank. She was likely already awake. Mary began to phone them and set it up as a conference call.

"We've got the travel agent's admission, the Facebook posts where Lois Alderston brags about the trip, and Rob's bank records," Pen said when she came on the line. "But is it really enough? The judge seems to have friends on the inside. How can we know law enforcement will investigate him, based on our word?"

"I don't know. Maybe it is a weak case." Mary's voice dropped.

"Alderston—wasn't that the judge's last name?" Amber asked. "It's suddenly ringing a bell. Hold on."

A scurrying sound came over the line as Amber rummaged through papers on her desk. "How on earth did we miss this?" she said, almost breathlessly. "Intrepid Dog Pictures actually did pay off one investor, with interest on the money. Guess who?"

"Layton Alderston." Pen's voice was almost a whisper.

"Exactly. That should nail him, shouldn't it?"

"I'm calling CNN," Mary said. "Right now."

"Wait—wait!" Sandy said. "We still need to get Rob back here to town for the supposed gala. Agent Daniels is lining up his team. We can't do anything that would give Rob a heads-up, would warn him not to come."

"She's right," Pen said. "We must think this through very carefully. There's too much at stake, and it's only forty-eight hours more."

Mary grumbled a little, but all in all she had to agree.

Chapter 69

Venue is set. Guests seem to be an especially generous crowd. Looking forward to seeing you there tomorrow night.

Rob read the message twice, his pulse rate picking up. Less than forty-eight hours and he'd be sitting pretty. After a frustrating day, as he tried repeatedly to reach Mary, he needed this good news from Sandy. He texted her back: Great news. See you there, six p.m. Give me the address again.

After a week in Mexico, it was good to have someone he could communicate with. Mary, the realtor—what a loser. Get the sale then never return a call. The locals were friendly enough, but frustrating to deal with. No one stressed over anything. Plenty of them offered suggestions when he asked about the various beach communities in an effort to get back out to his new property.

"Oh, you mean Cholla Bay?" followed by directions that took him to some way hell-and-back little hamlet.

"Oh, maybe it's Puerto Privada," which turned out to be just another condo complex.

He'd even walked into the office of Beachside Realty, expecting to see Mary there at a desk acting too busy to take his calls, but the people in the office drew a blank when he described her. And another blank when he described the house he'd bought. No one seemed familiar with it, and he could only assume he had the name of the agency wrong. When he had more time, he would visit them all, if that's what it took. Or he would drive around and find the house on his own. At least he had his legal documents with the lawyer's signature on them.

That night he packed his things, and Saturday morning vacated the condo. The investor meeting, the gala, was the only thing on his agenda through the weekend. He'd booked a room and a massage at the Westin and entered the address for the west-side venue in his GPS. He would get to Phoenix in time to check in, maybe take a nap—he liked to be fresh and at his best for the presentations—then change into his tux. Sandy would meet him there and help set up the slideshow and trailer. Plus, she'd offered to introduce him personally to a couple of the wealthiest investors.

He sang along with the radio and talked to himself during the road trip. When he got to the border, he had to present his passport to the US border officials and to state how long he'd been in Mexico. It was the first official trace of his being away, but the agent was giving him the steady eye, so he answered truthfully.

The gala. He focused on that for the next three hours.

It would be the last of these moneymakers. *I promised myself I'd do this until I got my needs taken care of, my future all set, then I'm out of the business.* He pictured the huge beach mansion and imagined himself on the upper deck, tanning to the deep color of the locals. He would learn the language, blend in, and nothing could touch him after that.

His inner glow continued as he checked into the luxury hotel and enjoyed his massage. By the time he'd changed into his tuxedo, he was ready to face his crowd of admirers with complete confidence. He tapped the address for the venue on his GPS and headed out, allowing plenty of time for traffic. Nothing would ruffle him or derail the plan.

Forty minutes later, he was pulling up in front of the Phoenician, and it looked like everything Sandy had promised. Great part of the city, classy building. Cruising past the front, he could see a brightly lit ballroom, all set with tables and place settings, which must surely be for their party. Guests in long gowns and formal wear milled about. He looked around for Sandy but didn't immediately spot her.

The parking lot was crowded and a beefy van was pushing him to move along. He drove up and down the aisles until he found a spot, the damn van following along—as if Rob was expected to give way and let it take one of the precious few parking slots. He whipped into the one vacant spot and killed the engine. The stupid van stayed right behind him.

He picked up his computer with the presentation software on it and opened his door. Immediately, four men surrounded the Land Rover. One presented a badge.

"Robert Williams?"

Rob nodded automatically, before he thought better of it.

"You are under arrest for tax evasion, international money laundering, and financial fraud. You have the right to remain silent—"

Someone grabbed his computer bag and handcuffs clamped onto his wrists. Rob didn't hear the rest of the words as the agent droned on. Bright lights flashed into his eyes, seemingly from nowhere, and questions were shouted at him from all directions.

Rob ducked his head. What the hell—?

Chapter 70

Sandy hung back until the black van with Rob in it pulled away. Four media vehicles followed, like vultures catching the scent of roadkill. Agent Daniels stepped out of another black car nearby, his phone to his ear. He ended the call and thanked Sandy for her help with the apprehension.

"I don't know where those guys came from," Daniels said with a nod toward the media vans.

Sandy didn't say anything. "Rob Williams won't get away with it again, will he?" she asked.

"Not this time. Federal charges are much more serious, plus we've got a lot more evidence than in the previous case. *And,* he doesn't have a judge in his pocket this time."

"How will that go?"

"Williams will definitely do time in federal prison if

convicted on these charges. It's not a slap-on-the-wrist type of thing. These are all serious crimes."

"And the judge?"

"I can't comment on that. It's an ongoing investigation."

Sandy felt some disappointment that everything couldn't be neatly wrapped up in one swoop, but Pen had assured her that real crimes and justice did not play out the way they appeared to in hour-long TV dramas. She handed something to Agent Daniels.

"What's this?" he asked.

"You'll see."

He looked at the phone, checked it, and saw that the contacts list contained only one name. Another agent gave a shout and Daniels needed to leave. Sandy watched him get back into the black car. She looked around the parking lot where she now stood alone.

She needed to be with her friends.

Ten o'clock Saturday night wasn't typically the time for friends to gather around the television, but it was where the Heist Ladies found themselves. They'd met at Gracie's house, where the kids were already in bed, and Scott joined them to catch the nightly news. He sat close to his wife, their hands clasped together.

Sandy had already given the scenario, up to the point where the media showed up. "It was very fortunate there was a big wedding reception in the ballroom there tonight. I watched Rob drive up and give a long glance toward the lights and the crowd. I couldn't have staged it better if I'd had the power to."

"Ooh, wait—here it comes," Amber said.

"In breaking news tonight, a California movie producer is arrested here in Phoenix on charges of tax evasion and international money laundering. And the interesting part is, he's not really in the movie business. The whole story right after this message ..." The newscaster flashed his very white smile and the video cut away to a hype-filled ad by a local car dealer.

Gracie muted the volume. "Is there any way he can skate out of it this time? Please say no. Families like ours can't take a whole lot of this. I'd really like to believe we protected others, his future victims."

Sandy relayed what Agent Daniels had told her. She glanced over at Mary, who'd been fairly quiet, although smiling widely. Just then the newscast resumed and Gracie turned the sound back up.

"In our lead story ..." The announcer went on with the same set of facts the ladies already knew. Video showed Rob being led to a government vehicle, his wrists cuffed, his tuxedo rumpled as the agents grabbed him by the elbows. Across the bottom of the screen, large letters followed the suspect: *Movie Mogul Fraudster?*

The announcer's way-too-pretty female cohost spoke up, delivering the enticing bits about how Williams was suspected of bilking hundreds of people out of millions of dollars using fake movie trailers and investment schemes.

"They certainly obtained a lot of material on him, very quickly, didn't they?" Pen commented.

Mary and Amber exchanged a glance but didn't say a word. The entire news story finished in fifteen seconds. Gracie shut off the TV and the room grew quiet.

It was over.

Chapter 71

Almost over.

The lead story the next morning on all the national cable and network channels focused on the Movie Mogul Fraudster, and it captured the nation's attention.

"Probably because it's a refreshing change over the usual rash of murders and abductions, and doesn't involve dozens of people being brutally murdered," Gracie told her husband over breakfast.

The phone rang almost immediately and she saw it was Pen. "If you aren't watching Channel 10, turn there quickly," she told them. "They just showed the judge being led from his home to a police van."

Apparently the network had managed to be first with the scoop—Judge Layton Alderston was now accused of being involved with the notorious Movie Mogul Fraudster.

Channel 10's investigative reporters had learned that the judge had invested in Robert Williams's scheme, and was one of the only such investors to have received his money and the promised dividends from the supposed film, although it was now proven no such film had been made.

The announcer continued: "We have obtained additional evidence showing Judge Alderston allegedly received a bribe in the amount of twenty thousand dollars, allegedly to dismiss the original case against Williams in California district court." Across the screen flashed images of Lois Alderston's Facebook posts bragging about their wonderful suite on the cruise ship.

As her husband was led away, Lois appeared on the front porch in her robe, hair askew, weeping. The cameras swept in.

"I knew it. I knew it! I found credit card receipts for hotels I knew nothing about, vacations disguised as business trips." The reporters became ravenous, throwing more questions her way. No doubt the family attorney was having a stroke by now.

Even Gracie cringed a little. "Is it a good idea for her to be talking so much?"

"The IRS, they were always on us about taxes," the judge's wife wailed. Someone finally had the good sense to pull her away from the cameras.

By the end of the day, the story had gone international, as the BBC picked it up, along with news agencies in a dozen or more countries.

Pen had received a call from Maisie Brown. "You asked me to let you know if I had any new information about Robert Williams," Maisie said. "I don't know if this is news to you or not, but my bank account magically grew a few days ago. All my investment money from Rob is back!"

Pen caught the subtle 'or not' in Maisie's statement. She congratulated Maisie and said nothing more.

Later that afternoon, Mary heard from Abby Singer with a similar update. She'd just finished teaching a martial arts class at the gym and was wiping sweat from her forehead when the call came. It reminded her of an important task. She left work and drove up to Roosevelt Lake, where she rented a paddle boat from a concessionaire. Eighty yards from the shore, she paused and pulled an item from the small pack strapped around her waist. She handled it with a kerchief and wiped it completely clear of fingerprints before dropping them into the chilly water.

So, *this* was why they called them throwaway phones, she thought with a smile. Her only tie to Rob Williams and the Mexico real estate transaction vanished.

* * *

Six months went by before they gathered at Pen's home to hear the verdict. Rob Williams, convicted on all counts, sent to the federal prison near Pima, a zillion miles from nowhere; Judge Alderston had been disbarred early on— now he too would do federal time on corruption charges. His poor wife and her lawyers would still have to deal with the taxation authorities.

As the case came back into the limelight, people around the country began to figure it out.

"Some kind of angel was looking out for us," one New York couple said.

"We got our money back, along with a note from Robin Hood, thanking us for our patience," said another, who came forward at Easter in Oregon.

"This Robin Hood saved me from losing my home," a

widow from Baltimore told her local news station.

"My husband has terminal cancer," came the story out of Dallas. "Getting our retirement money back will keep me out of poverty."

Amber had found the various news clips online and compiled the quotes into a little file on her computer. When the elation over their success had been toasted with champagne and the cheers died down, she opened the screen and showed them the effects of their hard work.

"It was all worth it," Gracie said with tears in her eyes. "I'm so happy to see it wasn't all about me and my family. We really did help a lot of people."

"We did." Amber wrapped her in a hug and the rest joined in.

Thank you for taking the time to read *Movie Mogul Mama*. If you enjoyed it, please consider telling your friends or posting a short review. Word of mouth is an author's best friend and is much appreciated.
Thank you,
Connie Shelton

* * *

**Sign up for Connie Shelton's free mystery newsletter at connieshelton.com
and receive advance information about new books, along with a chance at prizes, discounts and other mystery news!**

**Contact by email: connie@connieshelton.com
Follow Connie Shelton on Twitter, Pinterest and Facebook**

Connie Shelton is the author of the
USA Today bestselling Charlie Parker and
Samantha Sweet mysteries and her newest—
The Heist Ladies. She's known for a light
touch when it comes to sex and violence in
her stories, but is much more lavish with
food and chocolate. She and her husband and
two dogs live in northern New Mexico.

Books by Connie Shelton
THE CHARLIE PARKER MYSTERY SERIES
Deadly Gamble
Vacations Can Be Murder
Partnerships Can Be Murder
Small Towns Can Be Murder
Memories Can Be Murder
Honeymoons Can Be Murder
Reunions Can Be Murder
Competition Can Be Murder
Balloons Can Be Murder
Obsessions Can Be Murder
Gossip Can Be Murder
Stardom Can Be Murder
Phantoms Can Be Murder
Buried Secrets Can Be Murder
Legends Can Be Murder
Weddings Can Be Murder
Alibis Can Be Murder
Holidays Can Be Murder - a Christmas novella

THE SAMANTHA SWEET SERIES

Sweet Masterpiece   *Sweets Begorra*
Sweet's Sweets   *Sweet Payback*
Sweet Holidays   *Sweet Somethings*
Sweet Hearts   *Sweets Forgotten*
Bitter Sweet   *Spooky Sweet*
Sweets Galore   *Sticky Sweet*

Spellbound Sweets - a Halloween novella
The Woodcarver's Secret

THE HEIST LADIES SERIES
Diamonds Aren't Forever
The Trophy Wife Exchange
Movie Mogul Mama

CHILDREN'S BOOKS
Daisy and Maisie and the Great Lizard Hunt
Daisy and Maisie and the Lost Kitten